Fleur McDonald has lived and worked on farms for much of her life. After growing up in the small town of Orroroo in South Australia, she went jillarooing, eventually co-owning an 8000-acre property in regional Western Australia.

Fleur likes to write about strong women overcoming adversity, drawing inspiration from her own experiences in rural Australia. She has two children, an energetic kelpie and a Jack Russell terrier.

www.fleurmcdonald.com

Also by Fleur McDonald

Red Dust
Blue Skies
Purple Roads
Silver Clouds
Crimson Dawn
Emerald Springs
Indigo Storm
Sapphire Falls
Suddenly One Summer
Fool's Gold

FLEUR McDONALD

The Missing Pieces of Us

ALLEN&UNWIN
SYDNEY • MELBOURNE • AUCKLAND • LONDON

For the people I love, who believe in me

This edition published in 2018
First published in 2017

Copyright © Fleur McDonald 2017

Allen & Unwin
83 Alexander Street
Crows Nest NSW 2065
Australia
Phone: (61 2) 8425 0100
Email: info@allenandunwin.com
Web: www.allenandunwin.com

A catalogue record for this book is available from the National Library of Australia

ISBN 978 1 76063 336 3

Dear Diary,

Australia? I'd never heard of it until the day Mummy told me we were going to live there. It sounded as foreign as it was far away.

Our life in London wasn't especially hard, with Daddy having a secure job in the factory. Mummy looked after the house and I had friends at school. We went to church on Sundays, and for a while I attended Sunday school, but now that I'm nearly sixteen, I don't have to. I'm even allowed to take communion with the adults.

My brother and sister, Eddie and Anne, were settled in school and had friends too—it seems strange to take them out of the life that they know. I suppose they'll adjust more quickly than me, being so much younger.

Our life was so nice. I don't understand why we had to change it.

I liked that I could walk to Granny's for tea and cake. I

liked that I could walk to the shop and spend a twopence on some sticky sweets, and I liked that my family would take a picnic to the park every Saturday afternoon when Daddy wasn't working. Eddie and Anne loved feeding the ducks at the pond, and I loved watching the people. So many of the men are trying to dress like The Beatles; I don't know if Australia has even heard of The Beatles.

One afternoon I came home from school and Mummy was sitting at the kitchen table with Granny. Eddie and Anne were sitting there too, eating biscuits and drinking milk. Mummy's eyes were red and it looked as though she'd been crying, but she seemed happy. It was an odd combination.

When she saw me, Mummy gave me a big smile and asked me to sit down. She said there was important and exciting news. Then she told me we were moving to Australia in two weeks' time. I'd heard about the Ten Pound Pom scheme— I'd seen adverts but never thought we would be the ones to leave.

That night, Daddy talked about sunny blue skies and jobs galore. They wanted strong, fit and healthy men down in Australia.

As we were getting ready to leave, Mummy and Daddy laughed together so much. He'd swing her around and dance with her. From my bedroom I'd hear them talking, full of plans and ideas. A house with a backyard and maybe even a puppy. I like puppies. I'm sure Daddy said that just so I would stop crying.

I didn't want to go. I didn't want to leave Granny and all my friends. I didn't want to leave my life.

There wasn't a choice.

Mummy and Daddy packed up our belongings and sold our furniture, leaving the house cold and empty. When we walked out of our home for the last time and the door slammed shut, I heard it echo around inside. It gave me the shivers.

On the docks, Mummy cried when she hugged Granny. When we walked on board, I heard her say to Daddy that she was frightened she'd never see her mother again. He hugged her and promised we would. That made me weepy too. I couldn't imagine not seeing Granny ever again. Or not seeing my friends, my teachers, even the postman! I'd taken for granted that these people would always be there. I'm nearly a woman, but I cried like a child for all the people I may never see again.

When the ship's horn sounded for the first time, the crew ran around like ants scurrying for crumbs. They wound in the ropes, cranked handles and yelled instructions to one another. Then we were cast away. Out to sea. Our old lives disappearing with the smooth glide of the ship.

That night, many of us went to the top deck to watch the lights of Hastings fade into the distance. Daddy stood with his arm around Mummy. Eddie and Anne were sleeping in the cabin, so it was only me standing with my parents. They were busy making friends with the other passengers, so they didn't see me cry again.

All I wanted to do was jump overboard and swim home.

We've been on board for more than a week now. The mood is one of excitement, hope and expectation. Everyone is enthusiastic and can't wait for their new lives to start. I think it's only me who's been sad. I'm still homesick. I've already written letters to Granny and all my friends back home, which I can't post until we get to Australia.

Fortunately there's a lot of fun to be had on the boat, with swimming pools and games and new friends. And I've met a boy, and even though I still don't want to go to Australia, he will make the journey very nice.

Chapter 1

Lauren jolted awake, her breath coming in short, sharp gasps. Sweat drenched her body. Her heart was beating so fast, she felt as though it was going to escape from her chest. She forced herself to take deeper breaths. It had just been a dream. A nightmare. The one she'd been having her whole life.

She was always somewhere shadowy. Great walls rose around her, keeping her prisoner. In the claustrophobic darkness, her shallow breaths took in the moist, icy air that constricted her throat, making her struggle for oxygen.

Rough hands held her down. When she pulled away, other hands kept reaching for her, clawing at her flimsy nightdress, her hair, her arms. She tried to flick them from her, to duck around every outstretched arm and run towards a sliver of light in the distance. Stumbling onto some stairs, she somehow knew that she was only moments from safety.

Then she felt the hands again.

Just as terror threatened to overtake her, she woke up.

Lauren hated the dark, empty feeling that the dream always left her with. As if she'd been visited by a spirit who had sucked the soul from her, leaving her as just a body. A shell.

Rolling over, she looked at the clock. 3.39 am. Damn! Why couldn't it be later? She knew that although she was exhausted, she wouldn't be able to get back to sleep.

Beside her, Dean snored gently, oblivious to her turmoil. She snuggled closer to her husband, putting her arm over his waist, trying to absorb some of his warmth. His snoring stopped, and he sleepily pulled her arm to his chest and muttered something unintelligible, then started to snore again.

Before Lauren could stop them, tears pricked her eyes. Waking from the dream always left her needing Dean's comforting and steady presence, as well as a cry. She didn't just feel scared of the reaching hands; she was terrified by the absence of love within the bubble of the dream. Dean had suggested that she dreamed like this because lack of love was her greatest fear—quite possibly, he was right. Her friend Holly, who worked as a psychologist at the same school, had suggested the same thing.

Lauren wasn't looking for the heated, passionate type of love; she was content with the reliable, unconditional, never-ending type. Perhaps that was why the dream persisted: to make sure she never forgot that love was to be given, and it was her job to love as much as she could. Like her adoptive parents loved her. Like Dean loved her and their two children.

For a long time, as a selfish teenager, she'd assumed that her birth mother hadn't loved her enough—which perhaps was why she'd developed this fear. But as she'd grown older and read more about the history of adoptions in Australia, she'd realised that lack of love may have had nothing to do with it. Her birth mother might have been forced to give her up.

Lauren brushed away her tears, slid out of bed and stood still for a moment, gazing fondly at her husband. The same warm feeling she had when she'd watched her babies sleep rose inside her. She'd once tried to describe how it felt to Dean: 'It's like my chest becomes mush and my whole body glows.' She had averted her eyes at the last minute in case she'd said too much.

All he'd answered was, 'It's just love, honey,' and hugged her tightly.

Watching the rise and fall of Dean's chest calmed her. It was a long-standing family joke that he could sleep through an earthquake—which he'd actually done once, though only a small one.

She padded across the carpet to the window and watched moths swarm around the streetlight that stood in front of their two-storey brick house. Their suburb in the Perth Hills was always quiet at night: no noisy cars, horns or kids out too late. She and Dean had bought here because they wanted to raise their children in a community-based suburb, where they knew their neighbours and looked out for one another. Somehow in the busyness of life, that hadn't happened—they only knew their neighbours to wave to. The house was very old, built in a time when one bathroom and one toilet was all that was needed: a constant source of annoyance now. But it had been cheap, and they'd all come to love their home.

Lauren turned from the window and decided not to worry about sleep—it definitely wouldn't happen again tonight. She made her way down the stairs, avoiding the creaky step, third from the top. At the bottom, she ran her gaze over the family photographs lining the hallway. They documented Dean's and her life from their wedding day, to the births of their kids, to last Christmas when their whole family—Dean's mum and dad, her parents and all the grandies— were together. These photos made her smile; they gave her a sense of belonging.

She walked down the hall, passed the doorway into the lounge and opened the door to the study. Relief washed through her as the dazzling fluorescent lights lit up the room, chasing away the fragment of the dream. After she sat down in the chair, she turned on the computer, opened the browser and clicked her shortcut to Ancestry.com, the website she'd been using to investigate her family history. Well, the history of Dean's and her adoptive parents' families.

For as long as Lauren could remember, she had known she was adopted. 'We wanted a child very badly,' she remembered her mother saying, 'and then we were able to choose you. You've made us very happy!' So, as a small child, Lauren had told everyone with pride that her parents had *chosen* her, not really understanding the implications and significance of what she was saying.

Nineteen years ago, when she'd found out she was pregnant with her first child, Lauren had been hit for the first time by a longing to find her birth mother. And as the nurse had placed Stuart in her arms, an overwhelming instinct to protect him had settled in her chest and never gone away. Lying in the labour ward—her own squirming baby, with a good set of lungs, in her arms—Lauren had wondered if her birth mother had felt similar emotions; and if she'd experienced a deep sense of loss as a nameless nurse snatched Lauren away before she'd even held her. These same feelings and questions had arisen when Lauren's daughter, Skye, was born five years later after four heartbreaking miscarriages.

But as Lauren had become a busy and tired mum for the second time, the longing to find her birth mother had faded quickly; the rigmarole of dealing with bureaucracy wasn't a high priority. At times she'd still thought about giving it a go, but either life had got in the way or she'd worried that it would upset her parents.

Lately, now that the kids were a bit older and weren't so dependent on her, she'd been thinking about it again almost every day.

Online, while her family slept, Lauren traced their ancestors back generations so her kids would have a record. She felt a thrill of anticipation as she saw all the little green leaves scattered on the family tree. The hints behind each leaf led her closer to knowing all there was to know about their families.

'Come on, Skye!' called Lauren, standing at the foot of the stairs. 'You've only got half an hour before the bus!'

Silence from upstairs, as usual.

'Gotta run, honey!' called Dean, rushing out of the study, briefcase in hand, dropping a kiss on her mouth. He had a high-pressure job in IT. 'I've got an early meeting—one of our clients was hacked last night.' He was through the front door before he'd finished speaking.

'Don't forget it's your turn to cook tonight!' Lauren called after him, her eyes on his bum. *He has the cutest arse*, she thought. *Even in suit pants.*

With his muscly physique that he honed at the gym, dark brown hair and chocolate-coloured eyes, Dean was getting more good-looking as he got older. Not all men were that lucky—at a school reunion two years ago, Lauren had been shocked by the way some men had aged. Protruding bellies, bald heads and deep wrinkles had been the order of the day. But her husband was just like fine wine, she thought proudly.

She and Dean made a striking couple—his darkness against her fairness and stunning red hair. There had never been anyone else for either of them since they'd met when she was twenty-two. She and her teacher friends had gone to a gig at the Cottesloe pub, and Dean had chatted her up while she'd been ordering a round at the bar. The music had been heavy on the guitar and drums, but she and Dean had managed to have a yelled conversation. During a set break, he'd suggested they head outside to keep talking, and they'd spent an hour walking along the beach together.

Funny, she thought now, how they'd managed to find each other given the number of people who'd been there that night. And now she was forty-seven and loved him just as much as ever.

She heard the Commodore's engine starting, which set off the neighbour's dog.

She waited a few seconds and . . . right on cue, raised voices came from upstairs.

'Get out! I'm in here,' Skye whined before a door slammed.

'Could you hurry up?' said Stu. 'I'm busting for the loo.'

Rolling her eyes, Lauren took the steps two at a time and knocked on the bathroom door. 'Skye! Come on, sweetie, we do this every morning. You're pushing the boundaries again.' She turned to Stu, who was still looking bleary from sleep. 'What I wouldn't do for a separate toilet.' It was the same discussion every morning.

The bathroom door opened and her tall, lanky daughter came out. Skye's long red hair was wrapped in a towel and another was draped around her body. 'Sorry, Stu,' she said, not sounding apologetic at all.

'No, you're not!' Stu answered, walking into the bathroom. 'Skye, you're a feral!' he called out. 'Could you at least pick up the bathmat?'

With her hand on her bedroom door handle, Skye stopped and looked back as the bathroom door banged shut. 'What?' she asked Lauren in complete innocence. 'I only did it to annoy him.'

Exasperated, Lauren tried to stop herself from smiling at the look on her daughter's face. 'I know, but *why* do you feel the need?'

'Coz it gets up his nose.' Skye grinned cheekily.

Lauren shook her head and thought she'd better reinforce the rules that everyone knew but didn't always follow. 'You're unbelievable. Now, here's an idea . . . if you want more time in the bathroom, get out of bed a little earlier.'

Skye screwed up her nose and said, 'Ew!'

'I know,' Lauren said with a sigh, 'God forbid a teenager ever wakes up on time. Okay, I offer you a challenge for tomorrow: in and out of the bathroom within ten minutes, and no trace you were ever there.'

'What's the prize?'

'Me being happy,' Lauren said. 'Skye, you know none of us can get ready in time if you take longer.' She glanced at her watch. 'Now, if you're not careful, you'll miss the bus. I can't take you to school today—the car is full of all those art supplies I picked up yesterday for my class.'

'That's okay, Mum. You know I always make it. I'll be fine.' Skye's eyes shone wickedly as she went into her room, closing the door. A few seconds later, music started blaring.

Lauren smiled ruefully and went back downstairs. Sometimes it seemed the differences between her children were as large as their age gap.

She'd rarely had to worry about Stu, who seemed to have been born with built-in responsibility. Now in his second year at uni, studying accounting, he was early with his assignments and seldom missed a class—if he did, he made up for it later. To earn a little extra money, he taught kids at the Gooseberry Hills pool, and his employers couldn't speak highly enough of him.

Skye was the complete opposite. Always running late, always forgetting her homework. Lauren had lost count of the number of times she'd come downstairs after Skye had left for school and found her lunch still sitting on the kitchen bench. A few of the Year Nine teachers had expressed concern at Skye's scattiness.

Chalk and cheese, as Dean's mother always said.

Lauren walked into the kitchen and poured herself a coffee before reviewing the notes she'd made for today's lessons. She could have used more sleep, but she was still excited about her day: she loved teaching kindy. Loved seeing the kids with their little faces full of wonder. Loved their innocent questions about the world and their enjoyment of simple things—painting, reading, learning to write.

Her job at Gooseberry Hills School was the best teaching position she had ever held. She'd worked in both public and private schools, and she had learned early on that her colleagues could make the job satisfying or not. And the teachers at the Goose—pronounced 'Gooze'—were happy and cheerful, as were the children, mostly. The principal, Hamilton Walter, always encouraged openness.

Now when she glanced at the clock that hung over the kitchen sink, Lauren realised she'd have to get a move on if she wasn't going to be late—and Skye wouldn't let her forget that in a hurry! Lauren started to gather her notes and took another sip of her coffee as she glanced around for her briefcase.

Heavy clomping on the stairs indicated her son was on his way down.

'Could you bang on Skye's door, please?' she called to him.

She heard him clomp back up the stairs and bang on Skye's door. When he finally entered the kitchen, he said, 'It wouldn't hurt if she missed the bus. Might teach her some time-management skills.'

'Like you've never run late for something before. You're not her father,' Lauren reprimanded him mildly. He could be a bit hard on Skye. 'Nobody's perfect.'

'Alright, I'm *coming*!' Skye yelled at the top of her voice before jumping the last few steps on the staircase and barrelling past Stu, her bag on her back and ever-present earbuds in her ears. Lauren was sure she heard Skye mutter, 'Golden Boy,' to Stu, as she passed him, but there was no point in chiding her for it because she wouldn't hear. With a cursory flick of her hand towards Lauren, Skye raced out the front door, not even going into the kitchen to grab anything for lunch. The word 'goodbye' died on Lauren's lips.

She turned her attention to Stu, who was still wearing pyjama shorts, his curly brown hair flopping over his eyes. 'How are you today?' she asked.

'Okay,' he replied, checking the water in the coffee machine and grabbing a pod from the drawer. 'Skye's being a pain in the arse as per usual.'

After setting down her half-drunk coffee, Lauren picked up her briefcase and put it on the table, before stuffing all her notes inside and snapping it shut.

'Teenagers are changeable creatures. Beautiful one moment, a storm the next. Yes, yes, I know you're not like that at all, but you're one of the few.' Lauren gave him a slight smile. 'Actually, I do remember a year when all you did was grunt at me—so you weren't the perfect teenager either!'

Stu grunted, and Lauren laughed. She glanced at the clock again: there was just enough time for a quick chat with her son.

'What ages do you have to teach today?' she asked him.

'The three-year-olds,' he answered with a grin. 'Sometimes they can be cute, but more often than not, they're hard work. There's this one boy who's loud and rude, and his mother does nothing about it, just sits on the edge of the pool and drinks coffee while he kicks other kids under the water.' Stu spooned sugar into his cup and stuck it under the coffee machine nozzle.

'Some kids are hard work, but they're usually worth it,' Lauren said. It made her heart sing when she saw what a responsible man Stu was growing into. 'Look at you!'

'Ha, ha!'

Lauren watched her son as he sat down. His fluid movements were so much like Dean's, but there was an angle about his nose and chin that she couldn't attribute to either Dean's side of the family or herself. So where did that come from?

On some days, an expression would pass across Stu's or Skye's face and she'd want to know who they looked like; on other days, she didn't care. On some days, she wanted to share her children with her biological parents; on other days, she didn't. But no matter whether it was a 'yes' or a 'no' day, various questions had been plaguing her lately. Did she have any siblings out there? What about nieces and nephews?

When Skye had been smaller, after she'd learned what it meant to be adopted, she'd sometimes tried to match Lauren up with other women—usually those with red hair, freckled fair skin and blue eyes.

The first time had been at a netball match. Eight-year-old Skye had raced up to Lauren saying, 'Mum, Mum! You need to come and look at this lady.' Lauren had taken her daughter's hand and followed her. Skye had stopped in front of another girl's mum and said, 'See, Mum? She's got red hair and freckles like you. She could be your sister!' Then Skye had gazed up at Lauren, hope in her face. The other woman had jerked back in surprise, staring warily at them, and Lauren had done some quick talking.

Lauren had asked Skye not to do that anymore, but it hadn't stopped her. Over the years, there had been a substitute teacher, a lady behind a grocery store counter, a tour guide on an excursion, and a few others. But, thankfully, not for a couple of years now, so maybe Skye had finally grown out of it.

But for Lauren the question remained: how many people were walking around with the same blood as hers running through their veins?

Lauren still wasn't sure she could seek the answer to this question without hurting her parents. She loved them and didn't want to risk bringing them pain. Surely they'd think her searching for her birth mother was some kind of betrayal?

Dean had an opinion on this: 'If you want to find her, then do. All you have to do is talk to Connie and George. Just talk to them! Don't assume you know what they're thinking. You might be surprised.'

Maybe he was right. It could be all in her mind. But Dean had a black-and-white way of looking at life. His motto was: 'If you want to know the answer, ask the question; if you've got a problem with someone, tell them.' To Lauren, it wasn't that simple. Connie and George had taken her into their lives and raised her—a child who wasn't theirs! Surely that deserved loyalty?

'I'm going over to Papa's after work,' said Stu, breaking into Lauren's thoughts.

'That's nice of you, honey. You're very good to them,' she said, getting her lunch out of the fridge. It was nearly 8.15, and she needed to be in the car by 8.25.

Eight-fifteen also meant that her dad, George, would be sitting on the verandah, reading the paper, a cup of tea on a table next to him, while her mum, Connie, would be washing the dishes and sweeping the floor. Since they'd both retired, their morning regimen had been as reliable as the sun coming up. Apparently routine was part of ageing, which proved to Lauren that her parents were getting older. Not something she wanted to dwell on.

'You know, when I was over there last week, Papa mentioned that he's worried about you.' Stu put his coffee cup down and looked directly at Lauren.

'What? Why?' she asked. Although even as she said it, she realised that her exhaustion was probably evident to others.

'He says you haven't been yourself lately. You were supposed to ring them yesterday.'

Lauren hit her forehead with the palm of her hand. 'Hell! I forgot. I'll do it at recess.' She was so annoyed with herself. She'd always been a typical type-A personality: a woman who not only made to-do lists, but also added new items *after* she'd done them, just so she could cross them off. But lately, as more of her items went undone—mostly because she kept leaving her lists behind or even losing them—she realised that she wasn't as efficient as she used to be. Perhaps it was part of getting older, like the routine her parents had set. *God, I hope not*, she thought, making a mental note to buy another notepad.

'Papa thinks you're doing too much,' Stu said.

'Don't be silly!' scoffed Lauren before gulping down the rest of her coffee, rinsing out her cup and putting it in the draining rack. 'I'm fine. I've got you lot holding me together.' She leaned back on the bench, smiling. 'He's my dad, so it's his job to worry. But what on earth gave him that impression?'

'Oh, gee, Mum, I don't know,' said Stu, folding his arms. 'The big black bags under your eyes, or maybe you forgetting things you've never overlooked before—'

'Honey, that's all completely normal for a busy person. Sure, I'm tired, but who isn't? Working full-time is a constant juggle, but Dad and I are very lucky because we love what we do. And for me it's week six of the term. You know I get more tired as the term goes on.' She paused and gave his shoulder a squeeze. 'It's nice you're both concerned, and I love you for that, but I'm fine, honestly. Now, I've got to run or I'll be late to school, and Skye will never let me live that down!'

Chapter 2

Tamara rolled over and reached her hand out to the other side of the bed. Empty. She frowned and opened her eyes. Craig didn't usually get up before her.

The delicious aroma of coffee permeated the hallway, and then she heard the tinkle of the teaspoon against china, the clack as Craig set the spoon on the bench, and the floorboards creaking under his footsteps.

She stretched and sat up.

'Stay there,' Craig said as he came into the bedroom. 'You looked like Sleeping Beauty, so I didn't want to wake you.' He put the cup on the bedside table and bent to kiss her good morning. His beard tickled her chin.

'Sleeping Beauty?' Tamara said, her voice husky from sleep. 'More like Godzilla!'

'Not to me.' Craig sat on the edge of the bed and smiled at her.

'Get out!' Tamara swatted him and shuffled back against the pillow, sitting up and reaching for her coffee.

A stranger would never have guessed that Tamara's burly, tattoo-covered, earring-studded man was nothing but a big softy.

She heard a brisk clicking noise on the floorboards in the hallway, and then *whoomph*—a large dog who contained about a hundred breeds landed on the bed. Tamara's mug shook, coffee slopping out. Their brindle and black dog was face to face with her, his large tongue on her cheek.

'Whiskey!' snapped Craig, pulling him off the bed. 'How the hell did you get in here?'

'Ow!' Tamara flicked her hand to get rid of the hot coffee and put the mug down. She reached over to fondle Whiskey's soft ears. 'It's alright, bub, you don't have to go outside again, do you?' She spoke like she would to a baby, then asked Craig, 'Aren't we going for a walk with him this morning?'

'You looked too comfortable in bed and I've got to go into the construction site early. It's going to be so bloody hot today, I want to get the slab poured before ten. I'd like to keep the guys out of the midday sun if I can.'

'Okay,' said Tam, before turning her attention back to Whiskey. 'Well, it will just have to be you and me.' The dog thumped his tail on the floor.

Craig glanced at his watch. 'It's 7.30 already.'

Tamara knew what he was saying: she'd have to be quick. By the time she did all the normal morning things and had taken Whiskey for a half-hour walk, she'd be running against the clock for work.

He's trying to control you again, the Tamperer warned.

Don't be silly! He's letting you know the time so you can work out your own schedule, the Tam said.

Tamara had long ago christened the two competing voices in her head. While the Tam pointed out and reminded her of all the good things, the Tamperer was destructive. The Tam also gave her solid advice when the Tamperer didn't. Unfortunately, the Tamperer often had more to say and spoke much louder.

'If you're quick,' Craig said, 'I'll drop you at the park on my way to work.' He leaned forward for another kiss.

'Is that a challenge?' Tamara looked at him suspiciously.

'Take it as you like!' He raised his eyebrows and wiggled them.

She threw back the covers, got out of bed and went to select her walking outfit. As much as she would have loved to be one of those people who pulled on an old tracksuit and ran a brush through their hair before leaving the house, she couldn't bring herself to do that. She never went outside without perfect hair and makeup, and always wore the proper clothes. She felt naked without makeup on. Maybe someone would see something in her face she wanted—no, *needed*—to keep hidden.

Doctor Kerr had explained that this way of thinking was to do with her father, Evan, and his obsessive-compulsive need for everything to be in its place; it had just affected the way Tamara dressed and looked as well. This helped in her career, as she managed a fashion boutique at the local mall. But her need to appear perfect sometimes annoyed Craig. She'd often made them both late to social occasions because her hair wasn't right or her makeup had run slightly.

'You look beautiful,' Craig would say, using the quiet tone he'd perfected for this kind of situation—a cross between exasperation and puzzlement. He'd told her, more than once, that he didn't understand this part of her character.

It'll cause problems between the two of you, the Tamperer had warned. *Mark my words. He'll leave you over it.*

Don't be ridiculous, answered the Tam. *He loves you.*

Tamara would shake her head and try to listen to the Tam.

This morning she felt okay. 'Right, you can time me if you like,' she said to Craig, running towards the bathroom with Whiskey barking at her heels.

Craig followed her and grabbed her gently around the waist, pulling her to him. His beard scratched against her face as he kissed her again, this time for longer.

Whiskey let out a bark and Tamara shushed him. Playfully she let her hands wander over Craig's chest, across his shoulders and down his back so she could give his ponytail a tug.

He patted her arse and let her go. 'Five minutes,' he challenged.

'Fifteen,' she bargained.

'You'll be walking there yourself. I should have been on site already.'

She knew from his tone he wasn't being mean, just letting her know what he had to do. After throwing a quick glance at the clock on the bedside table, she raced into the bathroom and turned on the shower.

Seven minutes later, she was applying the last of her makeup. When Craig held out her sandshoes, she took them and slipped them on. While Craig called for Whiskey so he could chain him on the back of his ute, she ran to the laundry and grabbed the dog's lead from behind the door. When she got into the passenger seat of Craig's ute, she was only one minute over.

Craig laughed.

'What?' she asked.

'I can give you a month's notice that we're going out for dinner, and we'll still run late because you're getting ready, but when it comes to walking the dog, you're on time! Why?'

Tamara stared into the rear-view mirror and saw the excitement on Whiskey's face. He was leaning over the edge of the tray, looking enthusiastically at her, his large tongue hanging out. It seemed as though he was smiling.

'I like walking with him,' she said.

'Ah, but you don't like going out to dinner with me?' Craig asked, sounding amused.

'You know that's not what I mean!'

'I know. Just teasing. Trying to get a rise out of you.'

Tamara put her hand on his leg. 'Is it a house slab you're pouring today?'

Craig's large hand came down to cover hers and he drove one-handed. 'House over in the next suburb. It's a huge one—two hundred and thirty square metres.' He shook his head. 'When I first started this business, houses were only around one-fifty squares. Now we've got smaller blocks and larger houses.' He tapped his fingers on her hand and smiled at her. 'All the better for my bank balance!'

'I'd rather a smaller house with a nice backyard,' said Tamara.

'Me too. Anytime.'

A thought popped into Tamara's brain: how normal this was. She was having a normal conversation, in a normal car, inside a normal relationship. It gave her a feeling of satisfaction. Maybe she'd finally overcome her fears of commitment and of being a disappointment. She no longer felt unworthy, unlovable and unseen as she had when she was a child. Today, it appeared that the countless thousands of dollars she'd spent on therapy with Doctor Kerr over the past ten years had been worth it.

Yeah, well, you know where this relationship will end up, don't you? the Tamperer whispered.

No, said the Tam, *you've got it under control. Doctor Kerr has given you all the skills you need to deal with the emotions when they start. You've got this, and Craig loves you.*

But Tamara's smile slipped from her face. What if everything was so normal that she mucked it up?

She forced herself to focus on what Craig was saying now: 'Picked up a contract from a company that's going to build an office block. Starting that in a week's time.'

'That's so great,' Tamara said. *See? A normal answer!*

After Craig pulled up in front of the park, Tamara grabbed the lead, the thrower and a tennis ball, then got out and unclipped Whiskey from the back of the ute. Craig wound down his window and she leaned in for a kiss. 'See you tonight.'

'You certainly will.' Craig winked at her, and she smiled back.

Whiskey barked excitedly and tugged at the lead.

'Okay, okay, let's go!'

A few minutes later, out on the grass, Tamara took Whiskey off the lead and flicked the tennis ball from the thrower. As he chased after it at a gallop, she revelled in her conventional life, ignoring that pesky voice at the back of her mind.

Chapter 3

Heat radiated from the pavement, and Lauren found herself sweating within moments of walking from the car towards the school. She breathed in deeply then stopped, the smell of gum trees along the school fence bringing back a vivid memory. Laughter and the splash of water, and her dad's voice saying: 'Gently does it. When you land a fish, it's all in the wrist action!' She smiled as she remembered one of many summer holidays spent with her family and their friends in a houseboat on the Blackwood River. *What fun we used to have*, she thought, recalling the joy of diving into the cool river and the tug of the line when she caught a small fish. She hadn't liked to touch their slimy skin, so her dad had been the one to take them off her line and fillet them before putting them on the barbecue.

Lauren wished she could dwell on the memory, but those carefree days were over and she needed to get to work. Inside the school gates, a well-shaded lawn stretched out alongside the line of buildings. Children of all ages were milling about: from young ones struggling to walk under their heavy backpacks, to teenagers lying on the grass, chatting with one another or plugged into their earbuds, a few with books open in front of them.

The Goose was divided into sections. A playground for kindy through to Year Three was right next to the kindy classroom, and a line of trees cordoned off the Year Fours to Eights. In a quadrangle towards the back of the school, the rest of the years were mixed together.

A blast of happy chatter greeted Lauren as she walked out into the younger kids' playground. Some of her kindy kids were running around and playing, taking no notice of the heat. She stopped beneath a shade cloth to watch them. One group was hanging upside down from the monkey bars while another was kicking a footy. A boy tried to kick the ball and missed, falling flat on his backside. She smiled as she watched him get up and shake himself off, before he ran at the boy who now had the football.

In the split second before he tackled the other boy, Lauren called out, 'No tackling, Jarrod!' Jarrod pulled up and stared back at her, eyes wide. 'They're the rules,' she reminded him. The look on his face told her that he hadn't realised she was there. It made her want to giggle, but she couldn't. 'Firm and kind' was what she'd been taught at teachers' college—and 'be consistent'. These were the most important attributes to have when teaching, because they worked. Jarrod jammed his hat further down on his head and got back into the game.

In her mind's eye, Lauren saw her mentor, Fran, from her first practice teaching block. Fran had warned her: 'If they think they can get around you, Lauren, they will. Kids have a sixth sense. They spot any weakness within seconds and home in on it.'

Lauren missed Fran. Maybe death was like the famous passage by Henry Scott Holland. Lauren couldn't remember exactly how it went but it was about slipping into the next room. Of course, the next room didn't have a door to enter through. And Frán didn't answer when Lauren needed her to.

'Where's your hat, Will?' Lauren called to another boy.

'I forgot it.'

'You'll need to come and play under the shade. Remember: no hat, no play.'

'But that's where all the girls are!' Will protested.

'It might help you to remember your hat tomorrow,' she said.

Will's bottom lip stuck out as he slunk under the shade and leaned against the wall, crossing his arms. Lauren made a mental note to remind his mother to put a hat in his bag: Will never seemed to arrive with one, and Lauren didn't like the children sharing hats—it was one of the easiest ways to pass nits around.

Looking back to the playground, Lauren frowned as her eyes rested on Dirk Anderson, the only child by himself. Lauren would have loved to talk to Fran about him. He was sitting under a tree in the sandpit, grasping handfuls of sand before letting it run through his fingers. He repeated the action many times over, his head down, taking no interest in what was going on around him. When Zoe, Dirk's mother, had dropped him off out the front of the Goose the previous morning, she'd clearly been in a hurry, calling out to Lauren that he wasn't feeling very well before racing off. Zoe had been saying the same thing off and on for the past few weeks. Dirk didn't look any better today.

Lauren felt a fizz of annoyance. He would be much better off at home, in bed, being looked after by his mum, but she knew that wouldn't happen. She'd seen it all before. Parents would often bring sick children to school so they could go to work, to lunch, or do anything but stay home all day with their child. When it became obvious that a child shouldn't be at school, Lauren would phone the parent and hear comments like: 'Are you sure you can't keep her there until the end of the day? I'm at work. You've got a sick bay, right?'

Just as Lauren was about to call out to Dirk, she saw one of the most sociable girls in the class try to engage him in a game of chasies—but Dirk shook his head and remained in the sandpit. Worry churned in Lauren's stomach. He was changing, this little boy. It had been subtle at first but recently the difference in him had become clear. When Dirk first started kindy, he'd been such an outgoing, cheeky, mischievous child, and now he was withdrawn and quiet, avoiding eye contact and trying to make himself inconspicuous. He looked pale, tired and apathetic.

Lauren had been wondering if there was trouble at home, but it had only been a couple of weeks and she didn't want to seem like a panic merchant. Viruses could knock kids around for months!

Hoping her instincts were wrong, she put her hat on and walked over to him, greeting a couple of other children as she went. Squatting in front of Dirk, she handed him a bucket and spade. 'Hi Dirk,' she said gently. 'Looks like you could build a sandcastle with the pile you've got there.'

The little boy muttered hello but didn't reach out to take the offered toys.

Lauren felt her unease grow. 'Your mum said you aren't feeling well. Do you have a runny nose? Does your head hurt?'

Dirk shook his head and didn't meet her eye.

Digging into the sand, Lauren filled the bucket and held it out to him so he could tip it upside down and start making a castle.

Apparently without interest, he took the bucket and put it next to where he sat.

Lauren glanced at her watch and saw that it was about time for the bell to sound. 'You come and tell me if you want to lie down or need anything, okay, Dirk? I'm here to help you,' she said. When he gave a small nod, she touched him lightly on the head and got up, ready to pull the children into organised chaos.

The bell sounded, and with screams of delight the kids ran to their classroom door and scrambled into two rows. Lauren watched as Dirk just shuffled towards the line, hanging back from the group, his eyes on the ground.

'So, Fran, what do you think about him?' Lauren muttered. Sometimes it made her feel better to express her concerns aloud. She imagined Fran putting on her wide-brimmed straw hat and pushing it down over her wild grey curls. 'Well, lovie,' she might begin, 'Dirk seems a bit troubled.' For now, though, Lauren could only observe his behaviour, take notes and hope for the best.

Walking over to stand in front of the wriggling children, she smiled at their eager faces and bright eyes. They were anticipating the fun they'd be having today.

Through the classroom window, she could see Joy, her teacher's assistant, setting up easels and paint. Leading the children inside, Lauren told them to sit on the carpet.

'Good morning, class,' she said.

'Good morning, Mrs Ramsey,' they chorused.

'Don't forget Mrs Clark over there. She's setting up the painting for later on.' She gestured to Joy, who held a bottle of paint in one hand and a fistful of brushes in the other. Looking like a typical grandmother with her short grey hair tucked behind her ears and her sensible shoes, she put down the paint and waved to the children.

'Good morning, Mrs Clark.'

'We'll start with news first,' said Lauren. 'According to my roster, it's Jacob's and Dirk's turn.'

News time was always fraught with danger—as a teacher you just never knew what you were going to hear. About three years ago, a little girl had stood in this very room and said: 'My mummy and daddy had a big fight last night. Daddy came home from work, and Uncle Rod and Mummy were in the bedroom. He was very, very angry.' She'd sat down looking so pleased with herself.

Fran had told Lauren about many a news time gone wrong but the worst had been memorable: a mum had been in the classroom, doing 'mother's help', when a student had got up and said that his mother had hit his father the night before. The man had been the helper mum's brother.

Of course, news time could also be a lot of fun. Kittens and puppies made for a great show-and-tell—well, except when they piddled inside.

Today, Lauren said, 'Jacob, you can go first.'

The boy got to his feet, grinning with delight. 'Last night my sister brought home her new boyfriend. Dad said he's her third in three weeks! I thought he was nice because he kicked the footy with me. Any questions?'

No one said anything, so Jacob flopped to the floor.

Lauren was aware of Dirk fidgeting and looking uncomfortable.

'Dirk, it's your turn,' she said kindly.

He stood up, then looked at the ground as he spoke. 'The ambulance drove into our driveway yesterday. It had the flashing lights going. They were cool. Any questions?' Then, without waiting, he sat back down.

One of the other boys reached over to him. 'Was the siren going? Was it loud?'

Dirk shook his head.

'Well, class, I think that wraps up news time this morning,' said Lauren. 'Now we're going to paint something starting with the letter . . . G! Who can tell me a word that starts with G?'

Hands flew into the air again.

'Grown-ups!' one child yelled.

'Grapes!' said another.

'You're right! So, shall we start painting?'

'Yes!' shouted the kids.

One by one the children got their painting smocks from the art supply room, put them on and went back into the classroom where the easels were set up in two rows. A couple of children struggled with doing up the velcro at the back of their smocks, so Lauren went to help. As she straightened, she noticed Joy helping Dirk with his velcro. He pulled at the sleeves and then reached for a paintbrush.

As the children painted, Lauren walked around and looked at their artworks. 'What are you painting, Kia?' she asked.

'My backyard. I like playing on the swing.'

'And what starts with G in your painting?'

'Green grass!'

'Great job.'

Joy cleared her throat to get Lauren's attention. As she turned, Joy nodded over at Dirk. Lauren wound her way over to him to see what he'd drawn: an ambulance with round black wheels and red sirens.

Lauren needed to see his face, so she walked to the end of the row and down the other side, and positioned herself in front of him. He was staring at the page, lips pursed in concentration. She was about to comment on his painting when a large green blob accidentally dropped onto the page from his brush. He stared at it as if he was confused, then he frowned. Reaching up, he tore the paper from the easel and screwed it into a ball. Paint now covered his hands and he rubbed at them. 'Damn it!' he said loudly.

Well, now, there was an adult comment. He must have heard his parents say that. Lauren wanted to giggle at such a grown-up phrase coming out of a little boy's mouth, but she couldn't. And, really, none of this was a laughing matter.

'What happened, Dirk?' she asked softly.

'I messed up my painting,'

'That's okay, I can get you another sheet of paper. Maybe we should get your hands washed first, though.'

He looked up at her, and she was immediately struck by how pale his skin was against the black painting smock. She wanted to pick him up and cuddle him. To take him home and put him to bed. She wanted to help him. That was her job. She'd always had an overwhelming need to make children feel special and important, to make them feel wanted.

Taking a deep breath, she put her hands on his shoulders and nodded at his paint-splattered hands. 'Let's get you cleaned up, hey?'

Lauren caught Joy's eye and indicated that she should keep the other kids busy, then directed Dirk towards the storeroom. There was a large trough where the class would go to wash their hands. Turning on the taps and handing Dirk the soap, Lauren reached down to roll up his sleeves, first those of the smock and then the striped shirtsleeves underneath. With the heat today, she'd been surprised to see him in a long-sleeved shirt. Still, if he hadn't been feeling well . . .

She stopped, shocked to see purple bruises on his wrist. They seemed fresh.

'Oh, these look a bit sore,' she commented before she could stop herself, knowing she wasn't allowed to ask straight out how they'd happened. A teacher could never put words into the mouth of a child: the child had to tell you himself.

Dirk nodded but said nothing.

She washed his hands and dried them on a towel before asking, 'Would you like to paint again? Or perhaps you could do some drawing with pencils.' She led him out of the storeroom and over to another section of the classroom that had a set of tables covered in butcher's paper and coloured pencils. Dirk sat without speaking and picked up a pencil. This time he drew a sun in the corner of the page and scribbled the sky with a blue pencil. Nothing at all to do with the letter G.

Lauren was writing up notes at lunchtime when Joy approached her. 'Is it just me, or have you noticed a change in Dirk's behaviour recently?' she asked.

Lauren put her pen down. 'No, it's not just you.'

'What do you think it is?' asked Joy.

'I'm not sure. I think . . .' Lauren's voice faded as she tried to think of what Fran would say. Maybe: 'Circumstantial evidence doesn't equal real evidence.' Yep, that's exactly what Fran would have said.

Lauren told Joy about Dirk's bruises. 'We need to keep an eye on him,' she said. 'I started to keep notes last week when he kept falling asleep during story-time. The more I think about it, I reckon Dirk's been withdrawn for at least a month, but I'm loath to go rushing in and do anything official until I'm certain. Those bruises . . . they could be anything. Kids accidentally bump into things all the time.' But Lauren knew her words sounded feeble.

'Let's organise a chat with his parents,' Lauren said, her mind ticking over. That's definitely what Fran would have done. 'If you haven't got the information, you can't make informed decisions,' she'd told Lauren on more than one occasion.

Joy nodded. 'That's a good idea. And are you going to talk to Hamilton?'

'Not yet. I don't want to bother him before I know more.' Lauren sighed. 'I think it's time to talk to the school psychologist, so I'm going to see Holly. And I'll try to have a quick chat with Dirk's mum this afternoon when she comes to pick him up.'

∽

The staffroom was unusually quiet when Lauren found Holly behind the bookshelf in the corner, poring over a psychology paper. 'Light reading,' Lauren said with a laugh as she pulled over a chair and sat down.

Holly looked up, then took off her glasses, blinking a couple of times. 'Oh, it's you! Sorry, I can't see past my nose with these new things. Everything's blurry. They're just for reading.' She waved the paper at Lauren. 'Bullying in schools.' She pushed her mousey-coloured hair off her face.

Lauren always thought Holly was extremely pretty in a conservative psychologist sort of way—large black-rimmed glasses and a solemn expression—but when she smiled her face was transformed.

'Anything new to report?' Lauren asked.

'Every year, all the experts come out with new and often conflicting ways to handle different situations. It's keeping my skills fresh and up to date.'

Lauren smiled sympathetically. She dug into her bag and pulled out a Tupperware container full of last night's chicken curry. After swallowing her first mouthful, she said, 'I need your opinion on something.'

'Professional or otherwise?' Holly asked, putting down the paper and concentrating on Lauren.

'Professional.'

'Shoot.'

'A boy in my class keeps being brought into school even though his mum says he's not feeling well. I've noticed recently that he's quiet and withdrawn, then today I saw bruises on his arms.' She pointed at her own wrist. 'He was the only child in the class wearing long sleeves on such a hot day.'

'I see. Do you know much about the family?'

'A little. His father is some highfalutin' international business-man. I get the impression he isn't home a lot. And his mother, Zoe, is a stay-at-home mum. His records say that he's an only child. That's all the information I have.'

'Have you spoken with the mother yet?'

'I plan on trying to catch her at pickup this afternoon.'

Holly sat back and stared at Lauren. 'What are you thinking? Abuse?'

'Maybe. I don't know. The bruises looked to large to be made by fingers . . . but I've never seen bruises made by fingers, so I can't be sure. And why the long sleeves?'

'Hmm. It's best not to jump to conclusions too quickly in these situations,' Holly cautioned. 'There could definitely be other reasons for the bruises. He might be sick, or there might be some upheaval at home. Something other than physical abuse.'

Lauren nodded. 'I know.'

'Have you kept any records?'

'Yeah. Just for the past week. Joy has noticed a change in his behaviour too, independently of me.'

'How long has it been going on for?'

'Hmm, look, I really can't be sure. Definitely the past month, but the change was hard to spot until it was so—' she made quotation marks with her fingers '—"in my face" that I couldn't miss it.' She frowned and put aside her lunch, her appetite gone. 'I'm cross with myself that I've taken so long to figure it out. I'm trained to see the signs, for God's sake.' She let out a breath.

'It sounds like the changes were very gradual. Don't beat yourself up over that.' Holly paused. 'Do you know if anyone has moved in with the family or there's been any other change in the family structure?'

'I have no idea.'

'Maybe that's a question for Zoe when you talk to her. But look, in my experience, if there's any type of abuse happening, she's not going to open up to you immediately. If there's nothing to worry about, it might make her wary of you—quite possibly, she won't understand why you're singling her out.'

'I've never had to do this before,' said Lauren. 'I've come close a couple of times, but just as I've been going to make a report to Child Protection, information has come through explaining the kid's behaviour. It's an enormous responsibility. What if I get it wrong?'

'You're going to need to be very careful,' Holly advised. 'As you know, the safety of the child is more important than anything else. You've done all your Personal Development training, but nothing prepares you for the heartache of seeing a beautiful, innocent child hurt.' She put her hand on Lauren's arm.

Holly had once told Lauren that her need to so fiercely protect every child who came under her care might stem from being given up as a baby.

Now Holly said, 'I'm only telling you this as a friend. As a professional, you know I'd be saying that you can't get emotionally involved, but realistically it's hard not to. Go ahead and talk to Zoe this afternoon, and depending on what she says, you might need to report to Hamilton.' She gestured towards the principal's office.

Lauren nodded. 'I'll make sure my notes are all together. And I took photos of Dirk's bruises while the kids were all holding up their paintings.'

'That's good. Don't go in without evidence to back everything up. And, I know Joy will already understand this, but it's imperative that the reporting is completely confidential. It wouldn't hurt to mention that to her.' Holly brushed her hair out of her eyes. 'Promise me you'll try not to get too personally involved. I know your history.'

'Of course I won't,' Lauren said. 'I'm a professional.' She packed up the remains of her lunch, trying to bring her emotions under control. 'Thanks again, Holly. I've got yard duty, so I'd better get out there. And let's grab a drink soon?'

'Certainly! It's been too long.'

Chapter 4

Skye sat with her back against a tree trunk and thumbed through her mobile phone. When it dinged, she saw that Billy had Snapchatted her. She stared at the notification as a thrill ran through her body. Keeping her thumb on the screen, she looked at the picture he'd sent until it disappeared. Ten seconds wasn't enough. She wanted to study it, commit every detail to memory.

Billy had sent her pictures like that before, though nothing this graphic. They made her insides feel all fluttery and squishy. Her friends called them 'dick pics', but that sounded so revolting. It wasn't revolting between her and Billy. It was . . . well, she wasn't sure what it was, but it wasn't disgusting.

Although she would never tell anyone, Skye had been trying to work out if she wanted to sleep with him. Well, she *wanted* to—sex was a secret rite to womanhood, that's what her gran's Mills & Boon books said, anyway—but it made her nervous at the same time.

Billy had already had sex. 'But I really want to do it with you,' he'd said when he called her yesterday. Skye had wanted to say something smart and sexy back. Her bestie, Adele, would have known what to say straight away, but Skye couldn't think of anything. 'I want to do it with you too,' she'd blurted out. Then she'd wanted to shove her fingers down her throat and throw up, it sounded so stupid.

To be honest, she still couldn't believe Billy liked her. Skye had found that being a teacher's kid made other students regard her warily, like she was going to run back and tell her mum whenever they hadn't done their homework. Thankfully, she had a group of friends she'd grown up with, girls who didn't care that her mother was a teacher, but making new friends was hard.

So for Billy Gaston, a Year Twelve boy, to sidle up to her after the first basketball game of the season and tell her that she looked 'pretty cute in those shorts'—well, she still had trouble believing it. She'd glanced over her shoulder to see if he was talking to someone else, her mouth going dry because there wasn't anyone behind her. Then she'd checked to see where his group of mates were—maybe they'd bet him to come and talk to her. She couldn't see them anywhere. In fact, she and Billy were alone in the long, dark corridor that led to the toilets.

'Yeah, it's you I'm talking to,' he said with a lopsided grin. Then he moved a little closer and she took a step back, still not able to find any words or make her tongue work. She was close enough to smell his deodorant and see dark flecks in his blue eyes. He was dressed in the basketball uniform of singlet and loose shorts, his arm muscles were well defined, and he smiled down at her with Colgate toothpaste advert teeth. Adele had once said that he was almost too good looking. *Not possible*, Skye thought at that moment. *He could never be* too *good looking*.

'I'm about to play,' he said with a nod towards the courts. 'Stay and watch?'

'Um.' She licked her lips. 'Sure. I don't have to go home yet.'

'Can I have your mobile number?'

'Mine? What for?' The words rushed out before she could stop them. *Oh. My. God.* She wanted to die. Had she said that? Adele would have tossed her head and asked what was in it for her.

Now, five weeks in, Billy rang every day. They never talked for long, and he always used a low, gravelly tone, not at all like his normal voice that she'd heard in the schoolyard. Once Skye had asked if he was practising his sexy voice on her, and he'd got all offended. She wasn't sure why; it had been a reasonable question.

They managed to see each other at least once a week—Skye had to lie to her parents every time. There'd been movies with Adele and studying with Jasmine. She knew she'd have to start getting some different excuses. Her parents would catch on soon enough.

She and Billy hadn't done much. He'd driven them to a deserted quarry where they'd sat under the trees, having fries and milkshakes from Macca's. She liked asking him about his family and plans for the future but he hadn't told her much; Billy preferred to ask the questions.

They'd missed out seeing each other over the weekend because she'd been dragged to her grandparents' place. He'd been teasing her ever since with pictures of his biceps and his six-pack—and then, today, a very erect dick. She wondered how much it would hurt when they finally did it. Everyone said it hurt.

Everyone except Adele, who'd lost her virginity last weekend with a boy called Neil. *What kind of a name is that?* Skye thought. '*I lost my virginity with a boy called Neil!*' She almost laughed out loud, thinking back to when Adele had arrived at school the day before. She couldn't wait to tell the girls in their group every detail, bragging about how good it was and saying that it never hurt at all.

'What did he do to you?' Jasmine had wanted to know.

'Played with my boobs then . . . You know . . .' Adele wiggled her eyebrows suggestively and pointed to 'below' while the others oohed and ahhed.

Skye thought that she might be lying. Adele could be a good liar, but Skye had known her since their first day in kindy and had worked out that when Adele scratched her elbow, she was telling a great big, fat pork pie.

When Adele had said it didn't hurt, she'd scratched her elbow.

Skye looked around the quadrangle, trying to catch sight of Billy.

Their first kiss had been under the stairs in the school gym, after she's watched that first basketball game. It was dark and musty but Billy was freshly showered and smelt of soap and deodorant.

Not the most romantic place to get your first kiss, Skye thought as his warm lips were pressed on hers. Then she forgot to think and concentrated on the feelings shooting through her.

'No one can know about us,' he'd told her. 'What would your mum say?' He was standing with his arm on the wall above her shoulder and his face close to hers.

'Who cares what Mum would say?' she said, when they came up for air again. 'She doesn't run my life.'

He tangled his fingers in her long red hair and pulled her into him. 'I'm not in your mum's good books—she seems to have a set against me for some reason. And me being seventeen would be a stopper for her too.' He kissed her again as she wondered why her mother had it in for him.

Skye was dragged out of this memory when her phone vibrated with another message. It was Billy: 'Gonna send me one back?'

Her hands began to shake. *A picture of what? My boobs?* She looked down at her chest, which was pretty flat. Nothing much to show off.

Another photo landed on Snapchat. Holding her breath, Skye opened it.

'What are you doing?' Adele asked.

Skye jumped and put her phone face-down. She felt her face flame hot and hoped that her friend hadn't seen the photo. She wasn't ready to share anything about Billy yet, and she had the feeling that now Adele wouldn't *want* her to. Adele was enjoying her time in the spotlight for being the 'first one' in their group to sleep with a boy.

'Nothing,' Skye said. 'A text from my cousin. You know.' She shrugged, picking up her phone again and pretending to look at the screen.

Adele flopped down on the grass, chewing her ever-present gum and casting a suspicious glance at Skye. 'Jumpy today. You feeling guilty or something?'

'As if. Just didn't realise you were there. Gave me a fright.' A change of subject was needed before Adele pressed her for more information. 'Oh, hey, did you hear what Chris said in Mrs McIntosh's English class today?'

Adele paused. 'No.'

'*So* funny. Mrs Mac goes: "Chris, where's your English book?" and he gets all, like, looking down at the desk and muttering and stuff. She leans forward and says, "Chris, I'm having trouble hearing you." He looks up and says, "I dropped it in water last night. Tried to dry it out with Mum's hairdryer, but she told me that wouldn't work, so I tried ironing it and that didn't work either." Our whole class pissed ourselves laughing. Even Mrs Mac was doing her best not to laugh!'

'Chris is so funny. Remember that time one of the teachers asked where his homework was?'

'Yeah, yeah,' said Skye, her eyes shining.

'It's still in my pen, Miss,' she and Adele chorused, then fell about hysterically.

'Last night my brother asked my dad if he was coming to "give him another mini-lecture",' Adele said with a snort. 'I wish I was as smart with the comebacks as some people.'

'You're quicker than me,' said Skye, thinking back to when Billy had asked for her phone number. 'Hey, have you heard from Neil?'

'Nah, didn't think I would.' Adele shrugged as she snapped her gum. Then she scratched her elbow.

Skye wondered which bit she was lying about: the not-hearing-from-him or the not-thinking-she-would. Probably the second one. 'When are you . . . ?'

'Dunno. Who cares? Not me.' Adele continued to scratch.

Gotcha, thought Skye. *You're upset he hasn't been in touch.* Well, she could understand that. 'He's probably a dick anyway,' she said sympathetically. 'Not worth worrying about.'

'He's got one, for sure,' Adele answered, her tone laced with innuendo. 'You going to the mall after school?'

Skye shook her head. 'Nah, got stuff I need to do.' She was going to wait until everyone had gone home, then meet Billy at the back of the school in his car. He'd suggested they go to the abandoned quarry. Her stomach twisted at the thought.

'Damn,' Adele said. 'I was hoping you'd go with me. I've got a couple of shops I wanted to check out. Angelic Threads has a sale on, and I found some really cool t-shirts. There's a white one that says, *Sorry, not sorry*. Thought I'd be able to wear it for when Mum tells me off for something stupid.'

'I could do with one of them,' Skye said. Actually, she would have loved to check out the sale at Angelic Threads, her favourite store. 'But I can't go with you tonight. How about tomorrow?'

Adele frowned. 'Whatever. I might be busy then.'

Exhaling through her nose, Skye fought the urge to whack Adele. She was a good friend, but she was never happy if she didn't get her own way.

'So,' said Adele, 'did you hear about . . .'

Skye let Adele talk without listening to her. She looked for Billy again. Instead of seeing him, she glimpsed her mum on yard duty. Skye automatically went to wave, but remembered in time to pull her hand back down. She didn't need to advertise that she was a teacher's daughter. It was so embarrassing when her mum came over and talked to her group. Plus, her mum liked talking to Adele and Jasmine more than to her anyway—she asked them more questions about what they were up to.

Hoping her mum wouldn't see her, Skye turned her back slightly. Lately her mum had decided to pick on her about *everything*, saying things like: 'Skye, your room's a pigsty. Go and clean it.' 'Skye, you haven't wiped down the kitchen properly. Surely you know where the sponge is?' 'Skye, have you done your homework?'

Stu couldn't do a thing wrong. Talk about being the Golden Boy.

'Stu's doing so well at uni,' Skye had overheard Lauren say to her PE teacher last week. 'We're very proud of the way he's got himself a job and is studying so hard.'

'But Skye can't keep her room clean,' Skye had muttered to her mum's back, imitating her disappointed tone.

There was no point in cleaning it, anyway, because she'd never get any recognition. Whenever she took the initiative to clean the kitchen or bathroom, her parents never even thanked her. 'It's all about living and working together,' her mum would say. And the time Skye had mowed the lawn, her dad had a fit! 'You've mowed it too low,' he'd said. 'It's a hot day and now it'll burn.'

Well, fuck his lawn. Wasn't that great anyway.

Of course, if Stu had done it, they'd have been all over him with praise, thanking him for fitting it into his busy life. Bloody Golden Boy.

Skye had a suspicion that her parents hadn't ever wanted her. There was such a big age gap between her and Stu. Adele had pointed it out a couple of months ago, and it had all seemed to make sense. But her parents had completely denied it when she'd asked them: 'Of course we wanted you. What gave you the idea we didn't?'

The age gap, she'd wanted to reply. *And the way Stu can't do anything wrong and I can't do anything right. The way you both pick on me.*

Actually, that wasn't fair. Her dad was okay, when he wanted to be. He'd talked her mum into letting her go to the movies on Saturday, so she could meet Billy. Not that her dad knew that: he thought she was meeting Adele.

'So, what do you think?' Adele looked at her expectantly.

'Um . . .'

'You are *so* out of it today.' Adele shot her a dark look. 'You weren't listening, were you? I found the coolest shorts at that surf shop in the mall. They're having a sale too. See?' Adele was holding her iPhone out with the photo app open.

'I really like them,' Skye said after she'd inspected the very short black shorts with small white pom-poms dangling from the hemline.

'I thought you would. But these are the ones I thought would suit you.' Adele slid the screen across to show shorts with a 3D red, pink and white print and a higher waistband. 'They'll match your hair for sure.'

'Hey, they're wicked,' said Skye, enlarging the picture.

'So, we going?' Adele had a triumphant look on her face.

'Where?'

'To the mall, you idiot.'

'Oh. Yeah. Tomorrow . . .' Not that she'd have any money to buy the shorts because, again, her mum was being a bitch and not paying her the pocket money she'd been promised this week. All because she hadn't cleaned the bathroom and vacuumed the lounge. Vacuuming was a waste of time—there was never any dirt in the house, and they didn't have any pets, so what did it pick up?

'I'd really like to go today,' Adele said.

'Told you, I can't,' said Skye. 'I've got stuff on this afternoon.'

'Like what?'

The bell sounded and Skye leapt to her feet. Adele hated it if she didn't know everything that was going on. 'Just stuff for Mum. God, she's being such a pain in the arse. I'm sure her real father was a dictator of some sort.'

Chapter 5

Angelic Threads had been humming all morning, but by four o'clock the customers had thinned out. Tamara was sitting in the back eating her very late lunch, waiting for the after-school rush. There was a sale on, and yesterday she'd had eight girls put items on hold until they could bring their mums in to check their choices.

Adele Blyth was one of them, and she'd told Tamara that she'd be back this afternoon with her friend Skye. Tamara smiled—she loved it when teenage girls came in. She understood what they wanted because she kept an eye on the latest trends. And she tried to guide the girls, in a cool aunty sort of way, towards what looked good on them. She would reassure them that there were fashionable clothes to suit every figure.

Her memory of who had bought which items was spot-on, as it was for names and faces. She could always greet her regular clients with their name and questions like 'How did that maths exam go?'

Adele and Skye were especially memorable. Adele favoured the nineties gothic look, but without going over the top. Tamara was particularly happy with what Adele had chosen to put on hold, because she'd managed to steer her away from black for once. Skye was fine featured and quieter than Adele, a bit unsure of herself. Her red hair made her stand out in a crowd and Tamara often noticed her hanging out in the mall with her friends. Tamara enjoyed helping them both—it was always great to make a teenage girl smile.

There was nothing about Tamara's job that she didn't like. When she glanced out through the two-way mirror at her store, she felt a surge of satisfaction. Angelic Threads was looking its best. The coat-hangers all faced the correct way, and there were no garments on the floor. She liked everything neat and tidy: all the clothes arranged by colour, sizing and type. At home, she liked her own clothes in the exact same way.

The shop's beeper sounded as a deliveryman appeared at the door. Tamara greeted him. She couldn't wait to see this season's collection. A fresh start—just the sort of thing she liked.

Once the three big boxes of new clothes were sitting in the back room, Tamara washed and dried her hands, then took out a Stanley knife and slit open the brown tape that held the first box closed.

The beeper sounded again: someone had entered the shop.

'Damn,' she muttered. Shutting the box, she fluffed her hair and smoothed her top before pasting on a smile and entering the shop to help her customer.

An elderly woman stood at the counter. It had been twenty-seven years, but Tamara recognised the same neat bun, out-of-fashion clothing and set features. Although her hair was greyer now and her shoulders slightly more stooped, Angela Thompson's expression hadn't changed.

'Mum,' Tamara said. With the counter between them, neither of them moved to embrace each other. Then, clumsily, her handbag knocking against the counter, Angela moved forward, one arm outstretched as if to draw her daughter in for a kiss on the cheek. Tamara shifted enough to leave her mother's gesture flailing in mid-air. Angela dropped her arm and glanced around, looking uncomfortable.

'What are you . . . ?' Tamara couldn't help gaping at the woman as if she was a hallucination. 'How did you find me?'

An image flashed through her mind of leaving the house in Whitfield Street.

'Hello, Tamara. How are you?' Angela set her handbag on the counter.

Tamara looked down at it, noting the black vinyl peeling at the corners. Old, used and well worn. Pretty much like the woman standing in front of her.

Angela glanced around again. 'How long have you worked here?'

'For twenty-something years. I started as a junior assistant and now I'm the manager.' Tamara needed Angela to understand what she'd achieved.

'Congratulations,' Angela said with a ghost of a smile to show that she was genuine. 'You've done well for yourself.' She nodded to emphasise her words.

Pride washed over Tamara. *No thanks to you or Dad*. The silence stretched out between them.

Three women entered the shop and started flicking through the racks. Tamara desperately wanted to ignore them and find out what the hell her mother wanted. A rush of worthlessness pierced through her. In one short moment, by walking into the shop, had her mother taken away all the work she'd done with Doctor Kerr?

A customer brushed past Tamara. 'Excuse me.'

Swallowing hard, Tamara tried to pull herself back from the edge of the abyss. 'Are you looking for anything in particular?' Her tone was uncharacteristically short. 'It's nearly closing time.'

'Just browsing,' the woman answered. The other two didn't even bother to respond.

'I guess you're wondering why I'm here,' said Angela.

'Not really,' Tamara lied. Of course she wanted to know! Why make contact after all these years, given the way they'd parted?

She's come to remind you of how invisible you are, the Tamperer whispered. *How unworthy.*

'I've got some bad news,' Angela said gently. 'Is there somewhere we can talk? The back room?'

'No.' Tamara glanced at her watch. 'I'm the only one here. My last junior left a few days ago and I haven't had a chance to replace her.'

'Oh.' Angela paused. Her face seemed to sag in defeat. 'Is there somewhere we can meet after you finish?'

'Just tell me, Mum,' Tamara insisted. She had to know.

Sadness and pain flitted across the older woman's face. 'I didn't want it to be like this,' she said. 'Your dad died two days ago.'

Tamara felt as though someone had punched her in the stomach. She couldn't get enough air.

'I thought you'd want to know,' said Angela, tapping her thumbs together.

Tamara tried to think of the appropriate response—her brain was fuzzy with all the cutting words Evan used to yell at her. They echoed so loudly, she wanted to put her hands over her ears and block them out. Things like: 'You'll never amount to anything!'

'Stupid, that's what you are. Plain stupid.' 'I'm so disappointed in you.'

Then there had been the first major blow-up. She'd been hanging around the train station with a group of kids who were smoking and drinking. One of the boys had a can of spray paint in his hand, so when the cops had rounded them up that time, there had been no way out for Tamara.

Evan had brought her home in a cold silence and then got stuck into her. 'We've given you a home, and this is how you thank us? I guess I shouldn't have expected anything else of you. You've been trouble since you were born. Crying and squawking so none of us could get any sleep. Then, nothing but disruption.'

Tamara remembered glancing at her mum, trying to catch her eye, hoping she'd make him stop. But Angela hadn't been any help—she'd just stood there with her hands over her mouth as if she was stopping her own tirade.

'God knows we've tried to make a difference to you,' Evan ranted. 'To bring you up right, give you a good start in life. And you repay us like this.'

Until she was a teenager, Tamara had tried to be a good girl, tried to make her parents love her. As a young child she'd snuggled against them at night, but they'd responded by pushing her away. When she was a bit older, she was often sent to bed early for making too much noise, for talking too much or for her room being untidy. It never was, though; her dad was just a clean freak. 'A place for everything and everything in its place,' he would say.

On other nights, Tamara took herself quietly to bed while her parents watched TV in the darkened lounge room. It was always loud, so they never heard her crying.

She did her chores diligently and tried to do well at school. Unfortunately, she wasn't the brightest child in the classroom—a fact that Evan never let her forget.

When she was thirteen, Tamara decided that, no matter what she did or how hard she worked at school or home, making her parents love her was impossible. There wasn't any point in trying. So instead of being hurt, she got angry. She used to chant to herself: 'You are the only one in your school whose parents don't love you.' Then she would ball her small hands into fists and pummel her thighs.

Turning thirteen brought her a whole new understanding of life. An older boy told her she was pretty, and those few words made her the happiest she'd ever felt. She wanted him to keep saying nice things to her. Which he did, especially when he wanted something. So, later, when he put his hand down her pants, she let him. If something so little meant he kept telling her he loved her, that she was beautiful and that he would never leave her, then she'd do whatever he wanted.

Wagging school with her boyfriend and smoking cigarettes had been the start of a downward spiral, which graduated to drinking and sex. She craved his words and kisses more and more; surely they *proved* he loved her. Still, she was happy to take any boy's attention. By the time her parents threw her out at sixteen, she had a reputation.

Tamara hated thinking about that time in her life. She wasn't proud of it. The memories made her feel unhappy and out of control.

'I'm sorry,' she said to her mother, appalled that her nose was beginning to tingle with the tell-tale sign of tears. She sniffed and lifted her chin, imagining that she did *not* care.

'Excuse me?' A lady holding a dress elbowed her way in front of Angela, glaring at her as she pushed by. 'Excuse me? Can I try this on? Where are your change rooms?'

Tamara saw dejection in Angela's face as she dropped her head to her chest and tried to make herself invisible. She looked as though she'd shrunk inches.

'Of course you can,' Tamara told the rude customer in a soothing voice. 'If you'd like to come this way?' She ushered the lady to the change rooms and held the curtain back for her. 'Let me know if you need another size,' she said with a smile.

'Yes, if you're not too busy talking about your personal life,' the woman snapped, disappearing into the curtained-off space.

Heat rushed to Tamara's face as embarrassment and anger threatened to overwhelm her. How dare the customer say that. She'd just been told that her father had died! It was a bloody miracle she was acting normally.

Tamara's watch told her it was now past closing time, which meant that she was actually doing the customer a favour by letting her try the dress on.

See? Doctor Kerr has helped you, the Tam said. *Although you're feeling all this now, you'll get through it, you always have. Stay strong.*

Closing her eyes, Tamara tried to follow Doctor Kerr's advice, progressively concentrating on every part of her body from her scalp to her toes. Her psychologist had told her time and time again that she needed to learn to sit with her feelings so she didn't run out and overindulge by drinking, eating or picking up men. Occasionally drugs had found their way into her life, but she never really had the money to indulge the habit. She'd preferred men, because even though loving words spoken in the heat of the moment were cheap, she felt good whenever someone liked her enough to sleep with her.

But she'd been getting better. She didn't do those things anymore. She was with Craig now. As she kept breathing deeply, her shoulders dropped and her head grew clearer. She stared at a spot on the carpet as she counted to twenty.

'I need another size up in this, please,' said the customer, thrusting the skirt through the change-room curtain.

'Certainly. I'll be right back,' Tamara said, feeling much calmer as she took the garment from the woman and headed back to the sale rack.

'Tamara?' said Angela, standing in her way. 'Please. I know you didn't leave on the best of terms, but I'd like it if you would come to the funeral.'

What Tamara heard was: 'Please come, please come, please come.' The Tam wanted to give her mum a comforting hug; the Tamperer wanted to shove her out the door. Push her out of her life forever. How dare Angela waltz back in and upset the fragile equilibrium Tamara had built around herself.

'Funeral . . .' The word faded on her lips.

'Yes, on Monday afternoon,' Angela said, picking up her handbag. 'Two-thirty at the church on Mundairy Road.' She looked at Tamara unhappily. 'Not that your father was one to believe in a higher power, but I feel we should give him a good Christian service. Someone needs to save him.' She put her hand out to touch Tamara, but pulled it back quickly. 'Think about it,' she said, before leaving the store.

Tamara put her hand to the part of her arm that Angela would have touched.

'Did you find one?' asked the customer, peering around the curtain and jolting Tamara back to her work.

'Uh, yes. One moment. Here we go.' She walked to the change rooms and handed it over.

segmentheaderFLEUR McDONALD

'Oh, this doesn't fit either,' the lady said without even trying it. She came out and went to her two friends. 'Come on, girls, it's after five. Time for a wine.' As the ladies left, Tamara stared after them, unseeing. Her feet, as if of their own accord, took her to the front of the store to watch Angela leave the shopping centre.

It's time to go home, Tamara's brain whispered, trying to counteract the barrage of emotional memories that had hit her as soon as her mother had walked in. The horrible sensation of never being loved, never being seen and never being understood made it hard for her to breathe. Her hands shook. As she methodically counted the till and balanced the day's takings, she knew she wasn't the same woman she'd been an hour ago.

Everything had changed.

So, how could she go home? It was just like she'd thought this morning: things with Craig were too good. She was becoming too normal. She'd known her insecurities would have to rear up again soon. And now, here they were.

Go home, said the Tam.

Home. Well, where the hell was that? the Tamperer replied.

You've got a home. With Craig. Go home to him, the Tam repeated.

No, no, no, the Tamperer whispered. *You're on a hiding to nothing, going back there.*

54

Chapter 6

Sliding her key into the lock, Lauren opened the front door, stepped inside and closed her eyes, enjoying the air-conditioning. As the sweat on her top lip dried, she revelled in the sensation for a couple more seconds before laughing quietly at herself. She was about to go for a run, so she'd soon be hot and sweaty again; no point in trying to stay cool now.

Throwing her handbag and briefcase down in the study, she pulled her shoes off and, hooking her fingers into the heels, took the stairs two at a time then jogged into her bedroom. She stripped off her clothes and dropped them into the laundry basket behind the bathroom door, then reached for her gym pants and top.

Passing the mirror, she caught a glimpse of herself and stopped. She knew that she'd lost a bit of weight—her waistbands were looser than they had been six months ago—but the dark rings under her eyes took her by surprise. This was what Stu had been talking about. What was happening to her? Why was she this tired? Why did she keep having that stupid nightmare?

And which of her biological parents was reflected in her own eyes?

The last question took her by surprise. They'd been doing that lately—popping up unexpectedly. But she knew that wasn't unusual. In her online research, she'd learned that questions about different physical and personality characteristics were common for adoptees.

Staring at herself a bit longer, she wondered if her birth mother was a redhead or if her biological father had the same blue eyes.

She heard the front door open and shut, then footsteps in the hall. 'Hi babe, I'm home!' Dean called up the stairs.

'Hey, yourself. I'm in the bedroom!' Lauren went out to meet him on the landing. After twenty-three years together, her stomach still flipped every time he smiled at her.

Of course, like all couples, they argued sometimes, but not about anything major. Not since the time when they hadn't spoken to each other for days after disagreeing about their house loan. Neither had been willing to give in, so for three nights they'd gone to bed with their backs turned to each other. Finally, Dean had made her talk and they'd moved past that. She hoped it would never happen again. Now, if one of them didn't agree with what the other was suggesting, they always made the time to sit down and talk it through.

'How was your day?' Dean murmured against her lips.

'Busy. Stressful.' She pulled him closer. 'I'm worried about a boy in my class. Yours?'

'Flat out, like you.' He pulled away and gazed down at her before putting his hand to her forehead and smoothing the worry lines away. 'You're going for a run, aren't you? Don't worry about the little boy now. Leave that at school. You can run all that stuff away. Are you tired?'

'I look that way, don't I?' She walked into the bedroom to pick up her iPod and headphones from the bedside table, along with the sun cream. She handed it to Dean. 'Can you rub some of this onto the back of my shoulders?'

'Getting towards the end of term, I guess.' He squeezed some cream into his hand. 'Turn around.' He paused. 'What's this?' he asked, running his finger over a small lump on the back of her arm.

'What is it?'

'Maybe a little pimple, but it's sort of brownish. I haven't noticed it before. When's your next dermatologist appointment?'

'In a few weeks. I'll see if they can squeeze me in earlier.'

'Sounds like a plan. The sun loves a red-haired, fair-skinned chick. All those sun kisses you've got across your nose.' He gently turned her face to him and kissed her freckles.

'Hmm, but I don't love the sun.'

As he smeared the cool cream onto her back, Lauren shivered slightly before his hands warmed her. She tightened the iPod holder around her upper arm and slipped the device into it, before holding out her hand for Dean to squeeze some more cream into her palm. She rubbed it into her face, checking in the mirror for white smudges. She was so careful about putting on sun cream; surely the pimple was nothing.

Dean set down the tube and wiped his hands before taking off his tie and shirt.

Their eyes met in the dressing-table mirror. Lauren raised her eyebrows.

'What?' he asked with half a smile.

'Nothing. Just perving.'

He laughed and tugged her towards him. 'And you're looking

good too. You know what lycra does to me,' he added, running his eyes over her body.

'Ew!' She crinkled her brow.

He sighed theatrically. 'But it will have to wait. I have dinner to make, you need to de-stress, and we have children due home at any moment. The joys of parenting.' He kissed her again.

'I know! Actually,' she glanced at the clock on her bedside table, 'Skye should have been home by now. I wonder where she is. Have you heard from her?'

'No, not today.' He gave her bum a gentle slap. 'Go on, off with you, before I lose control.'

'Is that a promise?' Lauren looked up at him coyly, enjoying hearing him laugh.

∽

For a while there was nothing but Lauren, the pavement, her breathing and her music. It pumped through the headphones, filling her mind, and she ran in time with the beat. Hey Violet was her band of choice at the moment—their highly energised music made her feel as though she could run forever.

Sometimes that was exactly what she wanted to do. If Skye had been particularly awful or there was a problem at school, her run gave her time when she didn't have to think about how she was going to fix the problem. The track she followed was the same as always: through the park, across the bridge, towards the freeway. It was just footstep after footstep, breath after breath, beat after beat . . .

Until she turned for home. It was then that worries crowded back in again.

Dirk was first. Poor little man. Her mind replayed the conversation that she'd had with Zoe at afternoon pickup.

'I'm concerned about Dirk,' Lauren had said, once they were in her office.

'Why?' asked Zoe, looking at her passively.

'He's very tired, and you keep telling me he's not well.'

'Oh, we've had that many colds go through our house in the past few months. Can't believe how unwell we've all been, and it's not even winter!'

Lauren leaned forward and spoke quietly. 'Zoe, the bruises on Dirk's wrists that I saw today—they're not caused by colds.'

Zoe gave a little laugh. 'Oh, them. One thing about Dirk is that he bruises so easily. He probably just bumped himself when he was playing outside.'

Lauren couldn't understand why Zoe was laughing about it. Surely there was a problem here? But she hadn't wanted to ask more without someone else present. So she'd nodded and smiled, telling Zoe that she was relieved to hear Dirk was going okay before steering the conversation into small talk.

Taking a ragged breath, Lauren wiped a hand over her forehead as she kept running on autopilot. Even if Zoe was telling the truth— and really, other than the bruises and the long sleeves, she didn't have reason to think otherwise—there had to be a reason why Dirk *did* bruise so easily. Didn't there?

And what about the ambulance? Of course, she should have cleared that up! Her apprehension about Dirk was sitting like a stone in her stomach.

From the back of her mind, she heard Fran snort. 'Kids are nothing but rough and tumble,' she would have said. 'You're making a mountain out of a molehill, Lauren. And be careful that Dirk doesn't take over your whole mind.'

Is that what Lauren was doing? Overreacting? Obsessing?

She remembered her words to Holly: 'I'm a professional.'

Yes, she thought, *let's keep it that way.*

The song changed and its drums brought Lauren into another memory—this song had started her argument with Skye on the weekend. The two of them had driven to Connie and George's for a visit, and Skye had been given control over the car music. Despite her preference for the loudest possible volume, the journey had started off well, both of them singing along and laughing whenever Lauren sang a wrong word.

Then 'I Can Feel It' started, and Skye changed as quickly as a cold front sweeping across the city. 'Don't pretend you know the words,' she sneered as Lauren started to tap the steering wheel and bounce in her seat.

'I'm not pretending,' Lauren said, looking at her daughter, not understanding. 'Why would I—?'

'This band is a bit too modern for you, Mother.' Skye's sarcasm put Lauren's teeth on edge.

'What's got into you?' she asked. 'We were just having fun.'

'Is *that* what you call it?' Skye turned away and stared out of the window.

Then Lauren snapped. 'Oh, for God's sake, Skye. Your behaviour is appalling. One minute you're lovely to have around, the next you're horrible. This isn't how your father and I raised you to be.' She turned to look at her daughter's profile, which was set in anger. 'Anyway, you might think I'm a dinosaur, but I'm not. I'll prove it, shall I? The song is "I Can Feel It" by Hey Violet.' Lauren started tapping her fingers again and singing along. 'Satisfied?'

From the corner of her eye, she saw Skye shift in her seat. Her face had darkened, resembling a thundercloud about to burst. Lauren had hoped to make her laugh, but she saw her daughter's lips form what looked like the words 'fuck you'.

'Sorry?' Lauren asked in a tight voice. 'I didn't catch that.'

'Nothing.' Skye crossed her arms and turned her back to Lauren.

A new song began to play. This time Lauren didn't know the track or the artist. Not another word was said during the drive to Connie and George's place, and by the time they arrived, Lauren was anxious for a talk with her mum.

'I don't know what to suggest,' Connie said as they wandered around the backyard, pointing out new agapanthus blooms. 'You were our only one. None of our friends had any major trouble with their teenagers.' Connie snipped a couple of summer roses to take back inside. 'Do you think she's taking drugs?'

A heavy feeling sat in Lauren's gut as the question penetrated her brain. Instantly, without thinking, she answered no. She scratched her arm in distress and felt the small pimple back there. Quickly she took her hand away—she didn't want to make it bleed on her white shirt.

'Can you be sure?' Connie asked. 'After all, the TV shows and newspapers all say the same thing: their behaviour changes. They become withdrawn and secretive, don't they? From what I see, that's all happening here.'

Lauren crossed her arms. 'She hasn't got any money, Mum. How could she buy drugs?'

Connie turned to Lauren and smiled reassuringly, and Lauren couldn't help but smile back. Connie was getting older—she was nearly eighty. Not able to imagine what she'd do when her mum and dad weren't around anymore, Lauren quickly put that thought from her mind. They were both active and spritely, so she shouldn't have even been thinking along those lines. They'd been her rock for forty-seven years.

After reading horror stories of adopted children being treated as second-class citizens, Lauren had often questioned what her life would have been like if she'd ended up with a different family.

Connie gave her arm a gentle squeeze. 'I'm not saying that she *is* on drugs. She's most likely being a normal, pain-in-the-neck teenager. You just need to keep loving her, but with boundaries in place. It's all you can do.'

How does Mum always know the right thing to say? Lauren thought now. *I never seem to. Look how I reacted to Skye that day.*

She slowed to a walk as her street came into view. Tonight she'd try to have a proper chat with Skye. She wished that, back in the car on the weekend, she hadn't reacted so quickly and sounded so irritated. She had to be patient with her daughter.

At her front gate, she pulled off her headphones, put her hands on the fence and stretched out her calf muscles. A few more cooldown exercises and she was ready for a shower. 'I'm back!' she called as the smell of dinner hit her from inside.

'I'm in the study, catching up on a couple of work things!' Dean called back.

'I'm off for a shower. Is Skye home?'

'Yeah, she's in her room.'

❧

Lauren tapped on Skye's bedroom door and waited for her to answer before opening it. 'Hi,' Skye said from her bed. She was stretched out, one earbud in, the other trailing over her shoulder. Her legs rested high on the wall.

'Comfortable?' Lauren asked. It didn't look that way.

'Yup.' Skye turned around and sat up.

Lauren noticed that she slid her iPhone under her leg as she did so. Was she hiding something? 'What have you got there?' Lauren pointed at the iPhone.

'Nothing, just my music,' Skye said protectively.

'How was your day?' Lauren tried again.

'Fine. Nothing different. What about yours?'

'It was okay. Very busy, you know—reports, keeping an eye on kids, talking to parents. I've got a lot of responsibilities this year.' She thought if she talked more, maybe Skye would too.

But her daughter just crossed her arms and flopped down on the bed.

What? Lauren wondered. *What did I do wrong there?*

Skye had completely shut down. Lauren could see it in her face. It was as though she'd been receiving a lecture for ten minutes and didn't care anymore—she wasn't going to listen. Why?

What Lauren wanted to do was sink down on Skye's bed and talk to her—really talk, not just exchange monosyllables. Ask her why she didn't want to open up. Ask what was bothering her. Tell her that her parents loved her more than life itself.

But Skye wasn't inviting that. Not at all.

Lauren remembered what it was like to be a teenager. All the mixed-up feelings and uncertainty. Being stuck halfway between childhood and adulthood. It was no man's land—a world swimming with emotion, passion, hatred. Every tiny feeling was exaggerated and intense.

If only she could tell Skye that she remembered. But no teenager could ever believe that their parents had been young before them, so Lauren just let her hand rest on Skye's upside-down head and hoped her gaze conveyed everything she wanted to get across to her daughter.

Then, as she left the room to have a shower, her thoughts returned to Dirk and his mother. She couldn't seem to help mulling it over. She'd need to do everything she could to protect that little boy. He was partly her responsibility.

'Hey Dad, what's goin' on?' Stu asked as he came through the kitchen door and slapped Dean on the shoulder. He smiled at Lauren, who was slicing a capsicum for a salad. 'Hi Mum. Mmm, something smells good.'

'Nothing special—just spaghetti and meatballs in tomato sauce,' Dean said, stirring the rich red mixture in the saucepan.

'How was your day, Mum?' Stu asked as he tried to grab a piece of cucumber she'd cut, but she knocked his hand away.

'Get away with you! Dinner's nearly ready. Great. And how was yours?'

Stu gave a detailed description of how a little girl he'd been teaching had had an 'accident' in the pool, and the powers that be had needed to 'shit, sorry, *shut* the pool down'. The laughter around the kitchen filled Lauren with happiness.

She looked at Dean, and they shared a secret smile. This is what she thought being a family was all about—being friends too. Now all they needed was for Skye to join them.

As if Lauren's thoughts had summoned her daughter, she heard a door slam and footsteps on the stairs. Stu made a frightened face and said, in an exaggerated whisper, 'She walks . . . Which beast will we face today?'

'Stu!' Dean growled at him just before Skye came in. 'Give it a rest.'

Skye threw herself into a chair at the table and slumped forward, her head resting on her arms, a pout on her face. 'What's for tea?'

'Hi family, it's good to see you. How are you?' Stu said.

Skye fixed him with a hard stare.

'Spaghetti and meatballs,' Dean said. 'Are you hungry?'

Silence filled the room, and it became quite clear that Skye wasn't going to respond. Stu exhaled and got up from the table with a grumpy sigh.

Lauren glanced over from the bench where she was still preparing the salad.

'Skye?' Dean asked.

'What?'

'It would be nice if you could answer my question.'

'Like any normal person,' Stu put in.

'Get stuffed, Golden Boy.'

Lauren quickly raised her hands and moved between them. 'Steady on, kids. You're at each other's throats, and you haven't been in the same room for five seconds. At least try to last a minute, please!' God, this was the last thing she needed tonight—bickering between the kids. All she wanted was to have a nice meal with her family, then watch TV and go to bed. She hoped she'd be able to forget her anxiety about Dirk when she was asleep. Maybe it was making her more snappy than usual.

She looked at Skye. 'How about you answer the question?' she said evenly.

Skye shrugged. 'Yeah, I'm a bit hungry, okay?'

'Now that wasn't so hard, was it?' Dean said.

Lauren put her hands on her hips. 'If you weren't fourteen, I'd send you to bed without any dinner. Really, Skye, you could be civil.'

After dinner, when Skye went back to her room and lay on her bed, she wondered if she'd seemed any different to her family. Could they tell what she'd been doing with Billy? She was sure her mum had looked at her strangely as everyone had sat down to eat. What would her mum do if she did, in fact, actually know? More to the point, what would her dad do?

And why had her mum come into her room earlier? That had just been weird. Usually she was too busy rushing here, there and everywhere to do more than put her head in the door and say hello. Why had she stopped to talk today? Especially considering that she then rambled on about how busy and responsible she was. Skye didn't care: she already knew that. Meanwhile, her mum might have guessed that something had changed, but really she had no clue.

A couple of hours ago, Billy had skipped basketball training so he could pick her up behind the school. He'd loosened his tie and untucked his shirt. To Skye, he looked like the ultimate Bad Boy. A Bad Boy who liked *her*—a teacher's daughter!

Billy's best mate, Tristen, had winked at her this afternoon, when they'd passed each other in the hallway between classes. Skye hadn't understood why. Was Tristen saying that he knew what was going on between Billy and Skye, or was he flirting with her? She'd thought about asking Billy, but he was never keen to talk about his mates or his life outside the time he spent with her—he just wanted to kiss.

Sometimes that annoyed Skye. She wanted to talk about school gossip and where the two of them would be in a couple of years. She wanted to joke about teachers and schoolwork. But aside from the way Billy kept asking her to hide their relationship, she did most of the talking and he did most of the stroking.

Tonight, he'd dropped her off at the bus stop closest to her house. He would have taken her right to her front gate, but he thought it was too dangerous. 'Your mum and dad might be home, and they can't see us. I'd get into trouble.'

'I can make my own decisions,' she said. 'Mum and Dad won't stop me.'

Billy put his hands on her face and stared straight into her eyes. 'Listen to me. You can't say anything to *anyone*. Promise me.'

Grudgingly, she promised. But why should she have to? Hadn't he told Tristen? An insistent little voice whispered that if Billy really loved her, he wouldn't mind being seen with her. She still had a horrible, nagging feeling that she wasn't 'cool' enough for his mates and that this was all some kind of joke.

But, no, it couldn't be—Billy loved her. He'd told her so. And she *loved* him. She needed to tell those little utterings in her head to shut up.

When Adele had made a flippant comment about Billy and a heap of others in his group being 'fuckboys', it had taken everything in Skye's power not to say anything. *He isn't!* she wanted to scream. *You don't know the real him!*

'I heard,' Adele had leaned over and whispered, 'Billy's mate, Dicko, made it with two tarts last weekend. As if any girl would go near that lot.'

Skye had wanted to put her hands over her ears. But she hadn't, and she was very proud of her self-control. That made her more mature than the others. She was mature enough for Billy, wasn't she? Once she'd proven it to him, he would finally agree that she could tell her friends.

Lying on her bed, she remembered the way he'd run his hands over her neck and shoulders and then across her breasts. She hadn't wanted to tell him that she felt funny about that—all excited and scared and apprehensive and guilty. So, instead, she'd taken deep, shuddering breaths and concentrated on how it felt.

She'd read about sex in all her gran's secret Mills & Boon novels. One day, when the two of them had been searching for a piece of family history in her grandparents' shed, Skye had opened a box full of thin, small books. The covers featured ladies in beautiful dresses, swooning into the arms of handsome men. 'Don't tell your grandfather,' Gran had whispered. 'These are my little secret—my escape from real life.' She held a gnarled finger to her lips.

After that, whenever they'd visited Gran and Gramps in Margaret River, Skye had snuck down to the shed and slipped a couple of books into her backpack, reading them furtively back at home. Even at fourteen, she knew that Mills & Boon romances never happened in 'real life'. But it was fun to read the graphic parts and learn.

Skye had also watched a bit of porn on her iPhone. She'd googled it when nobody had been in the house, because she was sure her mum would have got that self-righteous look on her face if she'd walked in. The one she always got when Skye did something she didn't approve of—the one she rarely used on Stu.

Anyway, those porn videos were a bit yucky. Skye couldn't imagine how that kind of sex would feel nice, but the women's moans made her think it must be okay. Watching it had given her a funny feeling between her legs. When she touched herself, she couldn't believe the pleasure that rippled through her whole body. But she was sure it would be a hundred times better when she and Billy did it together.

Tonight they'd come very close. They'd parked under a deep grove of trees in the abandoned quarry. Skye was so nervous; she pressed herself against the door of the passenger seat. 'Hey, I won't hurt you,' Billy said. 'I love you.'

It was on the tip of her tongue to say that she was scared, but she didn't. She wanted him to think that she was a woman of the world, one who could match his seventeen years, even at fourteen.

Billy was the perfect gentleman. He held the back-seat door open for her as she climbed in and looked up at him, all muscled and ripped in his school shirt. His shaggy brown hair made him seem even sexier. His top buttons were undone, his tie pulled open at the neck. She wanted to reach up and grab it, then pull him in, on top of her. Feel him on top of her . . .

But she didn't. She was too nervous.

He climbed in behind her and started to kiss her, his tongue poking lazily in and out of her mouth. Somehow, in a matter of seconds, he managed to get her school blouse unbuttoned and her bra off. His mouth sought her nipple, and she groaned like the women in the porn videos. She could feel him against her leg: he was hard.

A voice whispered in the back of her mind: *This is scary.* She shivered, even though she was so hot. *So* hot. The plastic seat was sticking to her bare back. Billy's breath was warm and loud in her ear as he tried to get her skirt up.

Then his mobile phone vibrated through the pocket of his shorts against her thigh. The fog of desire lifted. 'Shit,' he muttered and, for some reason, Skye laughed—maybe from relief. Billy's face was red, his eyes unfocused. 'Ignore it.'

She struggled to pull herself from under him. 'It might be important.'

'Not as important as you.' He leaned forward to grab her nipple between his fingers again. A thrill ran through her, but the phone continued to ring. She pulled away. Annoyed, Billy sat up. He glanced at the phone, then took her home.

On her bed now, Skye was filled with regret. She'd wanted to have sex with Billy more than anything in the world. As she trailed her fingers over her breasts and lingered on her nipples, where Billy's mouth had been, she let out a frustrated sigh.

She stuck in her earbuds and turned the volume up loud enough that she could disappear into the words and the pulsating beat. If she put it on her docking station, her mum would appear in two seconds flat, yelling at her to turn it down.

Skye didn't want to see her mother. Didn't want to see the disappointment on her face whenever she looked at her daughter.

Chapter 7

After she left work, Tamara had picked up a six-pack from the bottle shop and then driven around aimlessly, unable to focus on anything but memories and the voices in her head. She wasn't even sure how she'd ended up back here on Whitfield Street; she hadn't been by here in years.

Leaning against her car, she stared at the house where she'd spent such an important part of her life. Was it as frightening in real life as her memory had made it? Would it seem different now that her dad had gone?

The lights were out in the house—it was after ten. In the soft glow from the moon, the front garden looked the same as she remembered it. An ugly mission-brown brick fence bordered the footpath, with a white iron gate hanging in the middle. Tamara bet that it still squeaked, and her fingers tingled to push it open and find out. Geraniums, lavender and other hardy plants grew in garden beds around the edge of the fence. Looking at the brown buffalo grass lawn, she remembered how scratchy and itchy it had made her when she was a child.

Now what was making her itch was the swarm of mozzies that were keeping her company on this hot summer night.

Her phone vibrated against her thigh, but she didn't bother looking. It would be Craig, wondering where she was. She was late—so, so late.

Even though the sun had long slipped below the horizon, the pavement had held its warmth, making Tamara sweat. It reminded her of a summer's day when she'd been about six. She had longed to dive into the local pool, but Evan thought going there was a waste of money. So, finding shade under the black-spotted hibiscus bush, Tamara had sat with the hose trickling onto the soil. She remembered how beautiful the smell of the moisture on the dry grass had been, and how her legs had stretched onto the wet part of the lawn. That evening she'd been covered in a red rash, so her mum had smeared cream on her angry skin. 'You were a bit silly,' she'd told Tamara. 'Who sits on the grass? That's what chairs are for.'

Tonight, Tamara took another sip from the bottle of beer she'd brought with her, the refreshing liquid slipping easily down her throat. She stretched towards the front gate and her fingertips touched the cold metal. When she gave it a little shove, it swung open, letting out a long, low creak. Just as she'd imagined.

The dog next door started to bark, and Tamara jumped, her eyes flicking towards the front window. Angela was probably sleeping right behind it, in the master bedroom. The window stayed black. Tamara backed away, her heart beating fast.

'The body always remembers,' Doctor Kerr had told her during one session. 'You might forget, block it out, but your body will always remember.'

Right now, both her mind and her body were remembering just fine.

A vivid scene flashed before her eyes as though she was watching a movie. Her dad was pushing her on the bike she'd been given for Christmas. She was about six, wearing the pink skirt and white shirt, presents from her grandparents. Those brand-new clothes had been her favourites, because most of her clothes and toys were hand-me-downs from people Angela worked with or from op-shops; Evan said it was such a waste paying hard-earned money for new clothes and toys, which was why her bike was a bit rusty.

Tamara recalled how an unexpected shove on her bike from Evan had sent her careering onto the quiet street. She teetered on the edge before toppling over, the hot bitumen scraping the side of her knee and tearing her skirt. Tears streamed down her cheeks. 'Look what you've done to your new clothes,' her dad hissed. 'You can't wear them now!' He gave her a stinging slap on her shoulder. 'Angela, come and fix up your daughter!' he yelled. In comparison, her mum's hands were soft and caring as they hustled her inside, then cleaned and bandaged her wound before removing her clothes and taking them away forever.

'Tamara!' She heard Angela's shrill voice in her head as another memory started to surface.

On the front lawn, right here, in front of where she stood now. She'd been sixteen and had just arrived home from school, thinking of a boy with blond curly hair and brown eyes, and how he made her feel when he touched her down there.

'Your father wants to see you,' Angela had snapped.

'What for?' she asked, her defiance strong and loud.

'He'll tell you,' Angela replied, trying to hurry Tamara inside.

A smile crossed Tamara's face now as she remembered dawdling as slowly as she could to annoy them both.

Her dad had been sitting at the head of the kitchen table, her school reports laid out in front of him. 'I've had a phone call from the school,' he said, his face solemn. 'Want to tell me where you were today?'

Looking at him, Tamara weighed up her options. It was never a good sign when he started off quietly.

'Tamara?' Evan prompted.

'I didn't feel well,' she lied, looking at her feet. Subdued and demure worked best with her dad. She wanted to look him in the eye and tell him that she'd been at a boy's house and she didn't care about school.

'So, where did you go?'

'To the footy oval. I lay under the trees out there.'

'I see.' He linked his fingers together and placed them in front of him. 'You didn't go to the school nurse?'

'Nah. She always just gives you Panadol and tells you to go back to class.'

'I see,' he repeated.

'Can I go now? I've got homework.' She dared to look up, then wished she hadn't. He'd gone red with anger.

'Homework? Good, good.' He ran a hand over his balding head. Suddenly, he banged his hand down on the table, rattling the salt-and-pepper shakers. 'Homework, you say? Not sure I believe you. Unless you picked up your homework from Macca's at lunchtime?'

Remembering this scene as she stood outside her old home, Tamara instinctively raised her hands to ward off the blow that she'd expected. But it never came. Instead, her dad gripped her arm tightly and pulled her to the front door.

'Evan, no!' Angela lunged at him, trying to tug Tamara's arm from his grip.

He ignored her. 'It's time you looked after yourself,' he sneered. 'We've done it for long enough. Go on. Get out.' He shoved Tamara outside.

Shivering and sobbing, she heard a thud from inside the house, then a thin wail. The only other noise was the rushing traffic on the freeway a few streets away.

Where would she go? Could she ever come back?

She'd answered that question herself: she hadn't wanted to.

Now, twenty-seven years later, she was standing outside the same house, asking herself the same question.

Waking slowly from a deep sleep in the back seat of her car, Tamara couldn't work out where she was or what that noise was. Dimly she realised that it was her phone—and then everything that had happened the day before came flooding back.

Ignoring the phone, she rubbed her face and looked at her watch. 6.30 am. She struggled to sit up, groaning as her back protested. Reaching up to wipe some of the condensation from the rear window, she saw that the sky was a deep, clear blue. It looked as though it was going to be hot again.

He must be out of his mind with worry, said the Tam.

Why do you think he'd care? asked the Tamperer. *You're unlovable, remember?*

Don't listen to her, the Tam said. *He loves you.*

'Stop! Just stop!'

Tamara started to make a plan. First she needed to feel human.

Her toothbrush and toothpaste were in the middle console—in case of emergency, she always kept toiletry and makeup bags in her car, along with a change of underwear and work clothes. Second, she needed to find a shelter where she could have a shower. There used to be one a couple of suburbs over; she'd used it a long time ago. It was a place where no one would ask any questions and she'd be able to get ready for work before she called Craig. Hopefully it would still be operating.

Sipping from her half-full water bottle, she took two Panadol to dull her headache, then used the rest to wash her face and brush her teeth.

Putting her car into gear, she made her way to a fast food drive-through and ordered two large coffees and a hash brown. Grease would be good. Tamara didn't need to eat at the shelter—she had a good job and savings. She just couldn't go home to Craig yet.

She pulled up outside the shelter, relieved that it was still open, but stayed in the car to eat her hash brown and drink one coffee. She took the other one inside with her, then asked the woman at the front desk if she could have a shower.

'Of course. Need a meal?' the woman replied with a broad, kind smile.

'No, thanks. Just a wash.'

'No worries. Down the hall. Towels are on the trolley as you go past.'

Tamara finished her coffee and then headed towards the showers, clutching at her toiletry bag and work clothes, her eyes glued to the floor. From upstairs she could hear the murmurs of women who'd slept there overnight. Pain pierced her heart as she heard the wail of a newborn baby. 'It's alright, my lovely little one,' a gentle voice said. 'We're safe here.'

Tamara snatched a towel from the trolley and yanked open the bathroom door. She set out her toiletries neatly, then in seconds flat she stood underneath the steaming water, enjoying the sensation of it drumming on her head. Breathing deeply again, she practised the mindfulness exercises Doctor Kerr had taught her and, before long, she felt much calmer. As she soaped herself, she visualised washing away her negative thoughts, so she was clean and new.

After leaving a fifty-dollar donation at the front counter, Tamara hurried to her car. Even though Angelic Threads didn't open until nine, she always arrived early. Today, she couldn't wait to get there: work would keep her mind busy. She was bound to be flat-out because the sale was still on and she had new clothes to unpack.

In the car, she pulled out her phone. Twenty-four missed calls and voice messages—all from Craig. Twenty text messages. He must be going out of his mind. In his position, she would have been too.

Her fingers hovered above the keyboard, trying to work out what to type.

'Hey, sorry, I . . .'

No, that wouldn't work.

She tried again. 'Sorry about last night. Something came up.'

Something came up? Fuck. That was an understatement if ever there was one.

'Dear Craig,' she finally typed. 'Sorry I didn't come home. Something major happened. I'm not sure I can do this anymore. Please don't contact me. I'll contact you.' She pressed 'send', put the phone on silent and slid it into her bag.

There was still one major thing to take care of—she had to decide if she was going to her dad's funeral.

Something her mum had said when she'd left the shop kept coming to the front of Tamara's mind: 'Someone needs to save him.' The words had made Tamara stop and reflect. Standing in front of her old house, she'd realised that Angela had been the one protecting her from Evan, although it had rarely felt like that at the time.

That last memory of Angela trying to stop Evan had pushed Tamara to this realisation. She'd thought of her mum's softly spoken words when Evan wasn't home; the gentle hands fixing up the usual scrapes and bruises. And the very faded memory of a hand on her forehead at night, when she was half-asleep.

Was she still craving the mother she never felt she had?

Of course she was.

But Angela isn't a real mother, the Tamperer whispered.

Tamara entered the shop through the back door. It was only 8 am, but the phone was ringing. 'I bet it's head office in Melbourne, forgetting we're three hours behind, *again*,' she muttered to herself, before ripping the phone from its cradle.

'Good morning, Angelic Threads, Tam speaking,' she snapped. Although the person on the other end couldn't see her frown, they'd get the impression from her tone that this wasn't the best time to be calling.

'It's only me,' Craig said, his voice hoarse.

Clenching her fists, Tamara closed her eyes and took a few deep breaths. 'Why are you calling here?' The anger left her and she sagged against the wall.

'I wanted to know how you were, where you slept last night, what you're wearing today, and when you want to come home.

I care about you so much, and I miss you.' Craig sounded as though he'd rehearsed this.

'I've told you—' Tamara began.

'No, you haven't. You haven't told me anything other than you can't do this anymore. What the hell has happened for things to go so wrong so suddenly? You were happy yesterday morning when I dropped you at the park. Then you just never came home, without a word. I didn't get a say in it. *I love you.*' His voice broke a little.

Words were cheap, as she'd discovered during her forty-three years, and people rarely kept their promises, but she couldn't help allowing herself the ghost of a smile.

She and Craig had met at the Australia Day fireworks through a distant mutual friend. The heavy-set concreter, with his long ponytail, beard and tatts, had caught her eye, but back then she didn't admit to it. No, she preferred to keep her distance and date guys who weren't going to stay for long. No emotional attachment that way.

Craig had slowly won her over by turning up when she least expected him to, offering lunch dates; he seemed to know she was gun shy and lunch was much less threatening than dinner. Over the next year, they'd clicked.

She still hadn't really wanted to move in with him, preferring to keep her independence. He'd been so convincing that she'd finally agreed. One month ago, they'd started living together. It had come as a pleasant surprise that despite Craig's rough appearance, he was almost as neat and tidy as she was in the house.

Of course she'd still had doubts sometimes. But she'd always managed to pull herself together and use all the techniques that Doctor Kerr had taught her. She'd locked those horrible emotions away in a box where they belonged.

Now, they'd all spilled out. Everything had gone wrong.

He's being persistent. That counts for something, the Tam told her sternly. *Usually they up and go without another word. It's good he's still trying.*

The Tamperer spoke loudly over the top. *Don't be stupid. He'll be just like everyone else. You can't trust him to be there. And why should he put up with you? If he doesn't leave this time, he will eventually. Just like your father, just like . . .*

Tamara stopped and thought about Matt, the one bloke she'd lived with before Craig. He'd hit her more than enough times for her to leave, but she hadn't. She'd stayed because, in the end, it was easier to stay than to start out again. And she'd craved those times when Matt had told her that he loved her, needed her; that his life wouldn't be complete without her. The honeymoon periods would last for a few weeks—then the abuse would start again. But she'd lived for those honeymoons.

Without warning, Matt had thrown her out and replaced her with another woman. Then and there, Tamara had promised herself that she'd never, ever love another man. Never, ever rely on another man. And, most importantly, never, ever let another man into her life.

She'd broken all of her promises when she'd moved in with Craig. *God knows what I was thinking.*

'I'm sorry.' She spoke more quietly than she'd intended. What she'd wanted to do was yell at him. Let all of her stuffed-up emotions spill out for him to see. Then he might be able to understand why she was doing this. 'I'm sorry,' she repeated, 'but you don't get a say. It's my life. I'll run it the way I see fit.'

'I don't even know what's started this.'

'My mother came to see me in the shop yesterday.'

'Your mother? I don't understand. You told me you haven't spoken in years.'

'Yes, that's right.'

After a brief silence, Craig cleared his throat. 'Tam, baby, please. Please come home.' His voice cracked on the last word.

Craig wasn't the type to beg. Yeah, he was as soft as a marshmallow on the inside and had always been tender and loving to her. But he'd never begged before. It was completely out of character for him: he was a strong, silent type who gave the impression to the outside world that he didn't care about much. His words sent waves of emotion through her—how lovely it was to be wanted.

She waivered . . . just for a moment, but fear of rejection overwhelmed every other feeling. She didn't know what to tell him. She'd need to pick up her things, but she wasn't ready to go back to the house, to see him again. Staying strong and not changing her mind were easy when she didn't have to see him.

'I'm sorry,' she said again.

She hung up the phone and closed her eyes, surprised by the prickle in her nose. Why would she even contemplate crying over a man?

Get yourself together, the Tamperer told her.

He might really love you, the Tam said. *He might help you. You know, he didn't have the easiest childhood either.*

At least his parents loved him, said the Tamperer. *Your own parents kicked you out, and then Matt replaced you. You're fucked up, and Craig deserves better.*

Her mind replayed the night when she'd been thrown out of her house. The fierce hatred in her dad's voice, the rage in his eyes, and the way his hands had made those sharp, threatening movements.

All of this coming after the calmness he'd portrayed when she'd first come home. That had been Evan through and through: a quiet white-hot anger, then pure fury.

Shit, what time is it? Her eyes flicked to the clock on her office wall: 8.24.

She did a quick breathing exercise, then made a coffee and walked out into the dimly lit shop. She loved being in here before it opened, when everything was neat and tidy, in order and clean. The soft cotton and linen shirts appealed to her, with their crisp, clean lines and subtle colours, as did the plain skirts and pants. Anything with a classic look. She would prefer to return the bright colours, lace tops and ripped pants to the warehouse, but they were popular with the teenage girls.

That thought made her wonder what had happened with Adele and Skye. Why hadn't they come into the shop after school? Still it was so lucky they hadn't been there to watch her learn of her father's death.

Speaking of which . . . Tamara forced herself away from the clothes racks and went back to the counter to write a list of the pros and cons for going to Evan's funeral. But when she stared at the empty page, she realised it represented exactly how she was feeling about his loss. She had no feelings, one way or the other.

What did she feel about Angela, though?

If Tamara was fair, even though her mum had done a terrible job of protecting her from Evan, Angela hadn't been cruel.

Another memory surfaced: Tamara's ninth birthday. No one had remembered it. As she walked out of school that afternoon, trying not to cry, she heard her mum calling her name. Angela was sitting inside her car at the gate, wearing a wide smile. She waved Tamara towards her and told her to hop in. They drove to a little café on the Swan River, where they ate ice-cream and drank iced chocolate.

At the end of their private party, Angela pulled out a present and pushed it across the table.

'For me?' Tamara asked, disbelieving.

The small square-shaped box was wrapped in pink paper and tied with a pink bow. It was like nothing Tamara had ever seen.

'You'll have to hide it, Tam,' her mum said, without smiling. 'Just like you can't tell him we've had our own little celebration. Everything about today is our secret, okay?' Reaching across the table, Angela gripped her hand so tightly that her fingers left an imprint.

Tamara held her breath as she pulled off the wrapping paper and opened the red velvet box. Inside lay a silver necklace with a heart charm. Transfixed, Tamara picked it up and let the coolness of the chain run through her fingers.

Then she saw it—her name engraved on the heart.

Standing beside the register in her store, Tamara wondered how she could have forgotten for so long. *What happened to that necklace?* Maybe she'd hocked it. Ah, no, that wasn't right. She'd dropped it in a rubbish bin, on the street, as she walked along aimlessly, trying to work out where she would sleep that night.

Her dad hadn't cared. Her mum hadn't followed her.

But now Angela was back in her life, extending an olive branch. Doctor Kerr would probably have told Tamara that this was an opportunity to get closure. Going to her dad's funeral might help with that, although it would be tough.

She'd also need to get her things from Craig's place and talk to him—help him to understand why they needed to break up. She imagined him sitting in the lounge room by himself, Whiskey at his feet, staring into space. He'd done that when his mother had died. Not moving, not talking, not drinking. Sitting and staring.

Slowly, Tamara put down the pen and walked towards the front of the shop, where a grey skirt hung on a mannequin. Unclipping it, she took it off and checked the size. It would fit. And a top? She knew every piece of clothing within the four walls of the shop. There was a deep purple cross-over blouse on the sale rack. Paired with the grey skirt, it would be fine to wear to a funeral.

Chapter 8

At Dean's insistence, Lauren had rung her dermatologist's clinic first thing in the morning. She'd asked for an appointment as soon as possible, and the receptionist had told her that there had been a cancellation at ten: 'Can you pop in then, love? Otherwise you might need to wait another month for your regular appointment.' Lauren had checked with Hamilton, who'd given her the go-ahead, and now here she was at the clinic.

'I can't believe it's been five months since our last appointment,' Michelle said as she led Lauren down the brightly lit passageway towards her office. 'Next minute it will be Christmas again!'

'I hope not,' Lauren said. 'I've only just recovered from the last one.'

She'd been seeing Michelle for more than ten years and they had a professional relationship, but it was hard not to know a little of each other's personal lives given they had been patient and doctor for so long.

Michelle got out her magnifier. 'So, why did you call to make an earlier appointment? I'm guessing you've got a concern.'

'Oh, it's probably nothing. Dean wants you to check a pimple on the back of my right arm.'

'Okay, slip your shirt off and put your arms up—you know the drill.'

With gentle hands, Michelle ran the magnified lens over Lauren's skin. Wanting to distract herself while Michelle concentrated in silence, Lauren looked around the room. Nothing had changed much since her last visit—the photos of Michelle's husband and kids sat in the same spot on the desk, and bookshelves still lined the far wall. The fake green plant sat in the same corner.

'How long have you had this for?' Michelle asked.

'I couldn't tell you. I was vaguely aware of it for a week or so, but didn't take much notice until Dean pointed it out.' Lauren paused. 'What is it?'

There was another silence while she felt Michelle's fingertips holding the top of her arm. 'Um, I'll have to wait for the pathology report before I can tell you anything. With your history—you know, all the basal cell carcinomas I've removed—I don't want to do a biopsy. I'll just cut it out. I can do it now, if you've got time?'

'Yeah, sure.'

'Jump up onto the bed and lie on your side. I'll give you a local. I don't think you'll even need stitches with this.'

Up on the bed, Lauren felt the prick of the needle and tried hard not to jump. Needles didn't bother her the way they did some people, but they always stung a little. Funny, she thought, Dean hated needles—so much so that he avoided going to the doctor in case he needed a blood test—but the kids were all like her.

'How's your family history research coming along?' Michelle asked as she bent over Lauren's arm, her voice muffled behind the mask and her gloved fingers sticky against Lauren's skin.

'Good. I've traced Dean's family back to the early 1800s—it's so interesting! His great-great-great grandfather was distantly related to the Duke of Wellington. I'm still working on Dad's side: I'm missing a few pieces of the puzzle there.'

'Can you feel that?'

A small amount of pressure on her arm, but no pain.

'Nope.'

There was a rustle of Michelle's gown and a clink of instruments on the tray. 'How interesting to hear you call it a puzzle. I guess that's exactly what it is.'

'Absolutely, I'm always looking for the missing pieces.'

'And what about your birth family?'

Lauren took a deep breath. 'I still can't get past the fact that it's not fair to search for my biological parents while my mum and dad are alive. It probably sounds strange—'

'Not at all. They brought you up. I'd imagine it might seem ungrateful if you try to find the woman who gave birth to you, even though she didn't raise you.'

'That's exactly it,' Lauren said. She focused on the plastic plant in the corner as the pressure increased. She'd had this done many times before, so she knew what to expect, but it still didn't feel great.

'Have you talked to them about it, though? Maybe there's no need to worry,' said Michelle.

Lauren paused, not sure how to word her answer. 'I haven't,' she confessed. 'I don't want to hurt them. They're old. It seems better to wait until . . .' Her voice faded as she realised that if she did that, there was a chance her birth mother would be dead too.

She tried to put herself in Connie's position. She'd loved and raised Lauren from the moment they'd brought her home. She'd been the one who cleaned up Lauren's vomit, wiped her bum, been at prize night and everything in between. Could she understand Lauren's need to learn where she'd come from?

'You know, it's not about getting a new mum,' Lauren finally said as Michelle put on the bandage. 'It's about finding out who made me. My genes and that sort of thing. Some days the need to find her is overwhelming, and on others it's not there at all. That's probably the main reason I haven't bothered Mum and Dad with it yet. Well, that and disrupting everyone's lives. Such an upheaval.'

'I can only imagine. Have you thought about explaining it in those words?'

'No,' Lauren said quietly. 'It's really only occurred to me right now that this is the reason I need to meet her. If she's still alive. Maybe she has recurring skin cancers too.'

'Well, have you wondered what you'd do if you found out that she was dead? How would you feel to have a name and a family history, but not a person to talk to? You can sit up now.'

Lauren swung her body around and sat up. 'I've gone over it in my head a million times, and I can't give you an answer.'

Michelle gave her a reassuring nod, then put the sample into a bottle and labelled it. 'I'll send this off now, and we'll get the results in a couple of days. Keep your arm dry for the next forty-eight hours, then you can remove the dressing. I'll call you with the results.'

'Thanks so much, Michelle.'

Michelle smiled. 'Take care, Lauren. It was good to see you. I hope you can find a way to work through everything.'

When Lauren walked into the kindy classroom just after 11.30 am, the children were absorbed in tracing dotted letters. The first thing she noticed was Dirk's absence. 'Was there a phone call or note?' she asked Joy.

'Haven't heard a word. And we can't ring, can we?'

'Not on the first day. If he's away for a week without us hearing anything, I could make a phone call and ask what's going on.' Lauren shrugged, trying to ignore her worry. 'Other than that, there's not much else we can do.'

❧

During lunchbreak, Lauren flopped into a comfy chair in the staff-room, pulled out her phone and checked her messages. 'Loved last night, babe!' Dean had texted two hours ago. She laughed to herself.

From across the room, a harassed-looking teacher called out to her, 'Would you mind doing my yard duty in the quadrangle? I need to tutor one of my Year Twelves before an assessment next week.'

'Sure, no worries.' Lauren got up and stretched, then tucked her arms back in quickly as the bandage pulled her skin. Fishing around in her handbag, she found an apple and took it out to eat in the sunshine.

As she walked to the quadrangle, Lauren realised that this would be a good opportunity for her to check on Skye. She hadn't seen her this morning before she'd left for school, which was uncharacteristic. Maybe Skye was hanging around with a different group—that would explain her strange behaviour lately. More than likely, though, Skye's group would be sitting together as usual, all staring at their phones. Probably texting each other instead of talking face to face.

Lauren had to walk to the back of the quadrangle to find Skye's group. They were leaning against the school fence, half hidden by a hedge. If Lauren hadn't been looking for them, she would probably have missed the group. What were they doing all the way out there? How strange—they usually hung around the pine tree near the side entrance. Then she realised that Skye wasn't with them. Now that was even stranger, although maybe her daughter had just gone to the toilet.

She'd have loved to go over and chat, but they were probably like Skye, not wanting to be spoken to by adults—especially a teacher. These girls were so different to the kindy kids, who would seek attention from Lauren and Joy at every opportunity. Earlier in the year, Dirk had always wanted to show them his bugs. Every recess he'd found slaters or ants and brought them back to the classroom, a look of pleasure on his face. Lauren had joked that he might become an entomologist when he grew up.

For about the thirtieth time, she wondered why he was away. Did it have anything to do with her speaking with Zoe the day before? She hoped not.

Blinking, she looked back at the group of girls. Adele straightened her shoulders and flicked her hair as if trying to get someone's attention—a boy's, perhaps. It didn't seem possible that they were all fourteen already. Surely it had only been a few short years since their mothers had held them as babies for the first time. Now here they were on the cusp of adulthood. They had the bodies of women, but not the maturity to handle them.

A little pang of love formed in Lauren's chest. They were good kids with the world at their feet. They were smart and growing up in a time that celebrated rather than denigrated women. She hoped they'd all succeed in whatever they chose to do.

One girl dug into her bag and held up an item of clothing. From where Lauren was, it looked like a t-shirt. The girl showed it off, holding it against her body before placing it on the ground. Another item came from her bag, and then another.

Jasmine grabbed a light-blue shirt from the pile. Looking around, she slipped off her school shirt and put it on, testing to see if it fitted her properly. A bout of laughter erupted from near the hedge, and Lauren saw Jasmine, still wearing the non-uniform top, standing up and dancing in time to silent music. A few moments later, she flopped back onto the ground with a grin while the other girls cheered.

God knows what they're doing, Lauren thought.

Lunchbreaks had certainly changed since she'd first started teaching. Fran had always said that the way to keep kids out of mischief was to occupy them with swings and slippery dips and games. But that was for kindy and primary children: teenagers were a different breed. Especially this generation, who loved their smartphones and talked more through social media than they did to one another.

Lauren had spoken to Skye more than once about the dangers of Facebook and Twitter. Then, a few weeks ago, Dean had told her about two newer social media sites, Instagram and Snapchat, which allowed you to send photos that were automatically deleted ten seconds after they'd been opened. It sounded awful. When Lauren and Dean had asked Skye about it, she'd denied having the app on her phone. And because Skye kept her phone password-protected and within easy reach at all times, even when she was sleeping, there was no way of checking. Of course, Skye had brushed off their concerns with the innocent enthusiasm of a teenager: 'It'll never happen to me.'

Watching Skye's friends, Lauren hoped that it wouldn't happen to any of them.

She heard someone calling her name and turned around. Joy was walking towards her, holding out a message slip. 'Zoe just rang to explain that Dirk's sick.'

'Oh, great, thanks. But I'm not sure that makes me feel any better.'

'No, me neither,' said Joy. 'Listen, I've got to go set up the easels again, but let's talk more later.' When Lauren nodded, she hurried off.

Glancing back at the girls, Lauren noticed Skye running across the grass to meet them. *God!* She'd forgotten she was even looking for Skye; Dirk had taken over again. Lauren focused on her daughter now. She was red-faced and her hair was untidy, and she greeted Adele and the others with an embarrassed wave.

'Where have you been?' Lauren heard Adele call out. Skye answered, but Lauren only heard Adele's response: a high, disbelieving pitch. Had Skye just done something against the rules?

The bell rang. *Damn*. She had to get back to the classroom.

'Oh. My. God!' squealed Adele as she looked at the silver stud at the top of Skye's ear. 'You didn't? Oh, wow, your mum's going to kill you.'

Skye reached up to touch it. 'She won't notice. Too busy.'

Last night, Billy had surprised her by calling around midnight and saying a lot of sexy things. They'd talked about piercings, and he'd said that studs in the top of the ear were really wild. His last girlfriend had one. 'Makes you look like you don't give a fuck about society. Rebellious. That's really attractive,' he'd whispered into Skye's ear, his deep voice sending shockwaves of desire through her.

She hadn't slept much after that, and she'd got up early, packing a change of casual clothes and racing out the door without seeing anyone. Just before her final morning class had ended, Skye had asked to go to the toilet. With a shudder of apprehension, she'd glanced over her shoulder as she slipped through the gate and out onto the road. She was sure someone would pull up a car next to her and ask why she wasn't in school.

The mall's sliding doors opened smoothly, letting out a blast of cold air. She walked inside, surrounded by the hum of voices and smell of food. Butterflies brushed through her stomach as she wound her way through the food court to the ladies' room, where she quickly changed out of her uniform. Storing her schoolbag in a locker, she took the escalators to the tattoo and piercing shop. She'd forged a note from her mother saying she had permission to get the earring.

A few weeks ago, Jasmine had tried to get a tongue piercing, but she'd been told that she couldn't because she was under sixteen. 'Need a note from your mother, giving you permission,' said the manager, who had bright purple hair and multiple piercings. But when Skye walked in, that lady wasn't there, and the younger girl didn't even ask for a note. She just told Skye to sit in the chair, then squeezed the trigger. Pain rushed through Skye's body. Her eyes watered and she gasped.

So she'd done it. From now on at home and whenever her mum might see her at school, she'd have to let her hair down. But she'd wear her hair up when she met Billy again, so it would be the first thing he saw.

Chapter 9

In the shopping centre carpark, a horn blared and Tamara jumped back to the footpath. She'd stepped out without looking. She held up her hand in apology to the astonished driver who'd almost run her over.

'*So* out of it,' she muttered.

It was the end of the day and she still hadn't worked out where to go for the night. She had her toiletries and makeup, she could get clothes from the store, and she could buy underwear and anything else she needed—but she wanted her own things.

She got into her car and started the engine, but then turned it off again. Was she ready to get her things from Craig? She leaned forward and rested her head on the steering wheel. The sun shone heavily through the window, heating the car until she had to start the engine again and turn on the air-conditioner. Then, with more force than was necessary, she shoved the gearstick into reverse and backed out, before turning blindly onto the main road. With no idea where she was headed, she switched the music on very loud and just drove. She was homeless again.

Her mind went back to the time right after her dad had kicked her out. It had been winter, one of Perth's coldest. The rain had come down in sheets—torrential, unforgiving and heavy. At first she'd sheltered in some public toilets. Curled up in the corners, pulling her jumper around her, trying to keep out of the wind. Her fingers and nose had been freezing, and the smell had made her want to choke.

A couple of days later, after the shock had worn off—actually, more out of necessity; Tamara didn't think the shock had ever worn off—she'd realised she needed to take charge of her life. No one was going to do it for her.

Tamara's favourite place to steal from was a busy fruit and veggie shop on the corner of two main streets. Its owner was an old man who always put trolleys of goods out the front. She perfected the act of walking past nonchalantly while he was busy with customers, and plucking two apples at a time from the display.

Later, one of the other street kids recommended a place that was like a hostel, but kids didn't have to pay for it. Tamara checked it out—a shelter that supplied one meal a day and a shower. There Tamara met her two closest friends on the streets: Grind (because he ground his teeth at night) and Neva (because that was her name). They were inseparable; they rode trains without paying, shared their spoils, and pretended that they weren't dying on the inside. Three teenagers brought close by shared circumstances and a hatred for authority figures. Three teenagers who should have been at school learning maths and English, rather than how to live on the streets.

But a few months after Tamara's arrival, Neva was caught shoplifting; it was her third offence, so she was shipped off to a juvenile detention centre. And a few weeks after that, Tamara was caught stealing brandy from a bottle shop. It was her third time too.

The shopkeeper cornered her one afternoon. 'What's in your bag?' she demanded in a harsh voice.

'Nothin',' said Tamara, heat flooding her cheeks. Despite her bravado, her stomach was churning. The thought of being sent to a detention centre frightened her. She'd have a bed, clothes and three meals a day, but the authorities would have taken away her freedom. Didn't they know, even though she was a street kid, that she still had rights? She and Grind were willing to take their chances outside.

'Bullshit,' the lady in the bottle shop said, her arms crossed tightly in front of her. 'I saw ya put it in your bag. Back pocket. Five hundred millilitres of St Agnes. Still want to argue?'

Tamara toyed with the idea of slinging her bag to the ground and running, but somehow she was frozen to the spot. Grind had been waiting outside, but he would have run as soon as he'd seen her get caught. That was their deal: *Don't hang around, get away. If I can catch up with you later, I'll know where to find you.*

The shopkeeper was scowling at her. 'Open. The. Bag.'

In slow motion, Tamara lowered her bag to the floor and unzipped it. She reached in and pulled out the bottle of brandy. When the shopkeeper held out her hand for it, Tamara gave it to her.

'Come with me.' The lady somehow grabbed Tam's elbow in a vice-like grip and put the bottle back on the shelf in a single movement. 'Parents?' she snapped.

'No.'

'Where do you live?'

No answer.

The lady turned to Tamara, getting in her face. 'Where do you live?'

'Nowhere.'

'Thought as much.' She dragged Tamara through the shopping centre and stopped in front of a brightly lit clothing store. 'Stella will sort you out. Stella!'

A large woman looked up from behind the counter. 'What? What now?' she asked in a heavy European accent.

'Got another one for ya,' said the shopkeeper, giving Tamara a sharp push towards Stella. 'I don't want to see you in my shop again.' She shook her finger at Tamara as if she was shooing along an unwanted animal.

'Have you breakin' the law?' Stella's grasp on English wasn't good, but Tamara understood what she was saying. 'Eets alright. No police. No police here. I ask Mary, daughter of my cousin, to bring me girls who need my help. You will work, yes? You must work. Come.'

Tamara followed the woman, while a fight went on inside of her head. *Run!* said one voice. *It's all a trick. She'll turn you in. Don't believe what she says. No one is that kind.* But a softer voice told her to stop running: *It's time to stop relying on yourself. You need an adult.*

Stella had radiated no-nonsense dependability. 'Now, where you live?'

'Nowhere,' said Tamara, wanting to bury her head in Stella's ample chest to cry away the pain of the past six months.

Tut-tutting, Stella rustled through a great sheaf of paperwork on the counter and picked up the phone before speaking rapidly in a language that Tamara didn't understand.

Her desire to run was still intense. As Tamara looked wildly around for an escape route, the smallest details jumped out at her: the glare of the fluorescent lights, the clothes hanging higgledy-piggledy, coffee rings on the counter.

'You go now,' Stella said, after crashing the receiver back into its cradle. 'You go here now. Guesthouse.' She wrote an address in bold letters and handed it over. 'You be back here tomorrow. Eight-thirty. Do not be late.'

Tamara stared at her. Did this woman really expect her to come back? She'd just given her a ticket out. She could run now. Find Grind. Go back to the life she knew and understood.

As if Stella could read her mind, she said in her halting English: 'You will come back.' A statement, not a question. 'The way you live now . . .' Her hands waved in the air. 'Eets not good. This will be better. Much better.'

Now, behind the wheel of her car, Tamara felt a rush of gratitude. She sniffed and blinked back tears, cross with herself for getting so sentimental. But God knows where she would have ended up if it hadn't been for Stella.

That first night at the guesthouse, Tamara found out that her new boss had paid for a week of board and lodging. It included three meals a day, a hot shower and a soft bed in her own room. After that, Tamara would be responsible for the bill. Stella would pay her a wage to work full-time in her shop and Tamara would be expected to arrive on time, look tidy and work hard. 'One rule,' the guesthouse owner had told her. 'No visitors.' That had put an end to her plan to find Grind and smuggle him in.

Tamara kept driving, singing along to the music. She tapped her fingers on the steering wheel and smiled, remembering how Stella had used to wag her finger. 'Now, my chicken,' she would say in her soft voice. 'Those blouses? They are not in the right spot. You must shift them. See here?' Scooping up shirts, Stella would shift them to another spot. 'Ah, yes. Much better, much better,' she'd mutter. 'They are nice here. You can see better, yes?'

Tamara would nod and agree, although she could never see the difference. The shop was overstocked and nothing hung in order.

Tamara found that she liked clothes—she'd never had the chance to handle so many new things before, so this was exciting. The fabrics were soft and luxurious against her hands. When no one was looking, she would bury her face in them, breathing in the new smell. She'd take all the shirts and place them on racks in the right sizes, then colour code them. Slowly, the shop became neat and tidy.

Tamara learned about customers: some were nice, others were horrible, but it was always good to remember regulars, no matter what they were like. She also became proficient at reading body language.

The only downside of Tamara's job was the till. Stella had tried to teach her how to reconcile the takings at the end of each day, but Tamara couldn't make her brain understand.

'Don't worry. Eet will come,' Stella would say. 'Eet will come.' She'd been right, but it had taken a long time.

When Stella retired a few years later, she recommended that Tamara become the manager of Angelic Threads. And she'd been there ever since.

❧

Blinking, Tamara realised she'd come to a stop in front of Craig's house. Whiskey barked and ran to the fence, putting his paw up and hanging his head over. Pain pierced her heart with such intense force that she put her hand to her chest.

Then Craig was at the front door, and there was no going back.

She walked through the yard and followed him inside. He shut the door, then turned to her. 'I'm tryin' to get this right,' he said, his voice hoarse. 'So, because you're scared to love anyone, you chuck out the people who love you. You'd nearly got over this, but then your mum showed up and reminded you. That right?'

Hearing him say it made her feel as though she was the size of a pea.

You've got to stop running, the Tam pleaded. *Like you did all those years ago with Stella. She stopped you running then, and you need to stop running now.*

Tamara nodded at Craig. 'Yes,' she said. 'And also, well . . . my mother told me that my father died.'

'Oh, Tam. I'm so sorry.'

She froze. Couldn't breathe for a moment. 'It's alright. Actually, I've decided to go to the funeral.'

'That's brave of you,' he said, reaching out as though he wanted to take her in his arms. But then he stopped, his hands falling to his sides. 'Is there anything I can do to get you to change your mind about us?'

Biting her bottom lip, Tamara tried to find the right words. 'I don't know,' she said softly.

Craig exhaled heavily. 'Do you love me?'

'I don't know! How can I know? Love's not something I've ever had. All I'm sure of is that if I begin to rely on you, you'll leave. Everyone always does.' The words had come out in a rush. She'd finally said it. Finally told him.

Feeling as if a weight had been lifted from her whole body, she raised her head and stared directly into his eyes. He didn't seem angry, just sad.

Whiskey flopped at her feet before rolling over with his legs in the air, offering his stomach for a scratch. She bent down to pat him.

'Okay,' Craig said. 'Let's try another question. Do you reckon we can sort through this?' He paused. 'Maybe a better question is: do you want to?' There was a heavy silence. 'Coz I do. I want to be there for you.'

Tam stayed mute. She couldn't form one damned word.

'Anyway, Whiskey misses you. He misses his walks with you.'

'I miss him too,' she said wistfully, stroking his velvet ears.

Craig grabbed a letter from the hall table and waved it at her. 'Your licence turned up today. Not sure if you want to change your address on it or just pay it.'

As Tamara reached for the letter, her stomach started to churn. Could she trust him? Go back to him? Was it that simple?

Of course not. He seemed to understand where she was coming from, but that didn't mean he'd be able to live with her. Not the way she was.

'Leave the address as here,' she answered softly, 'but we shouldn't live together at the moment. Like I said, I need space. I've got to try and fix myself. So I'll pick up my things and stay in a motel. Can you be patient with me?'

Relief made Craig's shoulders slump. He nodded, staring her straight in the eye again. 'I can do that. For as long as you need.'

❧

The motel room was clean and so were the sheets, but that was the best Tamara could say about it. Green curtains hung limply from the window, hiding the view of the city lights, and the bed sagged in the middle. A few Lipton tea bags, sachets of International Roast coffee and sugar packets sat on a shelf above the empty fridge, but there wasn't a minibar. Good thing she'd brought her own supplies.

She took the top off one beer and stashed the other five in the fridge. The cold liquid was welcome, but bed would be too, as soon as she unpacked some clothes. Methodically, she hung them in the wardrobe in order of colour, then lined her shoes up on the floor. Having things neat and tidy made her feel as if she was in control. Her emotions still had the ability to take her over, but at least she could control everything else.

After another sip of beer she stripped the sheets, replacing them with her own. If she was going to be here for a while, she wanted to be comfortable. Kicking her shoes off, she fluffed the pillows, grabbed the Thai takeaway she'd bought for dinner and used the remote to turn on the TV. Some mind-numbing soap was in order. She didn't want to think for a few hours: laughing while enjoying food and beer was on the agenda. Then blessed sleep that would help keep today's problems at bay.

Later, standing alone in the dark, Tamara looked through the curtains over Perth. There were thousands of pinprick lights twinkling at her. People in their houses, talking, fighting, loving. People who knew how to love. Or hate.

And Craig. Her Craig who loved her.

Chapter 10

Lauren hadn't been expecting a call from her dermatologist for a couple of days. So as soon as her phone rang at nine the next morning, Lauren knew she had skin cancer. Of course, Michelle couldn't tell her the details over the phone, but they made an appointment for 2 pm. Then Michelle told Lauren that she might want to bring Dean along—and that was when she knew it was serious and arranged to take a day of sick leave.

'Lauren, Dean, thanks for coming in at such short notice,' said Michelle. 'As I said on the phone, I have some important news. I put a rush on your results, Lauren, which is why they've come through earlier than usual. The lesion that I removed yesterday is malignant. I'm sorry to say that it's melanoma. What I'd like to do now is discuss what this result might mean and what we have to do next.'

Lauren's dermatologist kept speaking, but she couldn't hear the words over the whirring in her head. She was compiling mental lists. Was her private health insurance up to date? Had she paid the last lot of bills? And what about Dirk? She needed to make sure he'd be looked after. In her whole career, she'd never let a child down, and now wasn't the time to start. Dimly, she realised that she probably had her priorities wrong—that she should be focusing on her own kids. But she just couldn't think about them yet.

'Stop, Lauren,' Fran would have told her. 'Take a breath.'

Many years ago, the father of her good friend Jan had died unexpectedly. She remembered Jan saying that after she'd received the news, all she could think about was doing the shopping and making sure there was enough food in the house for everyone. Lauren wondered if she was going through her own version of that now.

Part of her knew there was no need to react with the dread she was feeling. After all, Michelle hadn't said it was terminal or anything even *like* that. It might be at an early stage—it might not have spread.

After all, she'd been so diligent about coming in for regular appointments. Her fairness had caused her to run from the sun, much earlier than anyone else had. To slather sunscreen on and don a rashie at the beach. But when she'd been a little girl, sunscreen hadn't been a big deal. No one knew the damage that the sun could cause— well, they did, but the TV campaigns hadn't been running yet. 'Slip! Slop! Slap!' was the first one she remembered—she must have been about twelve when Sid the Seagull first insisted that everyone slip on a shirt, slop on the sunscreen and slap on a hat. Why she was hearing that annoying jingle now, she had no idea. Shaking her head slightly, she tried to concentrate on what Michelle had to say.

'. . . need to operate. The pathology showed that there are still cancerous cells around the edge of the area I removed, so I haven't got it all. We need a buffer of about one centimetre from where the cancer cells were found.'

How would Stu and Skye take the news? God, how would Lauren even find the right words to tell them? Was there advice for this type of thing? There had to be books, blogs and information sheets—she must remember to ask Michelle for some.

And Dean, how would he cope with work and the kids as well as the house?

Dirk's little face jumped into her mind. *And me*, the vision seemed to be saying. *Don't forget about me.*

Oh, her birth mum! She had to find her birth mum before it was too late.

'What happens now?' Dean asked, his face pale.

'Today I'd like to go over Lauren's whole body again and make sure there aren't any other moles or lesions. I'm almost positive that I haven't missed any, but it's always best to be on the safe side.' Michelle's eyes were full of sympathy. 'In the media, melanoma is portrayed as large moles that change colour or suddenly go from flat to raised. This is often the case, but there are many other ways it can manifest. You're very lucky that Dean noticed it and that you listened to him.'

Lauren gripped her husband's hand tighter. 'I'm sorry,' she said to him.

He turned to her in surprise. 'What? What do you mean?' He took her face in his hands. 'What are you sorry for?'

'I'm sorry to do this to you. To scare you.'

'Babe, this isn't your fault! You didn't make yourself have cancer. You can't think like that. Anyway, as Michelle keeps saying, this might just be a small blip. There's nothing to indicate that it's life-threatening.' He squeezed her face gently, then turned back to Michelle. 'Is there?'

'Look, melanoma is a complex disease. It usually has deep roots and can show up anywhere. I'll be a lot more comfortable when the tests show that it hasn't spread from the original site into the lymph nodes or any organs. I'll get these bloods organised. You'll also need to have a CT scan. All of this will tell us what we're dealing with.' She folded her hands on her lap, and Lauren realised that Michelle was watching her closely. Probably trying to work out how she was taking it all.

Lauren wasn't sure. Numb and disbelieving were about as far as she could get, along with a little frightened. She stared at the familiar fake pot plant until she heard the printer whirring. Michelle was signing papers and holding them out to Dean. He took them and glanced over at Lauren, as if unsure what to do next.

'Do you want to get undressed and I'll check everything again?' Michelle asked Lauren. She realised that her dermatologist must be a veteran of these types of appointments. She couldn't remember the exact statistics Michelle had once told her; something like one in fourteen men and one in twenty-four women will be diagnosed with melanoma in their lifetime. So how many of them had Michelle needed to tell?

Now, being one of those patients, Lauren couldn't wait to get the all-clear. She ripped off her top and bra before Michelle reached for her dermascope and started to scan her skin. 'Dean, do you know much about melanoma?' she asked.

'Only what Lauren has told me over the years,' he admitted, watching the examination.

'There are five things I look for that might raise a flag with me. The first thing is moles that don't look the same on both sides: that's called "asymmetry". Then there are edges that are blurry or irregular—jagged, if you like.' She stopped and ran her finger over part of Lauren's skin, checking the height of a mole. 'Then there are colour variations within the lesion or mole itself.'

'What are you looking for now?' Dean asked.

'All of the things I've just mentioned, plus anything that's bigger than about six mils.' She straightened and smiled at Lauren. 'I know this is frightening. I can tell you, it's the unknown that causes the fear. Once we know what we're dealing with and we have a plan, it won't feel quite so overwhelming. Plans always help. Now, I just want to have a feel under your arm and see what your lymph nodes are doing.'

'Why do you do that?' Dean asked.

'To gauge of the size of them.'

Fingers pushed deeply into her skin, and Lauren smiled for the first time since the phone call. 'That tickles!'

'Sorry,' said Michelle, her face serious. She moved the dermascope to Lauren's neck. 'I'll check your groin too, just to be on the safe side.'

Lauren tilted her head under the pressure of Michelle's fingers. Her mother used to make a similar movement when she was brushing Lauren's hair, ready to put it in a ponytail.

When Lauren thought of Connie, she was struck by an idea. *Parents!*

'Is melanoma genetic?' she asked, the question rushing from her.

'It can be, but we don't know your family history,' Michelle said gently. 'If we could test your biological parents, then we might find that it's hereditary. Of course, you're also at risk of skin cancer because of your fair complexion.'

'Can we test my children?'

'We can,' Michelle said cautiously, 'but I think we're getting a little off-track—and too far ahead of ourselves.'

'Okay,' said Lauren, filing it away for later. She had one last question. 'Another thing is that I don't feel sick. Is that normal?'

Michelle paused. 'There are often no physical symptoms at the beginning of melanoma. And yours may not have spread.'

'But she's tired,' Dean broke in. 'She's always exhausted—look at the black marks under her eyes. Could that be part of it?'

'That's a question I can't answer yet. Another reason to request a full blood picture and find out where your body is at.' She picked up the phone. 'I'm going to make an appointment for you at the hospital, and we'll focus on your arm first.'

Lauren and Dean drove home in silence. She was reeling and couldn't think of anything to say that would ease the pain Dean was so obviously feeling. The fact that he was holding her hand as they drove was enough.

He flicked on the blinker and turned into their driveway. As she'd done a million times before, Lauren opened the glovebox and pressed the button for the garage door to rise. Once inside, Dean turned off the car. Lauren counted the ticks of the engine in her mind. *One, two. One, two.* Like the rhythm of a metronome.

As Dean turned to her and started to speak, she did the same thing.

'Sorry, you first.' Dean gripped her hand.

She swallowed. 'Okay, we've got to tell the kids. How are we going to do that? "Hi, kids, how was your day? Oh, by the way, I was diagnosed with cancer."' Tears welled in her eyes, and she took a deep breath before she continued, her voice stronger this time. 'I don't feel all that unwell, so I think we should make light of it—tell them what's happened, but that it's not a big issue. Continue with all the normal things. I'll go back to work tomorrow and go to the hospital when I have to. Let's just take each day as it comes, and live as normally as we can. Okay?'

Dean stared at her, his eyes full of love. 'You are so incredibly strong. I love you. And I think you're right: there are so many unanswered questions, and there's no point getting ahead of ourselves. Let's wait and see the results, then make a plan.'

'I don't see another choice, do you? My mind was going a mile a minute at first, but now that I've had a little time to process everything, it's like you said at Michelle's—probably just a blip.' She leaned over and kissed him.

'No, they've got the results wrong,' Skye said, her voice wavering. She was standing in front of Lauren and Dean in the kitchen, where they'd just delivered the news. 'Those results have to be *wrong*.'

The look of desperation on her daughter's face broke Lauren's heart. She reached out to comfort her, but Skye wrenched away, staring at her with wild eyes.

'Sweetheart, this isn't a big deal. I've got to have a few extra tests and a bit more cut out. Nothing more.'

'I *know* about melanoma,' Skye said. Her eyes were huge and she couldn't stand still. 'We learned about it in health. Once you've got it, it *never* goes away. Never! It can turn up anywhere. It *kills* you.'

'You're being a little melodramatic,' Dean interjected. 'Mum still has to—'

'I'm not!' There was just enough time for Skye to draw breath before she shouted: 'I'm *not!*' She stormed out of the kitchen, leaving

Dean and Lauren looking at each other, feeling as though they'd done ten rounds in the boxing ring.

'Bloody hell.' Dean ran his hands over his face and rubbed hard. 'I hope telling Stu isn't like that.' He started after Skye.

'Just leave her for the moment,' Lauren said, sinking into a chair at the kitchen table. 'We need to be here together when Stu shows up.'

Soon they heard a key in the front door and glanced at each other. Dean got up and grabbed a beer from the fridge, then held another one up, offering it to Stu as he came in through the door. 'That's what I like,' he said, grinning at them both. 'A-plus service, guys. But I'll take a raincheck, thanks. I need to study tonight.'

'Lauren, want a wine?' Dean asked.

Yes! Yes, she did. In fact, she could probably drink a whole bottle. But she shook her head. 'No thanks, babe.' She gave Stu a smile. 'So, how was your day?'

'Fine, I didn't drown anyone.'

'Well, that *was* an achievement!' Lauren joked. See? She could act normally.

Dean sat down and took a long swallow of his beer, while Lauren looked down at the table and fiddled with the glass of water that sat in front of her.

'What's going on?' Stu asked, looking from Dean to Lauren and back again. 'You're sitting here pretending something isn't going on. You're not doing a very good job of it.'

Out of nowhere, a bubble of laughter escaped from Lauren. The situation felt surreal and crazy, and there didn't seem to be any better option than laughing out loud. She didn't want to let her children know how frightened she was.

When Lauren was growing up, she never saw her parents discuss problems or fight. They'd shielded her from every little piece of emotional upheaval. As a mum, she understood the need to protect her children from distressing news, but she wasn't much good at hiding her feelings. She was a heart-on-her-sleeve type of woman.

She obviously needed to take a leaf out of Connie and George's book and try to be a bit less transparent.

'So what happens from here?' Stu asked, once Lauren had finished recounting the events of the day. He squeezed her hand. 'Is there a prognosis?'

'We're not at that stage yet,' Lauren explained. 'And fingers crossed we won't need to be—I'm really hopeful that it will be contained to part of my arm.'

'You'll be okay, Mum,' Stu said. He put his chin on her head and wrapped his arms around her. 'I'll do whatever I can to help.'

'I'm really lucky to have you. And, really, I shouldn't be out of action much at all.' Lauren smiled at them both. 'This is going to be one of those times that just makes us all a little stronger.'

'Does Skye know?'

Lauren nodded.

'How did she take it?'

She sighed. 'Not well, but it's just a matter of adjusting.'

Dean held her close that night. They were both taking comfort in each other. The future seemed uncertain, but they wouldn't let it get to them right now.

'I need to find my birth mother,' Lauren said. 'For the kids' sake, I need to know if this is a genetic thing.'

Dean squeezed her. 'Of course you do.'

'I'll talk to Mum and Dad as soon as I can.'

A silence stretched out, and Lauren thought that Dean had gone to sleep until he turned over. 'Skye's going to have trouble with this,' he said seriously. 'I'm surprised by her reaction.'

Lauren gave a snort. 'I'm not. I can never predict how she's going to react these days. So unlike the girl she used to be.'

'She's concerning me.'

'And me. We've just got to get through this time and we'll be able to concentrate on us as a family again.'

'Yeah.' It was said softly. Almost wistfully, Lauren thought.

Worn out, hugging Dean, she slipped into a deep sleep.

That night the nightmare returned. But for the first time, it changed halfway through. The hands holding her down morphed into soft ones, kind ones, poking and prodding. Instead of darkness, she was bathed in the glare of fluorescent lights. A scalpel glinted in Dirk's hand. 'Don't forget me,' he said. As she watched herself in the dream, Lauren felt the very real prick of a needle entering her arm. She woke with a jolt.

Dear Diary,

I asked him not to—no, I told him not to—and he still did. I didn't want it to happen, but he didn't listen.

What are Mummy and Daddy going to say when they find out? I can't tell them, but I need to tell someone.

It's easier to write it down. Then I can tear out the pages and throw them overboard. Let the fish eat them and pretend it never happened.

I'm so scared.

Everywhere I look, there are happy faces. People in the pool, sunbaking, reading on the deckchairs. It feels like one big party all the time.

But it's not. There are real things happening on this ship. Things that shouldn't happen. Bad things.

Daddy promised me that going to Australia would be a new start. A new beginning. But it's not now. It's tarnished; just like me.

I can't write this without crying. I still can't believe it happened. Never again. Just never. Again.

The deck is supposed to be a safe place. There are always clusters of passengers sitting on the chairs and hanging over the railings. People even sleep up there now. The captain told us that we could go up there and sleep if we weren't happy with our cabin. I was happy in the cabin, but some of my new friends wanted to try sleeping outside. Mummy was happy for me to go, just so long as there was a group of us. There were ten girls, and all the other people who were sleeping up there.

Ten. And it still happened.

The deckchairs are lined up next to one another. Quite comfortable, really. All ten of us in a row.

I had wanted to see the stars. From where we were, they shone so bright. I'd never seen so many before: big orbs and tiny little sparkles shining out from the blackness. And the moon. In all her glory, so large and full. The way the light glistened off the water was so beautiful.

At first it was very noisy. Everyone was commenting on the beauty of the night or the stars or the moon. But our chatter gradually died down. One by one, people fell asleep on the chairs.

I couldn't sleep so I watched the moon on the water.

The boy came and found me. At first he was gentle. Took me to the funnel area. I'd heard about it and what people did there. I'd never believed it.

He went from being gentle to forceful.

I never want to go near a funnel again.

Chapter 11

Stomping towards the bus stop, Skye couldn't wait to get to school. To get far away from the house with its long silences and whispers. Her parents had their heads so far up their arses, they couldn't see what she already knew was coming. They could call her a drama queen, or melodramatic, but she knew. Stu had told her off for saying the truth out loud, but she didn't care. The sooner they realised that what she was saying was right, the better.

She remembered her gran telling her that anger was often the cover for a real emotion, but then Skye shoved that thought aside. She wasn't anything else but pissed off. Not scared, not sad, not vulnerable. Of course not.

Last night, when the house was really quiet, she'd heard her mum's and dad's voices through the wall. Not what they were saying, just the murmur. She'd had a fleeting thought of how she would be so exposed without her mum around to protect her; to love her. 'Don't be bloody stupid,' she'd muttered, rolling onto her side and pulling the pillow over her head. She was fourteen, so she didn't need to be treated like a child anymore—especially by a mother who didn't have time for her.

Fiddling in her pocket, Skye found her earbuds and put them in. She flicked her phone from screen to screen until she came across the song she wanted. Music relaxed her; it filled her head with guitar riffs and drumbeats. When it was pumping through the tiny earbuds, she didn't think about anything else. Not schoolwork, not her dad, not her stupid Golden Boy brother, and certainly not her mum's illness.

Sometimes, the lyrics prompted a memory of Billy. Especially when Rihanna's 'We Found Love' started: the chorus talked about finding love in a hopeless place, and that was exactly how she felt when she was with Billy.

The bus pulled up with a hiss and a jerk as the driver stamped on the brakes. Students moved towards the doors like a flood. *They're sheep being herded along*, Skye thought. *Blindy doing what's expected of them.*

If she had her way, she'd be on a beach somewhere, not going to school. Lying under an umbrella, swimming in the sea, dreaming of her future. A future with Billy. A future as a successful music agent.

She'd mentioned to her parents one day that she wanted to be a music agent. Their laughter had been humiliating. 'Think you'd better try for another profession,' her mum had said. 'To get that type of job, you need to know someone, who knows someone, who knows someone. So it's not a job for you.'

Well, why not? If Skye worked hard, she could achieve anything. Her teachers told her that all the time.

Staring at the floor of the bus so she didn't accidentally catch anyone's eyes, Skye found a spot near the middle where she could stand up, keep looking down and hang on. Even though her music was pumping hard, she couldn't stop her thoughts from going back to the night before.

'I've got to have a few extra tests,' her mother had said.

Yeah, thought Skye bitterly. *Extra tests find* extra *things wrong.*

What did her mum expect they'd find? Of course they'd find something.

Melanoma was like a sheet of water spreading out across the flat ground. It crept quietly from one place to another. Then *BANG!* It was all through you, and there was no going back. When Skye had googled melanoma blogs the night before, she'd found a few 'good' stories—people who were still fighting the disease, ones who had a few decent years after the initial mole was cut out. But then it returned. Some fought for years, others for only a few months. But the result was still the same.

Skye tried to focus back on her music. The bus was packed this morning, and she could already smell the BO. When the bus jerked forward, everyone moved with the motion. An older man stumbled into Skye's back, making her lose her balance. Anger burned inside her.

'Sorry,' he muttered.

She glared and turned away, then realised he would now think she was the sort of teenager who was rude to adults. The sort who doesn't have any work ethic and believes the world owes them something—all the stereotypical things adults said about teenagers. *I'm not one of them. I want to make something of myself.*

She tried to take a deep breath, but her throat closed over. Her heart started to beat really fast and beads of sweat prickled on her forehead. There was no air in the bus. She needed to get off. But no

questions: 'Where were you yesterday, Mrs Ramsey?' 'I painted a new picture and I want you to see it!' 'Mrs Ramsey, I've got something to tell you!'

Laughing, Lauren gazed down at all the eager faces smiling at her. 'Let's sit in a circle and you can all tell me something that happened yesterday while I was away,' she said. 'Yes! All of you, not just the ones whose turn it is. Then, I've got some new worksheets for you. What do you say?'

There was a chorus of 'Yes!' before the children ran to the mat.

'Walk, please! No running.' Lauren turned her attention to Joy. 'Have you seen Dirk? Is he here today?'

'Yes, he's just gone to the toilet. He was off sick again yesterday, but his two days at home don't seem to have changed him at all. He still looks very tired.'

'It can take months to get over a virus. Two days' rest isn't enough. It makes me want to shake Zoe.' Lauren frowned and shook her head. 'I didn't mean that.'

Joy gave her an understanding smile, then went to cut up the fruit for the children's recess.

Lauren's stomach did a flip. She wasn't sure if it was her own situation or Dirk's that was unsettling her the most today.

The kids made room for her in their circle, shuffling along, and Lauren sat down. 'Good morning everyone,' she said.

'Good morning, Mrs Ramsey.'

'It's so good to see you all!' she said. Then she noticed Dirk walk in. 'Oh, hello there, Dirk. Come sit down with us.' She patted a space on the floor next to her.

As Dirk sat down, she noticed the bruises on his arms had begun to fade, but he still looked tired and drawn.

'Right, news time,' she said. 'Katie, would you start?'

The little girl sat forward and told Lauren about the painting she'd done the day before. 'Mrs Clark said it was the *best* dragon she'd ever seen!' she finished with a big smile.

'That's great!' said Lauren. 'Now, who wants to be . . . Oh, Dirk!' she cried as she saw Dirk's nose dripping blood all over his hands and t-shirt. She jumped to her feet, grabbed a handful of tissues and rushed back. Excited chatter erupted and a couple of kids squealed. Oddly, Dirk seemed calmer than the other children.

'Shh, shh,' Lauren soothed. 'It's just a nosebleed. He'll be fine. Joy?' She pinched the bridge of Dirk's nose and ushered him towards the bathrooms.

She could hear her teacher's aide trying to restore order. As the door banged shut behind them, high-pitched voices started to sing 'Twinkle, Twinkle, Little Star'.

'Okay, can you hold that?' she asked Dirk, taking his tiny hand in hers and showing him how to hold the tissue and pinch tightly at the same time. Grabbing paper towels from the dispenser, she ran the cold water tap, wet them down and placed them on the back of his neck, all the while making calming noises.

'Do you get many nosebleeds, Dirk?' she asked when the bleeding had finally stopped. 'I wonder if the heat caused it.'

'I've had a lot,' Dirk said as he wiped his nose with the back of his hand. It came away smeared with blood, but he didn't seem disturbed by that.

Lauren directed him to wash his hands before gently wiping his face. 'Feel better?' she asked softly, and he nodded, his eyes soulful and tired. 'Is anything bothering you, Dirk? You seem very worn out. I want you to know that you can talk to me about anything you need to. Okay?'

Again, Dirk nodded. 'My tummy hurts sometimes.' He gestured to his middle, and Lauren nodded. 'Okay, is it hurting now?'

'No.'

'Would you like to see the school nurse and lie down?'

'No, I want to stay with my friends.'

Lauren ran her hand over his hair. 'Alright. Let's go back, then. You'll have to take things a bit easy so you don't get your nose going again, okay?'

When classes had ended for the day, Lauren googled 'bruises, nose-bleeds, sore stomach, fatigue'. WebMD popped up and gave her the top few listings of what it could be.

'Haemophilia'? No. His nose wouldn't have stopped bleeding.

'Viral Syndrome'? Maybe. Maybe he just had a virus that was knocking him around. There were some nasty ones these days. Hope rose in her.

'Medication reaction'? Lauren hadn't been told if Dirk had been put on any medication, so she flicked through his file. His mother had written 'no' in loopy cursive when the questionnaire had asked if he was taking anything.

'Aspirin use'? Lauren shook her head.

'Pre-leukaemia'? She stared at the words until they blurred in front of her eyes. Leukaemia? Surely not.

Why not? she asked herself. He wouldn't be the first one.

Ignoring the argument going on in her mind, she clicked 'viral syndrome'. The website didn't say anything about nosebleeds.

Her cursor hovered over 'pre-leukaemia'.

A knock at the door. She minimised the screen and swung around in her chair.

'Hey, how're you going?' said Holly, walking into the office.

'Busy. Reports and stuff. You know how it is at this time of term.'

Holly nodded sympathetically, and Lauren wondered if she was here to check on her. She knew Lauren would be focusing on school rather than the diagnosis, and Lauren knew that Holly didn't think this was healthy.

'Want to grab a coffee before you head home?' Holly asked.

'Sorry, I can't. I need to check on Skye. She didn't take the news very well.'

'No worries. How was Dirk?'

Lauren recounted everything that had happened with Dirk that day, listing the symptoms she'd just run past Dr Google.

Holly straightened. 'Has he had a nosebleed here before?'

'I went back through his diary while the kids were at lunch—I write notes in each child's diary every day. That way, the parents know how things have gone. A nosebleed is the type of thing I would have documented. Couldn't find anything but Dirk says he's had a lot.'

'If those symptoms were all by themselves, they wouldn't concern me, but put together, they're definitely worrying.'

'I know,' Lauren said softly. 'I was just googling them.' She maximised the screen again. The cursor was still on the highlighted word 'leukaemia'. Looking over at Holly, she raised her eyebrows to ask the question.

'Dr Google has rarely diagnosed anyone correctly,' Holly warned.

'Okay, how about this?' Lauren typed in 'childhood leukaemia symptoms' and hit enter. 'Seven important symptoms of leukaemia in children' was the first hit, so she clicked on it: 'Bruising and bleeding.' 'Stomach ache and poor appetite.' 'Frequent infections.'

'Do you think,' Lauren asked slowly, 'that Zoe knows something's wrong with Dirk? When I spoke to her on Tuesday, she acted relieved when I told her about the bruises. It was as if she expected me to talk about something worse. I immediately thought of him being abused within the home, but maybe I was wrong.'

Emotions swirled at the bottom of her stomach and started to rise up. God, the unfairness of it, if he was ill! Right after her diagnosis, she'd had the thought that her melanoma was unfair, but then she'd managed to dismiss it: life wasn't fair. However, Dirk having cancer would take the word 'unfair' to a whole different level.

'Lauren,' said Holly, 'do you think you might be getting a bit too involved here? That's a pretty big leap. I agree that something isn't right, but leukaemia?'

'Well, give me a better answer,' Lauren said as she swung around on her chair to face Holly. 'It's all right there in front of you.' She pointed at the screen.

Holly looked steadily at Lauren before thoughtfully tapping her fingers against her mouth. 'Why don't you phone Zoe?' she said eventually. 'Ask her to come in for a meeting with us on Monday. We can put it to bed once and for all.'

Lauren could almost hear Holly add: *And then you won't have to be worrying about him when you should be concerned about yourself.*

∽

'Where have you been all day? And why haven't you replied to any of my texts? I thought we were meant to go to the mall this week.'

Adele nudged Skye hard with her shoulder as they walked out of class to their lockers. 'Are you okay?'

'Fine,' Skye responded shortly, although she knew Adele wouldn't let it slide. She never knew when to stop.

'Hey, I heard Sir talking to Teabag Tonkin about your mum while they were on yard duty. They didn't know I was behind them.'

Skye kept walking, her head down. 'Oh yeah?'

'Said she has cancer.'

'Adele!' Jasmine, who'd just fallen into step with them, looked over at her, horrified. 'You can't say *that*.'

'Why not?' Adele stopped and grabbed Skye's arm. 'It's true, isn't it? How are you coping? Why didn't you tell us? It must be a bit weird.'

Skye shrugged.

'What can you do?' Adele asked.

'Not much.' It was on the tip of her tongue to yell: 'I don't like this. Can it just *stop*?'

'Aren't you scared?' Adele wanted to know.

'It's not me who's dying. What's there to be scared about?'

'Oh. My. God. Is she gonna die? Shit, Skye!' Adele moved over to put her arm around her shoulders, but Skye shook her off.

'I said I'm fine.' This time she bit down on her tongue. The words 'I'm really scared for her' wanted to come out, but no way was she going to say them aloud.

'We're all going to die sometime,' Jasmine said, pushing in between the two girls. 'Leave her alone, Adele, can't you see she's upset?'

'Don't worry about it, Jas,' Skye said. 'It's okay.' She stopped walking and took a breath. 'Yes, Mum has cancer. It's melanoma.

Yes, she's gonna die, because everyone who gets melanoma does. Anything else you want to know?'

'Oh, Skye,' Jasmine started, 'you don't know that . . .'

'I read all about it on the internet last night.' Skye started walking again. 'Come on, let's get out of here.'

'Hey, I've got an idea to take your mind off it,' Adele said.

That was Adele all over, Skye thought: she'd find something else to do so she didn't have to think about what was really going on. Still, Skye had to admit that wasn't a bad idea right at this point in time. She hadn't heard from Billy for half a day, and a niggle of anxiety had twinged at lunchtime. He always texted her at lunch.

'What did you have in mind?' Skye asked Adele.

'A dare!'

'Adele, maybe not now, hey?' said Jasmine. 'Don't give Skye one of your wild, harebrained schemes. Right, Skye?'

Adele gave Jasmine the finger. 'Who made you all knowledge-able?' she shot back. 'I'm just keeping our lovely Skye busy.'

'For fuck's sake,' Jasmine said and walked ahead.

Skye's phone dinged. She took it out and saw a text from Billy. Stifling her smile, she stuffed her phone back so Adele couldn't see.

Adele leaned over and whispered a dare in her ear. Then she took a step away and crossed her arms, looking pleased with herself. 'Go on,' she said. 'Do it.'

Chapter 12

Saturday dawned bright and clear. Lauren was standing by the front window with a cup of coffee, watching light spread across the sky. She hadn't had the dream, but she'd woken at 3 am and lain there worrying about the melanoma—and about what she planned to do today. She'd called her parents the night before to say she was coming to visit. After her coffee and a quick breakfast, she put on her headphones and got a whole lot of chores out of the way. Dean was off at the gym, Stu was catching up with friends before heading to his job, and Skye was . . . at a basketball game? At the mall with Adele? She'd rushed out the door again without saying much.

In the early afternoon, Lauren drove to her parents' place. True to their routine, Connie was pruning roses and George was mowing the lawn. Lauren had called them after her diagnosis on Thursday to tell them the news, so they both gave her a big hug before they all went inside to have a cup of tea in the kitchen.

'I'm sorry, Mum and Dad, but I'm going to have to look for my birth mother,' Lauren said as she sat across the table from the couple who'd raised her from when she was three days old. *I just came out with it!* she thought. *Dean would be proud.*

Connie's wrinkled hands wrapped around her cup of tea and she smiled sadly, but George reached out and grabbed Lauren's hand, pumping it up and down.

'Of course you do,' he said gruffly. 'I'm not at all surprised, are you, dear?' He turned to Connie.

'No. No, I'm not.' She ran her palm across the tablecloth, trying to smooth out a non-existent wrinkle. 'What I *am* surprised at is that you haven't done it sooner.'

Lauren's phone beeped with a text message, but she ignored it. This conversation was too important. She was about to say something more, but Connie spoke first.

'Is it something you've always wanted to do, or mainly because of this health scare?'

That stopped Lauren. To lie or to tell the truth? She'd been raised to always be honest. Perhaps a small white lie wouldn't hurt.

'It's been on my mind for a long time, but there never seemed to be a right time. Whenever I started to think about talking to you, life would throw another spanner in the works and it'd get put on the backburner,' she answered, deciding on the truth. 'But now, it's on my mind all the time.' *If you don't count Dirk*, she thought. 'I've realised that I need to find her. I'm probably not at death's door, but what if I was?'

Her parents nodded, understanding in their eyes.

'You know,' Lauren continued, 'I've started researching the family tree online, just so the kids know where they've come from. I'd like to include my birth family in there too. I think I'd even be okay with not meeting my birth mum, but I'd like to know her name, her family and medical history, and if I've got any half brothers or sisters. That sort of thing.' Lauren swallowed hard. 'You know, I'm so grateful to you both. I doubt my life would have been as wonderful as it has been or I would have been loved as much if you hadn't decided you wanted to give a child a home. *You* are my parents—not some stranger. Not someone who I haven't seen for forty-seven years. Just because she gave birth to me, does not—' she gave a small, harsh laugh'—*does not* make her my mother. But Skye and Stu might have cousins. Maybe someone else in that family has had a melanoma too. They're the types of things I want to know.'

'Lauren, dear, we know all of that and we completely support your decision,' Connie answered, finishing her tea and pushing her cup to the side. 'You agree, George?'

'Yes, I do.' He smiled. The familiar wrinkles around his eyes deepened and, as always, Lauren couldn't help smiling back. It had been like that since she was a toddler—it had been their game. He would smile and say, 'Your turn.' She would smile. He would laugh and say, 'Your turn.' Of course, then she would laugh. He would do a little dance and hop on one leg. 'Your turn.' And she copied him.

Lauren breathed a sigh of relief. Why had she thought it would be so hard? And why had she left it so long? Her phone dinged again, but she ignored it. Nothing could be more important than this time with her parents.

Digging in her handbag, she brought out a document and laid it on the table.

'Do you actually know who my mum was? It's your names on the original birth certificate.' She held it up for them to see.

Connie and George shook their heads. 'That's not something we were ever told,' George said.

'That's right,' Connie said. 'The authorities were strict about the details they gave to us. In fact, there were very few.'

George reached across and took Connie's hand. He gazed at her for a long time before turning back to Lauren. 'I believe any adoptee's original birth certificate is sealed. You can request it from the proper authorities if your biological mother has put her name on the contact register. If she hasn't, I'm not sure how much information they'll give you.'

A deep sigh escaped Lauren as she stood up. She walked to the other side of the table and kissed both of their cheeks. 'Thank you,' she said. 'I love you both so much.' Of course, she knew all the things her dad had just told her; she'd done a lot more research than she was prepared to tell them about. In fact, she had already written her letter to the Department of Child Protection. Dean had proofread it for her, and now she had it in her bag, ready to post after she left her parents' house.

Connie reached up and patted Lauren's hand. 'We love you too, dear.'

George pushed back his chair and got up. 'Do you know when you have to go in for your next appointment? Does Dean need any help with the children? All you have to do is call, and we'll be right over. We're not so old that we're useless yet.'

Lauren smiled. 'You're both far from useless! And I'm scheduled for the next procedure on Tuesday,' she said with a shiver. 'At seven in the morning.' She walked over to the window and stared out. Everything in the garden was the same as it had been when she'd visited last. Her world was in the process of being tipped upside down, while everything else seemed to stay the same.

'I'm nervous,' she finally admitted. She hadn't said that out loud to anyone. Not even Dean. Lauren didn't want to let anyone know how concerned and frightened she was. She'd told herself sternly that as far as anyone she loved needed to know, she wasn't worried. Everything would be fine. But now, in the comfort of her parents' presence, the truth had slipped out.

'Your dermatologist seems to be very knowledgeable, and I'm sure she'll have everything in hand,' Connie said, but Lauren could see the pain in her face. Maybe she wasn't the only one cracking hardy.

'What happens after you've had the extra tissue removed?' George asked.

'I'll have more tests. A CT scan. Hopefully they'll find nothing.'

'Exactly. Hopefully nothing,' Connie said, determination in her voice.

Lauren nodded, smiling at her. If anyone could fix a problem through positive thinking, it was her mum.

In the car, Lauren slid the letter she'd written to the department from her handbag and read it one last time.

To whom it may concern,

My name is Lauren Connie Ramsey and I'm requesting information on my birth parents. Born at Subiaco Hospital on 12 May 1969, I was fostered to George and Connie Jenkins, of 32 Hunter Avenue, Gooseberry Hills, Western Australia, when I was three days old, until they adopted me twelve months later.

I have recently been diagnosed with a life-threatening

illness and would like to know if there were any other cases of this disease in my birth family. I would also like to know more about my biological family's history in general.

I'm undecided about whether I would like to meet any surviving biological relatives, but any information you have would be most gratefully received.

Lauren finished with every contact detail she had: phone, school fax, email and postal address. She'd even included a stamped self-addressed envelope.

After folding the letter neatly and sealing it in its envelope, she placed it on the seat next to her before backing out of her parents' driveway and heading towards the nearest post box. In the flow of traffic, she came to a stop at a set of lights. As if on their own, her eyes were drawn back to the letter. Impulsively, she reached over, picked it up and gave it a kiss for good luck. As the lights turned green, she saw the man in the next lane over staring at her as if she was quite strange.

She kissed the letter once more before she carefully placed it in the post box.

Back in the car, her phone beeped and she remembered the text messages she'd received while talking to her parents. 'Bugger, bugger, bugger,' she muttered, picking up her phone. When she read the first two messages, anxiety shot through her. They were from Skye. The first was short and to the point: 'Can you pick me up from the pool?' The next one, ten minutes later, said: 'Don't worry, I'm obviously too much of an inconvenience for you, since you can't be bothered answering.'

Dean just asked, 'Hi honey, how's your day going? Did you

talk to your parents? What would you like for dinner? Thought I'd cook. xx'

Lauren dialled Skye's number but wasn't surprised when it went through to message bank. She left a short message: 'Hi sweetheart, Mum here, sorry to have missed your text messages. I was with Nana and Papa, having an important conversation. Give me a call if you're still at the pool, and I'll come and pick you up.' As she hung up, she realised that her words were wrong. In the sort of mood Skye was in, she'd take exception to 'an important conversation' being the reason Lauren hadn't answered the phone.

Driving towards home, Lauren dialled the landline and listened to it ring out. Then she tried Stu, who picked up straight away. 'Hi sweetie, just wondering if you've seen Skye?'

'She was at the pool earlier, but I haven't seen her since she left an hour or so ago. I'm leaving now, so I'll be home in about half an hour.' He paused. 'What's she done this time?'

Lauren let out a small laugh. 'Nothing, Stu. Why do you assume that?'

'Because I know her.'

'I'll see you at home.' Lauren pressed the 'end' button. Trying the home phone again brought no answer, and she hit the steering wheel with the palm of her hand. Her body felt as though the world's weight was pushing down on it.

She wanted to grab Skye and shake her. Of course teenagers were self-centred and thought the world revolved around them, but couldn't Skye see that everyone in the family had been given a shock when the melanoma diagnosis had come through? It didn't give her the right to behave as she was.

If the melanoma was in Lauren's lymph nodes or had gone

further, how would Skye take that news and how much further would her behaviour deteriorate?

The streetlight glow edged the curtains in Lauren's bedroom and, once again, she was awake after the dream had assaulted her. This time it had been the old nightmare of being in the dark—still disturbing, but familiar. She reached for the air-conditioner remote to turn it off. It beeped softly and the low hum of its engine stopped.

Lauren got up and padded to the bathroom. As usual, she knew there wasn't any point in going back to bed. Her thoughts were in overdrive.

That afternoon, she'd driven home only to find that Skye still wasn't there—and she wasn't answering her phone. Leaving Stu in the house in case she arrived back, Lauren and Dean had driven to all of Skye's favourite haunts, checking clothes shops and fast food places. Lauren had suggested she go by herself so that Dean could enjoy a couple of hours watching the cricket with his mates, but he'd insisted on coming.

It was dark by the time they gave up their search and drove home. Lauren alternated between angry and extremely frightened, in two minds about whether to call the police. In her heart of hearts, she was sure that Skye would come home in her own time. But what if she didn't?

'She's had a shock with your diagnosis,' Dean said. 'She needs to be in the fold of the family, not out somewhere stewing on it by herself. She wouldn't talk about it when I tried to speak to her again this morning. I've tried and tried—'

'So have I,' Lauren interjected, then wondered if that was really true. She remembered sitting Skye down in the lounge room, but she'd still had one earbud in and refused to take it out. Lauren was sure she couldn't concentrate like that, so she'd thrown her hands in the air and walked out.

'We're not getting through to her, babe,' said Dean. 'I'm quite worried.'

He ended up driving around their neighbourhood again later by himself. Finally, he found Skye only a few blocks from their street, walking home.

They tried to talk to her when she came home. Dean asked her to sit down, tell them what she was thinking.

'My thoughts are private,' Skye said. 'That's the one thing you can never know.' She crossed her arms.

'Sweetheart, we understand if you're frightened or worried. We are too, but we're a family and we need to stick together. For Mum, for all of us.' Dean squatted down and looked her straight in the eye, while Lauren stood off to the side.

She couldn't make herself go to her daughter, and she wasn't sure why. Maybe it was Skye's indifference or anger—surely they were masking fear, but they were so hard to deal with. Again, Lauren thought how unlike Skye this was. She wondered if there was more to it than the cancer. But what? It wasn't as though Skye had anything to be worried about: she never needed or wanted for anything.

Now, tonight, somewhere in the back of her mind, a little thought jolted Lauren. *Your attention*, it said. *She wants your attention*. But Lauren dismissed it. Skye was getting plenty of that.

Lauren went downstairs and walked along the hall, stopping to look at the family photo that had been taken last Christmas. There was Skye with her long red hair hanging around her face, a wide smile and her arms slung around Lauren's neck. Things were very different now. As Lauren gazed at the photo, she decided to ask Holly to recommend a colleague who specialised in teenagers and cancer.

Lauren glanced down to see her fists clenched. Not good. Not at five o'clock in the morning. She shook them out and took a few deep breaths to calm herself.

After she turned on the computer, her fingers hovered over the keyboard, wanting to type 'melanoma'. What would Dr Google come up with? Timeframes? Symptoms? Holly was right, it was best not to do that. Lauren was sure it could only mess with her state of mind, and that was fragile enough as it was.

She wiped away the tears that had arrived from nowhere and leaned her head on the palm of her hand, thinking about the days ahead.

Tomorrow, she'd try to get some bed rest and read a good book. On Monday, she and Holly were finally meeting with Dirk's mum. And on Tuesday morning, she'd be back at the hospital for surgery. Michelle had said it wouldn't be tricky or hard, but it would make her arm a lot sorer than the previous procedure. She'd also explained that because she'd be taking out a bigger portion, the wound would take longer to heal and limit the use of Lauren's arm for a couple of days. The stitches could come out in ten days, as long as everything went according to plan.

Straight after she'd finished with Michelle, Lauren would have her blood tests and CT scan. They'd know so much more then. In a way, Lauren was looking forward to it. She was sick of the uncertainty. As Michelle had said, having a plan was always the best thing.

Chapter 13

Over the weekend, when she wasn't at work, Tamara watched TV alone in her motel room and tried not to think about the funeral.

On Monday morning she touched base with the temp who was running Angelic Threads in her absence. All sorted. She then spent even longer than usual getting ready. She applied makeup twice—the first time was less than perfect—then dressed in her pre-planned outfit and headed off.

When she arrived, all the parking in the churchyard had been taken. She was surprised that so many people had turned up to her dad's funeral: she couldn't remember him having many friends. Taking a side street, she finally found a space under a large gum tree, thankful for the shade. As she locked the car door, a breeze blew and rustled the leaves. A couple of dead ones floated down and landed on her car windscreen. A magpie warbled. She tucked her handbag underneath her arm and started to walk towards the church.

'Tam?'

There was Craig, dressed in black jeans and a black shirt, standing on the footpath in front of the church. His beard was freshly trimmed and his hair was combed back into a neat ponytail. Sunglasses hid his eyes and his hands were shoved in his pockets.

She was so astounded to see him that she couldn't speak. She had never told him when or where the funeral would take place.

'I called around to find out the details,' he said, by way of explanation. 'I couldn't let you go through this alone. Your dad was an arsehole, but that doesn't make it any easier. I should know.'

Tamara nodded, overwhelmed. They walked side by side into the church.

Considering the number of cars outside, there were very few people sitting on the pews. Angela was in the front row by herself, her shoulders back, staring straight ahead. Unmoving. Tamara's conscience twinged: maybe it would have been better if she'd sat with Angela. Whether she liked it or not, Evan was her father, and her mother was now a widow. Which left Tamara as Angela's only living relative—life would be lonely for her now.

But it was too late to sit at the front, Tamara decided, as music began to filter from above. The service would start soon.

Craig let her go into a pew first before following her. They were right at the back of the church.

Tamara scanned for the source of the music: small speakers had been screwed into the ceiling. Next to them a fan spun lazily, shifting the humid air. Filtered light shone in beams through the stained-glass windows, and the few people sitting in front of them fanned themselves with the Order of Service. At the front, on a trolley, lay a coffin with a wreath of yellow and pink roses sitting on top, along with a photo of her father. Tamara sucked in a sharp breath as she looked at the picture.

Evan had aged badly. His wispy grey hair was brushed in strands across the top of his skull, and his eyes stared at the camera with a weepy, dull expression. The skin under his eyes sagged so that his whole face appeared to droop. If she'd been a betting woman, Tamara would have wagered a whole week's pay that this was the only photo Angela had of him as an older man. He'd never been one to have photos in the house and despised any being taken.

Angela hadn't mentioned how he'd died, Tamara suddenly realised. In the shock of her mother's reappearance, Tam had never even thought to ask. Had he been sick? That would certainly explain the pallor of his skin.

The minister's silky robe rustled as he walked past, indicating the start of the service. 'Welcome, everyone, to this celebration of the life of Evan Thompson. It is customary to come before God and pray for the souls of our loved ones . . .'

The sound of his voice faded into nothingness. Tamara could feel Craig's leg against hers and hear the rustle of paper. Someone coughed and the fan whirled.

What she heard the loudest was her dad's voice in her head: 'Clean that room of yours. It's a pigsty.' 'Don't answer back!' 'Do as I say, or else.'

A burst of music made Tamara jump. Craig gently pushed his leg into hers to remind her he was there. It was over.

The funeral directors moved to the doorway, pushing the trolley with the coffin on top. Angela followed slowly, her head cast down, a handkerchief clutched in one hand. As she arrived at the end of Tamara's aisle, their eyes locked. The relief and emotion that crossed

Angela's face made Tamara swallow hard. A lump appeared in her throat that made it difficult to breathe.

❦

The cobbled stone courtyard at the back of the church had a large wisteria vine growing up through the pavers and a wall of graffiti. There were tables covered in white cloths and plates of sandwiches set out.

'Nice spread,' Craig said as he helped himself to a ham sandwich and glanced around. 'Pretty cool place for a church too.'

Tamara stood next to him, her high heels beginning to make her legs ache. In the shop, she always wore a medium height heel, not her extra-tall formal black shoes. Shifting uncomfortably from one foot to the other, she decided that enough was enough. She'd done her duty.

Duty? Is that what it was?

Remember the secret birthday party? the Tam prompted. *She tried to love you.*

Not very fucking well, the Tamperer responded.

You need closure, the Tam argued. *That's what Doctor Kerr would say.*

The funeral was enough closure, said the Tamperer. *Done and dusted.*

'Come on.' Tamara took the empty plate from Craig's hand and put it on the table. 'Time to go.'

'You haven't talked to your mum,' he said around a mouthful.

'I don't need to. She saw me as they walked out, so she knows I was here. I didn't come to be the prodigal daughter.' After taking a few steps towards the door, she stopped and waited until Craig caught up.

'Tamara?'

Her stomach dropped as she saw Angela in the doorway.

'Tamara, I'm so glad you've come.' Angela didn't move forward, but extended her hands towards her daughter.

Not knowing what to do, Tamara glanced at Craig, but he had faded into the background and was now talking with another mourner, his back to her.

Bugger him, she thought. *He's done that on purpose.*

She gave her mother an awkward smile. 'Thought I should.' She shrugged. 'No big deal.'

'It is to me.' Uncertainty crossed her mum's face. 'Who are you with?' she asked, gesturing towards Craig.

'Just a friend.' Tamara's tone invited no further questions.

'Oh.' Angela looked down at her hands, her fingers twisting together.

'Sorry about, uh—' What should she call him? He hadn't been 'Dad' to her for years. Still, that's what he was. 'Sorry about Dad. Had he been sick?'

Angela nodded. 'On and off. Trouble with his kidneys. But in the end he went to sleep one night and didn't wake up. In one way it was expected, and in another it was a very big shock.'

'Must have been hard on you.'

Angela pressed her lips together. 'It will get better now.' Another pause.

Tamara kept trying to catch Craig's eye. She had to get out of there.

'Tam, I need to talk to you. Explain some things,' said Angela. 'But here isn't the place. Would you come to dinner? Tonight?'

'Ah . . .' Tamara was torn. She wanted to hear what her mum

had to say, but her need to keep some distance between them was very real. She couldn't just forgive and forget the way her parents had thrown her out onto the streets. Did she really want to open the door for her mum to come back into her life?

Angela started to speak very quickly, as if she only had one chance to say what she needed. 'I didn't get to bring you up the way I wanted to. I'm sorry. I'm sure you realise Evan was very controlling and needed things done his way. He wasn't like that when I married him, but I soon found out it was easier to keep the peace than it was to live with the consequences. He got worse after we . . .' Her eyes filled with tears and she stopped speaking.

Bloody hell, Tamara thought. *I don't want to hear her sob story. She should have protected me.* Uneasily, she shifted from foot to foot again. 'Look . . .'

Her feelings must have showed on her face, because Angela pulled herself up straight and interrupted. 'I know I have no rights to you or your life. But as your mother, I'm not asking you, I'm *telling* you that I must explain some things to you.'

The desperation in her voice made Tam want to push her away. It was all too much. The past week had brought the death of her father, contact with her mother, breaking off her relationship, and then Craig's unexpected kindness. Goosebumps rippled over her arms and she shivered.

'So will you see me? Tamara?'

What did 'must explain' mean? What could there be to explain?

'Right,' said Tamara. 'Well.' There didn't seem to be any more words left in her vocabulary. 'Okay. Fine. Yes.' Once the clipped and stilted words were out, she couldn't take them back.

Angela wilted in relief. 'Would you like to come over for dinner tonight?'

Tamara nodded reluctantly.

෭

Later, when Tamara was sitting in her motel room again, her phone beeped with a text message from Craig. 'How are you?'

She responded straight away. 'Okay. Thanks for coming today.'

'Glad I was helpful. Be good to see you soon, I hope.'

She read and re-read his words, then closed the screen and clutched her phone to her chest, hating herself. Why had she thought that going to the funeral might help? She felt even more confused and shaken up.

But maybe dinner with her mother would be a good thing, even though she was dreading it. She just had to do her makeup again and find the right outfit.

Chapter 14

'Are you sure you're up for this?' Holly asked Lauren. They'd met up five minutes before their meeting with Dirk's mother and were waiting for her to arrive.

'Of course!' said Lauren. 'I hope we can resolve the issue with Dirk before my surgery tomorrow morning. A weight off my mind.'

'Okay,' said Holly. 'It's just that I can do this with Joy if you need me to.'

'No, no.' Lauren chuckled weakly. 'I'm fine.' Of course she wasn't feeling all that great, but she had to see this through. She *had* to.

When Zoe walked in, they all smiled and shook hands.

'Zoe, thank you for meeting with us,' said Lauren. 'I really appreciate it. This is Holly Young, our resident psychologist.' Lauren hadn't wanted to introduce Holly like that, worried it would frighten Dirk's mother, but those were the rules.

Something flickered across Zoe's face. She carefully put her handbag next to her chair and sat down. 'I'm not really sure why I'm here. Dirk is doing fine in his work, isn't he? I haven't heard otherwise. And I thought we cleared up everything else in our talk last week.'

'Oh yes, there's no doubt that Dirk's a clever boy. And he gets along with all the other kids in the class and is lovely to have around.' Lauren smiled to put Zoe at ease. Holly had told her to praise Dirk, then gently bring up the problems.

It seemed to be working because Zoe started to relax—her shoulders lost their stiffness and she smiled a little. 'Yes, he's a good boy. He's our only child.' She crossed her legs and sat back. 'We've tried to have more, but we can't seem to make it happen. I'm resigned to the fact now.'

'I'm sorry to hear that,' Lauren said quietly. 'Children are very important, aren't they? Nothing more important, really.'

Zoe started to look uncomfortable, and Holly kicked Lauren under the table.

What? Lauren wanted to say. *I'm only stating the obvious.*

A silence fell while Lauren composed her thoughts. Really, there wasn't a soft way to do this. It was going to be like Michelle telling her about the melanoma. 'Zoe, as much as Dirk is going well in class, we do have some concerns about him.'

In the chair, Zoe froze and her face became set.

'Last Tuesday I spoke with you about the bruises,' Lauren continued. 'You then took him out of school for two days due to illness. He had a nosebleed on Friday and it took some time for me to stop it. He told me that this isn't unusual.'

Zoe fixed her eyes above Lauren's head. It seemed to her that the woman wasn't listening. She'd shut off.

Lauren kept trying to get through to her. 'Dirk also mentioned stomach pains, and I've noticed he doesn't eat much. In fact, I reckon he's lost a little weight. Of course, that always happens if a child has a growth spurt, but . . .' She paused. 'He doesn't seem any taller to me.'

Again, silence filled the room. Zoe was chewing her bottom lip and had dropped her gaze to the floor. Everything in her demeanour worried Lauren. It also made her angry. This woman should have been doing something for her child—even something as small as putting him to bed for a week until he felt better.

'I don't think that this is any of your business,' Zoe finally said, although she didn't move from her seat.

Holly leaned forward slightly. 'I understand your thinking, Mrs Anderson. After all, we're just Dirk's teachers. However, we have a duty of care to each child in our classroom. That's why we're having this conversation.'

Zoe nodded, but then she pressed her lips together and stayed silent.

'I'm curious about something, Zoe,' said Lauren. 'When I asked all the kids to paint an object starting with the letter G, Dirk drew an ambulance instead. He said that it parked in your driveway?'

'Yes, that's right, to pick up our elderly neighbour who'd had a stroke. They don't have any car access. Dirk thought it was very cool. He must have just really wanted to draw it.'

Was that true? It sounded plausible.

Lauren also wanted to bring up how quickly Dirk seemed to get upset—after all, it had only taken a blob of green paint to make him angry. *Bugger it*, she decided. It was more important to bring it up than not. A child's welfare was at stake. 'Dirk became quite angry when he spilled some paint last week.'

Zoe's head jerked up. 'Well, all kids can be moody.'

Lauren shook her head. 'Don't you see?' Her voice rose a little. She noticed Holly giving her a sharp look, but she ignored it. 'It *is* important, because something so small never would have upset him earlier. You know as well as I do that he was a happy-go-lucky child.'

Overhead, a jet rumbled as it roared into the sky. The windows shook gently as it flew west.

When Zoe started to speak, her voice was soft, so Lauren and Holly had to lean towards her to make out the words. 'You're right. There's something wrong with Dirk. First the bruising started, and I made sure I watched him like a hawk. In the playground, he always seemed to give himself a little bump, but at times they just appeared. Then the nosebleeds started. I blamed the hot weather, but then he had one on a cooler day.' She shifted in her seat, and Lauren read trepidation in her eyes. 'Look, for a while I even suspected my husband of hitting Dirk. He didn't want to eat with us. He told me that his tummy hurt.' She took a shaky breath. 'Of course, the idea was dreadful, but better than . . .'

Out of the corner of her eye, Lauren looked at Holly, trying to work out what to do. Did Zoe think that Dirk was sick or that her husband was hitting him? Lauren wasn't sure. But Zoe was clearly putting in her head in the sand.

'Mrs Anderson, what are your plans to help Dirk?' Holly asked gently.

'What do you think I should do?' Panic radiated from the woman.

'I'm wondering what you think the problem is?' Holly prompted her.

'I don't know,' Zoe admitted. 'I really don't know, but I'm too scared to find out.' She put her arms around herself and held on tight as she looked at Lauren. 'There can't be anything wrong with him, there just *can't* be! He's my only son.' She shook her head. 'No, I can't do this. I'm sorry. I have to go.'

Disbelief coursed through Lauren. She swung around to look at Holly in horror. Without stopping to think, she turned back to Zoe and spoke loudly. 'You can't not take Dirk to the doctor because you're frightened. That's completely ridiculous! If he's sick, the sooner he gets medical treatment, the better. I'm sorry, Mrs Anderson, but you don't have a choice. You must get him to a doctor.'

'Unless you suspect that your husband is hurting your son,' Holly said gently, shooting Lauren an annoyed stare. 'Do you think that's a real possibility?'

Tears overflowed from Zoe's eyes. 'I don't think so.' She was trembling. 'I think . . . I think he's sick.'

'Whatever happens, whatever action is taken, we're here to support Dirk for as long as he needs,' said Holly, handing Zoe a tissue from the box on the desk.

They agreed on a plan of action: Zoe would take Dirk to her family GP the next day. After she'd thanked them, said goodbye and headed out of the room, Holly turned to Lauren and raised an eyebrow.

'I'm sorry,' said Lauren. 'I don't know what came over me.' She'd never sounded so unprofessional in her life! She was just glad it had worked out.

'That went better than it should have gone,' said Holly, echoing her thoughts. 'Lauren, it's okay, I completely understand this time— but that can't happen again.'

'I know,' Lauren said apologetically. 'I think you and Joy should take it from here. I'm going to focus on getting better.'

Chapter 15

What's the protocol when having dinner with your mother for the first time in twenty-seven years? Tamara wondered. Should she bring chocolate or flowers? A bottle of wine? No, her parents had been teetotallers. Occasionally her father would see something on TV about alcohol-fuelled violence and start on a rant about the evils of drinking. That was one of the reasons why Tamara had started— just to annoy him.

It was also why she'd be taking beer tonight. If Angela wanted to talk to her, she could bloody well accept her the way she was.

Deciding that flowers were a benign gift, Tamara stopped at a roadside florist on the way and picked up a bunch of brightly coloured gerberas.

Just before seven, she pulled into the driveway and turned off the engine. She saw the curtain in the front window move aside. Angela peered out into the street, then the curtain fell back into place. A few seconds later, the front door opened. Angela stood in the porchlight where a million midges attacked the unsuspecting lightbulb.

Frozen to her seat, Tamara stalled for time as she slowly gathered the flowers and beer. Finally, there was nothing else for it. She took the keys from the ignition and pushed the car door open with her shoulder, then kicked it shut with her hip.

'Hi,' she said, holding out the flowers to her mum as she stepped onto the porch. The smell of a warm potato salad floated out on the air-conditioned breeze.

'Thank you, they're lovely,' Angela said. 'Come in.'

The house had changed a lot. When Tamara had lived there, everything had been sterile. The kitchen benches were scrubbed and the floor was so clean it would have been perfectly acceptable to eat off it. There had been no photos, wall hangings or knick-knacks on the shelves to show the personality of the people who lived there. Now, a cheery calendar with inspiring quotes and sunrises was pinned to the fridge. A small statue of a kitten sat on the top shelf of the sideboard, and an indoor plant flourished in the corner of the kitchen.

'Do you want those in the fridge?' Angela asked, holding her hand out for the beers after putting the flowers on the bench.

'Thanks. Do you like beer? I didn't know whether to bring you anything,' Tamara said, still looking around in surprise.

'I have the occasional glass of wine now and then, but I've got some in the fridge.' Angela straightened up after putting the beer away and looked at Tamara. 'So, how do you feel?'

'I'm not sure. I'm here because you said you have something important to tell me.' She crossed her arms as if they made a full stop at the end of her sentence. Then, realising that her body language probably looked defensive, she made an effort to uncross them. She wasn't sure what to do with her hands—she wished she still smoked. In the end, she slid them into the pockets of her freshly ironed linen pants and leaned against the wall.

'I'm not expecting anything, Tamara,' said her mother. 'But I have to say my piece so you know the truth.'

'The truth?'

Angela filled a vase, arranged the flowers and took it to the table. 'You need to know some things about the past. I'll serve up and we can talk over dinner. Please.' With a movement of her hand, she showed Tamara into the lounge room. 'Take a drink and make yourself comfortable. I'll be in shortly.'

Tamara's chest fluttered with anxiety. In the lounge room, she drew in a sharp breath when she saw three photos sitting on top of the old-fashioned TV. Without thinking, she picked them up to inspect them closely. The first one had been taken on that Christmas Day when she'd been given new clothes. She was standing underneath the spotted hibiscus bush, next to a bike that had colourful plastic streamers attached to the handle grips. Her smile was so large, her blue eyes so bright. Her shoulder-length hair had been put into pigtails, and there seemed to be more pink ribbon than hair.

She hadn't even known this photo had been taken.

The next one was a professional school photo. How was this possible? She never knew her parents had bought one. She would always go along with her classmates to have her photo taken, but when the pictures were delivered to the school, none were ever handed to her.

Setting it down carefully, Tamara picked up the last photo. She remembered everything about this one. On her first day of Year Six, Angela had insisted on a family photo before Tamara left for school. After much whinging, Evan finally agreed. Angela had brought it home in a frame and proudly set it in the lounge room on the mantelpiece above the oil heater. Two days later, it was gone. Tamara didn't know the story behind its disappearance, but she guessed it had something to do with her. Everything always had something to do with her.

Hearing a noise behind her, Tamara turned to see Angela placing two plates on the coffee table between two rocker chairs and removing a magazine that had been open to a crossword puzzle. Tamara had never seen her mum do a crossword before. The salt and pepper shakers were already on the coffee table, and next to them was a bowl of nuts. Evan wouldn't have let them eat in front of the TV; dinner took place around the kitchen table in silence, so he could listen to the news on the radio.

'You kept these?' Tamara asked in wonder, still holding the family shot.

'Of course I did. Just because they weren't on display didn't mean I threw them out. Come and sit. It's nice to have someone to cook for.'

'Why didn't you have them out before?' The question was out of Tamara's mouth before she could stop it.

'Well, in that one of the three of us, Evan said you weren't smiling properly. The one when you were small I took when you weren't looking, so you weren't quite facing the camera properly, which meant the whole thing was off-centre. You know, your father didn't like it when things weren't straight. He was very . . . what's the word for it now? Obsessive something?' Her tone was matter of fact.

'Obsessive-compulsive?' Tamara put the photograph back down and went to sit on the rocker. 'There was never anything out of place.' Of course, as Doctor Kerr had pointed out, she was the same. Her mind flashed back to the motel room—everything was in lines or rows. A place for everything and everything in its place.

She was her father's daughter. How depressing.

'Yes, that's right,' said Angela. 'And the school photo was never able to see the light of day, because it wasn't his idea to buy one.' Angela spoke in a flat, expressionless tone, like someone reciting a monologue. 'Salt?' Tamara shook her head. 'Please start.' Angela gestured to the plate, and Tamara picked it up, took a mouthful and chewed. The potato salad was creamy and smooth, while the cold meat was succulent and juicy. Angela had always been a good cook.

With the lights on and Evan's foreboding presence gone forever, the house didn't trigger her fears as much as she'd expected. Sure, there were some not-very-nice memories here. And obviously this 'truth' needed to come out. But it gave Tamara a nice feeling to think that the photos had been kept and were out now.

How do you know she didn't put them out tonight? the Tamperer whispered.

'Will you tell me a little about you?' Angela asked tentatively.

Tamara put another mouthful onto her fork and thought about what she was ready to share. 'Not much to tell, really. Once Dad kicked me out, I lived on the streets for a while. Then I was lucky enough that a shopkeeper saw some potential in me and gave me a chance. I've worked at Angelic Threads since then.' She paused. 'So, how *did* you know where to find me?'

'I never lost you,' Angela answered simply. 'I always knew where you were. Actually, that's not right. I went looking for you. I made sure I took extra-long to do the shopping and walk through the places where you used to go. I even asked a policeman, once, if he'd seen you—I had these photos, you see, so I could show him. He hadn't, but he asked if I wanted to report you missing.' Her mouth twisted in a sad smile. 'But I couldn't. I looked for weeks before I found you—and then it was only by chance. You walked by the green grocer's while I was getting veggies for dinner.' Angela looked away, lost in memories. 'I was in the back, and there you were. Just in front of the window. I went running out, but you'd gone so quickly. Then I asked the owner if he'd seen you before. He was quite stroppy when he told me he knew you were stealing from his front stalls, but he couldn't catch you.'

'He *knew*?'

Angela nodded. 'So I suggested he let you take whatever you wanted, and I'd come in and pay him every week. That way, I knew you were eating well, not scavenging in rubbish bins like some urchin. I had to do *something*. Evan always kept a close eye on the household budget, but I managed to make sure there was enough to cover what you ate. He wouldn't have any idea what groceries cost. He just liked to make sure we were thrifty. Which is why you always had hand-me-down clothes, unfortunately.'

Tamara gave a wry half smile. 'I've made up for that,' she said. 'Now about—'

Angela held up her hand in a 'stop' gesture. She put her plate aside and met Tamara's eyes, a lifetime of regret and sadness in her expression.

'After that, I went back often to catch a glimpse of you at that corner. You'd be with other kids, a girl and a boy. Then you disappeared.' She paused. 'I still remember the day I saw you again: the third of April, three years later. I was walking through the shopping centre on my way to the dry-cleaning store with Evan's suit. I happened to look at a dress in the window of a shop, two doors down.' She stopped and took a breath. Her eyes had gone a little red. 'And there you were. Putting clothes up on the racks, helping customers. I was so proud. So you see, I never lost you.'

Tamara's appetite was gone. 'What?' she whispered.

'Did you really think I'd let you go without keeping an eye on you? That wasn't possible. Like I said, I should have spoken out a lot more than I did to Evan, but the die had been cast. I couldn't have left Evan—I threatened to, once.' She sighed deeply. 'But that's another story. And I truly believed you'd be better off out of this house. He was hurting you, and he could have done worse, so I had to let you go. Please understand! It's the hardest thing I've ever done in my life. I wanted—*needed*—you to be happy . . .'

Tamara widened her eyes, anger surging through her body. 'Are you *serious*?' she asked in a low voice. 'Happiness?' Her voice broke. 'I didn't get that with you two. I got criticism, taunts, little affection and even less love. All of that makes for a fairly unhappy childhood, and it—' Somehow she reined her emotions in and continued in a steady voice. 'It's made my adult life very difficult. And now you're telling me you sent me out on the streets on purpose? What sort of a . . .' She let it all out this time. 'What sort of a person does that?'

She placed her plate roughly on the coffee table and stood up, then watched as Angela's shoulders drooped and all of her strength seemed to vanish. In front of Tamara's eyes, her mother shrank and became a little old lady.

Tamara paced the room, desperate to leave, but also desperate to hear more.

Angela seemed to rally and stood up too. 'You can go ahead and blame me for the things that have happened in your life, but they would have been a whole lot worse if Evan had had his way. Please, try and understand.'

'Shit.' Tamara shook her head. She went into the kitchen and grabbed another beer from the fridge.

Angela followed her and stood quietly, watching. 'I need to tell you the whole story. It starts a lot earlier than when he kicked you out. It starts when you were born. And how you came to us.'

Tamara put down the beer and looked at her mum. 'What do you mean?'

Angela paused. 'Do you think you can come back in and sit down while I tell you? If you don't want anything to do with me afterwards, I'll accept that. I'll leave you alone, but I can't die without you knowing everything.'

Feeling numb, but still needing to know 'the truth', Tamara took her beer and did as she'd been asked.

When they were in the rockers again, Angela stared into the distance as she spoke. 'Evan and I tried to have children for many years and nothing happened. When tests showed the problem was with Evan and not me, that's when everything changed. I saw a story in the newspaper about the need for more foster-parents. I started thinking about adoption, so I made enquiries. It took me a long time, but I finally convinced him. Of course, we had to jump through hoops to be accepted—but once we were, I didn't think there could be any turning back.'

Her eyes flickered all around, never once resting on Tamara. All Tamara could feel was the thudding of her heart as she stared at the woman she'd thought for over forty years was her mum.

'On the day you were born, we got the phone call quite early. We had to meet the social worker at the hospital. I remember getting dressed in a hurry—we'd been sitting at the table having a cup of coffee. We knew you were due, but your birth mother—well, she'd gone over her due date. We'd been on tenterhooks for days.'

Angela stopped to take a sip of water.

'When you were brought in to us, I burst into tears. The happiest I'd been for so long. You were tiny and had eyes so, so blue. And when they handed you to me, your hand wrapped around my finger as tightly as anything. You were so precious.'

Her dreamy voice suddenly became harsh and bitter.

'I asked Evan if he wanted to hold you, but he took a step back. I remember it so clearly. His face went red then white, and his fists clenched. "What's wrong?" I asked. "I don't want this," he said. "I can't have a kid that's not mine." Well, I was flabbergasted. And frightened that he wouldn't let me take you home. I'd already fallen in love with you, so there was no way you weren't coming home with me.' She sighed. 'Of course when the social worker heard that, she got very worried. We'd already been through counselling, you see, to make sure we'd be able to cope.'

Tamara broke out in a sweat. She was sure her heart was going to come right out of her chest, it was beating so fast. And she couldn't breathe.

'I asked the social worker for a moment alone with my husband. "He's overwhelmed," I told her. When she left the room, I went up to him. We were almost touching noses. "Evan," I said, "if you don't sign those papers, I'll leave you."' Angela smiled at the memory. 'He scoffed at me for a couple of seconds, then he realised I was serious. "We take that child home today and give her a life," I said, "or you'll regret the day you ever met me." And then we took you home.'

Tamara put her face in her hands, trying to understand.

'Parenthood doesn't come with a manual,' Angela said, kneading the palms of her hands with wrinkled, arthritic fingers. 'You were a . . . "difficult" is a harsh word, but you had a lot of colic and tended to be unsettled. Evan wasn't used to noise of any sort. He'd look for any excuse to criticise me, my parenting. You. Even when you were still tiny, he said awful things about you. Of course, it wasn't all his fault. One of the only times I ever stood up to him was in the hospital. After that, he tried to make sure I never could. He'd cut me down, call me names, undermine me when we were out in public. It was easier to stay quiet than try to argue.'

Tamara couldn't believe what she was hearing. She tried to form words, but despite the beer she'd been drinking, her mouth was dry and her tongue was stuck to the roof of her mouth. Her first instinct was to deny everything Angela had just told her—and make her swear that it wasn't true.

But something about Angela's story suddenly made so much sense. Tamara had never been able to please Evan because she wasn't his. He'd never given her a chance, simply because she wasn't his child. In a warped way, that was comforting.

Angela started to speak again. 'You have to understand, he was a good man when we married. Not a soulmate, but he was steady and solid. Had a respectable job. Like my dad said, he was a provider, and all I ever wanted to do was marry and have children. I dreamed of a house with lots of kids, mess and laughter. People to cook for. To nurture.' She paused and looked over at Tamara. 'Evan had a few major disappointments and changed. People do that.'

Angela seemed to have run out of words. She sat there gazing at Tamara, twisting her wedding rings around on her finger. The silence grew uncomfortable.

'Are you going to say something?' Angela asked, a tremor in her voice.

Tamara opened her mouth, but nothing came out. She tried again. 'I . . .'

Angela put a hand on her arm. 'I'm sorry I waited so long to tell you.'

'I . . . I don't know what to say. Sorry. Um . . .' Tamara looked around at the house that was so achingly familiar and yet strange at the same time. 'Thank you for telling me.'

Angela dared to smile, just a little.

Chapter 16

'Where *were* you?' her dad's question from the previous evening echoed in Skye's mind as she leaned against the classroom wall in the sun. It warmed her and made her dozy. She was tired from not sleeping well over the past few nights. Not since she'd walked home from the pool on Saturday. For some weird reason, she kept remembering her dad's question, along with his look of hurt and confusion.

She hadn't meant to hurt her parents, especially her dad. She'd been annoyed that her mum hadn't checked her phone. Once again, something else had been more 'important' than her daughter. And after her mum hadn't picked her up from the pool, it had been quicker for her to walk to the air-conditioned shopping centre than to walk all the way home in the heat. Even catching the bus had been out of the question, because she'd run out of money and her ticket had expired.

Skye had wandered through the shopping centre and browsed in a couple of the clothes shops that Adele had said were having a sale. At Angelic Threads, she had peered in through the doorway to see if the blonde shop manager was there. Skye didn't know the woman's name, but she was cool. The type of cool that any teenager liked: someone who talked music and clothes with the girls when they went in. Remembered their names and what they liked. Told jokes that were actually funny.

For some strange reason, Skye had a longing to talk with her. Maybe she would listen to her in a way her mum couldn't. But Skye felt too awkward to go in.

Although the lady was busy with customers, she caught sight of Skye and waved, calling out, 'Hi there, Skye!'

Skye just gave her a small smile back and kept on walking.

Now, leaning back against the sun-warmed wall, she hoped she hadn't seemed like a cold bitch. Adele had told her she could be a bit standoffish.

She heard footsteps approaching and opened her eyes. *Speak of the devil.*

'Hey, there you are!' said Adele. 'Been looking for you.' She sat next to Skye. 'Geez, it's hot. Why are you sitting here?'

Skye shrugged. She didn't want to talk just now. The sun had almost put her to sleep. This way, she didn't have to think about the surgery her mum was having today. Her dad had been up early, and when Skye had come downstairs to get some breakfast, it had looked like her mum had stayed up all night.

Not that she cared.

They'd left to go to the surgery when she'd been in the shower.

She'd actually been tempted to not go to school today. She could have forged her mum's signature again, and she was sure the teachers would have understood. After all, her maths teacher had pulled her aside after class the day before, saying that if Skye wanted to talk then her door was always open. *Nice*, Skye had thought. Nicer than her own mum, anyway. She wondered if her maths teacher had a fourteen-year-old daughter at home she was ignoring so she could focus on kids from school.

Anyway, then Skye had remembered that the school might text her parents if she wagged, so she'd decided it probably wasn't worth the risk.

She would just have to get through the day while not thinking about anything. Big ask for someone with nearly a million different thoughts and emotions swirling around in her head. She wanted one of those things that Professor Dumbledore, from *Harry Potter*, had in his office, where he could put his wand to his ear and drain out all his thoughts. That would be perfect for her right about now— then she wouldn't have to feel anything.

'How's your mum?' Adele asked.

Great timing, Skye thought. Adele had always had a knack for bringing up the last thing Skye wanted to talk about.

Struggling not to show how much she cared, Skye shrugged. 'Fine, I guess. She's having surgery this morning. I heard Mum and Dad talking to Stu about it last night. And, get this, she's full-on wanting to find her birth mum now too, so she can meet her before she dies. But, I mean, who wants to bring more people into our family?'

Adele raised her eyebrows. 'Oh. My. God. They could be anyone. *We* might be related!' She giggled. 'Or . . . what if you ended up marrying your brother? I heard that long-lost siblings are *really* attracted to each other. Like, totally DTF.'

Jasmine flopped down next to them. 'You don't know if she's

going to die,' she said to Skye. 'Stop saying that. And if you get a new family, they might be the best people you've ever met, so you can go live with them instead of with your mum.'

'I don't need anyone extra in the family,' said Skye, shaking her head. 'I've *got* grandparents—ones I've known since I was born. I've got a brother, unfortunately, and I've got parents. Our family works fine the way it is. I don't get why she'd want to bring strangers in. What if they're druggies or horrible people?'

'Yeah, your family works fine,' Adele said sarcastically. 'I can see how you'd think that.'

Skye frowned at her. 'What do you mean?'

'Well, you're always bitching about how your mum's wrapped up in work and is never around when you need her. Sounds like your family's working great!'

Jasmine pushed Adele with her foot. 'Stop it. Don't be such a bitch.'

Skye looked down and thought about that. She wouldn't admit it out loud, but Adele had a point. Sniffing, Skye got to her feet. 'I gotta go.'

Adele jumped up and started to walk with her. Then she leaned in and whispered, 'So, are you gonna do it? The dare? Come on, it's been ages!'

'Time's got to be right, doesn't it? I'll text you when I've done it.'

'Going to be so good,' Adele said. 'So much fun!'

'Yeah, totally.' Skye didn't really think so, but she didn't want to look like a loser. 'Anyway, I gotta go,' she said to Adele. 'See ya.'

Skye walked towards the girls' toilets. While she was in the cubicle, her phone dinged with a Snapchat message: a selfie of Billy, his mouth exaggeratingly turned downwards. 'It's been 2 days. I'm so horny.'

Yeah, she knew that. She'd also heard Adele and the girls talking about Billy and his mates yesterday at lunch.

'Did you hear about Billy Gaston and his group?' Jasmine had said, flicking her long blonde hair to get everyone's attention.

Unable to stop herself, Skye leaned forward, hungry for any information about what he'd been doing. He hadn't answered her last two texts.

'God, what have those fuckboys done now?' Adele asked.

'They got pulled up by the cops coz they were breaking all the hoon laws!'

Skye's mouth dried up. Billy had told her he was going to study all weekend—he hadn't said anything about being caught by the cops. Maybe he hadn't been driving: all his mates had their P-plates too.

'Apparently they had a couple of girls from that boarding school, just down the road, with them as well.' Jasmine's voice had a spark of excitement, and Skye wondered if she liked bad boys too.

'Oh well, that explains it,' said Adele. 'Everyone knows that school produces girls who are—' Adele paused to give an innocent look '—rather loose-knickered.'

The girls fell about laughing.

Skye felt sick. What was this all about?

'The guys probably had their hands down the girls' shirts, and whoever was driving was trying to impress them.'

Wrinkling her nose, Skye said, 'Who'd do that sort of shit anyway? As if I want some guy grabbing at my tits in front of all his mates.'

Adele burst out laughing. 'You've got nothing but mosquito bites! Wouldn't be anything to grab.'

Skye's face went hot when a couple of her friends laughed, but Jasmine shifted over and put an arm around her. 'Adele, you can be a bitch sometimes.'

Skye grabbed her bag and stalked off to the girls' toilets. In the stall, she thought about Billy and those pretty private school girls who walked around as if they owned the world. They had so much confidence—they must have been born with it, because Skye had tried to copy their walk, but she couldn't. Her gran had told her that confidence was attractive.

All her gran's Mills & Boon covers came back to Skye, and she swallowed hard. Men gave in to women who were sexy and confident and had big boobs. Jealousy flooded her.

Leaving her bag in the stall, she checked the time on her iPhone: only five minutes before the bell would go. She looked in the mirror and ran her fingers through her hair, trying to achieve a sexy bed-hair look that would reveal her piercing; then took some lipstick out of her bag and tried to apply it the way the lady at the chemist had shown her. She smacked her lips together and threw her head back in what she hoped was a sexy pose. Staring at herself, she thought she looked pretty good.

Back in the stall, she took off her top and held her breast up with one hand, focused the camera, made sure her pose was right and clicked. Not giving herself time to think about it, she typed 'missing you, big boy' and hit send in Snapchat.

Once he'd seen the photo, Billy would want her more than ever.

The bell sounded. Skye quickly repacked her bag, took a paper towel from the dispenser and scrubbed at her lips before joining the throng heading for class.

At lunchtime Skye was sitting in the quadrangle by herself, holding her phone, waiting for Billy to reply.

When a group of older boys walked past her, their laughter made her look up in the hope that it was Billy. A couple of the boys glanced her way and winked at her.

She turned away, wondering what their problem was.

Then Holly was standing next to her. Skye could tell that she was trying to work out whether to sit down or not. *Don't!* she screamed in her mind. *Don't sit down.* She quickly scrambled to her feet to take the option away. 'Hello, Miss.'

'Hello, Skye, how are you?' Holly asked.

'Fine,' Skye answered quickly, plastering a smile on her face. She noticed that the school psychologist had a strange look in her eyes. Skye's stomach dropped—had Holly heard gossip about her relationship with Billy? She reached down to pick up her schoolbag and repack it, as if she had to go somewhere fast.

'Coping okay with everything?' asked Holly.

'Yep. In fact, I'm just on my way to do a bit of study in the library. I've got a maths test this afternoon.' Swinging her backpack up, Skye started to escape, but Holly kept up with her.

'I just want you to know that I'm here if you ever want to have a chat. Completely off the record, as such. I won't tell your mum what we talk about, but I thought you might need someone to speak to about everything that's going on.'

'Yeah, cheers for that,' Skye said awkwardly.

'No problems. I'll catch you later.'

'Sure.'

Changing direction from the library to the school gate, Skye glanced over her shoulder to make sure no one was following her.

Holly had disappeared into the crowd of kids, and there didn't seem to be any other teachers close by. Quickly, Skye walked out of the gate and down the street. She'd change out of her uniform in the mall toilets and damn well go and do what Adele had dared her to do, right now. That might put Adele in her place.

Then Skye would find Billy after school.

Chapter 17

Tamara had come to work in a daze after Angela's revelations. Well, maybe 'daze' wasn't the right word—perhaps 'stupor' or 'confusion' was more appropriate. Oh, parts of what Angela had said made clear and total sense . . . but the fact that she'd actually let Tamara out on the streets and then watched her like some guardian angel? Well, Tamara just found that odd, even with the explanation Angela had given her.

After Tamara had left Whitfield Street, she'd tried to remember if she'd ever sensed that Evan might actually hit her. She'd realised Angela had been right: the night he kicked her out he'd come very close. And now, thinking back, she would have bet next week's pay that after she'd left the house, he'd hit Angela. Sadness swept over her.

'Excuse me?' A woman's voice sounded at her shoulder, making Tamara jump. 'Do you have this in a size 12?'

Tamara took the white linen shirt and stared at it. For a second, she couldn't remember what to do next. Then it clicked. 'Ah, I'll check out the back for you.'

As she headed for the storeroom, she tried to shake the fog from her brain. Once inside, she let out her breath in a long *whoosh* and leaned her head against the wall. She wanted to splash cold water on her face, to shock the clouds of incomprehension away, but she couldn't. It would ruin her makeup, and she didn't have time to reapply it—she needed to serve her customer. Instead, she slapped her face a couple of times and did a few star jumps. Her sluggish blood started to flow, bringing more oxygen to her brain. Then she flicked through the racks holding the extra sizes and found an identical linen shirt in size 12.

'Here you go,' she said, bustling out into the store, a polite smile on her face. She held up the shirt for the customer to admire. 'Would you like to try it on?'

The lady nodded. 'It's lovely, isn't it? Crisp lines and classic.'

Everything went well from there, and soon Tamara was going through the motions of ringing the purchase up on the till and talking to the woman about how hot the weather had been. As Tamara farewelled her happy customer, she walked her to the door. 'Enjoy!' she said with one last smile, then turned to go back inside, just as a loud alarm went off from the surf shop opposite Angelic Threads. A thrill ran through her. Shoplifting was a shop-owner's worst nightmare. She glanced over and saw a young red-haired girl frozen just outside the shop. Fear was etched in her body—she looked as though she was about to run.

Tamara could imagine all the questions running through the girl's mind: *What do I do? Should I go back? Am I about to be arrested?*

'Don't!' Tamara called out, involuntarily.

The girl turned around, staring at Tamara through the throng of people who had stopped to see what the commotion was about. Tamara's face dropped as she recognised the teenager—Adele's friend, Skye.

Tamara walked towards her, reaching her at the same time as the shop-owner. Usually, Tamara would have said a friendly hello to this woman, Sarah—they'd worked opposite each other for ten years—but now Sarah was totally focused on Skye.

'What have you taken?' she asked angrily, yelling over the alarm. 'I get *so* sick of you teenagers doing this. Do you know I lose five per cent of my profit each year to you buggers?'

Someone in Sarah's shop switched off the alarm, making it a lot easier to hear. Sarah held out her hand to Skye. 'Give it back to me. Now.'

'I . . .' Skye didn't seem able to make her mouth work. She dropped her bag.

Sarah bent to unzip it and pulled out a pair of shorts with pom-poms hanging from the hemline. 'I'm calling security,' she said.

Skye looked at Tamara, her eyes wide. Trepidation mixed with distress. 'No,' she said, sounding panicked. '*No!* Please don't. I'll do anything . . .'

Suddenly Tamara was remembering how it had felt to be caught with the brandy bottle. Something in Skye's eyes, her voice, brought it all back so vividly that Tamara's stomach clenched. She'd never intervened with a shoplifter before, but this time she had to take action. 'Sarah,' she said, 'please wait a moment. I know this girl. She comes into my shop a lot and we've never had a problem.' Tamara glanced at Skye, who looked ready to cry. 'Just leave her with me and I'll sort her out.'

'God, Tam, you know how much shoplifters cost us! Let security make an example of her. At least she can spread the message to all of her friends.'

Tamara put her hand on Sarah's arm and spoke quietly. 'Look, we both know there are other ways to get the message out.' Over early morning coffees, she and Sarah had shared a story or two about their own wild teenage years. In fact, Sarah knew about how Tamara had come to work for Stella at Angelic Threads, and she'd said she thought it was a great idea to 'keep those buggers off the streets'. Tamara dropped her voice even lower, so that Skye couldn't hear. 'The girl's had a scare, Sarah. She's a good kid. If she wasn't, we both know calling security would make no difference whatsoever. Leave her with me, and I'll take care of it.'

Sarah seemed to waver, then she turned to Skye and shook her finger at her. 'If I catch you in my shop again, I'll call security whether you've taken something or not. You're banned. Don't *ever* come back in here again.'

Skye nodded. 'I promise,' she answered quickly.

'Go. Get out of my sight.' Sarah pinned Tamara with a hard stare. 'You make sure you fix this.'

'You've got my word,' Tamara said.

Sarah, still holding the shorts, went back into her store, muttering.

Tamara put her hand on Skye's shoulder. 'Come on, let's go.'

Skye walked alongside her into Angelic Threads. Tamara shut the door and put her 'Back in Five' sign up, then led Skye into the storeroom. The girl sat on an office chair and stared at the floor, fiddling with the silver stud at the top of her ear. Tamara had once had a piercing like that.

Again, she remembered being caught in the bottle shop. It was as if she was standing above herself, watching it happen in slow motion. She remembered the suffocating feelings of terror and shame. The threat of the juvie centre.

Being taken in by Stella had been the turning point in her life. Now she could help this girl in the same way Stella had helped her: give Skye a chance. If she wanted it.

'My name's Tamara Thompson, but you can call me "Tam",' she said, sitting opposite the girl. 'I've always liked chatting with you and Adele and your friends, and I know you're a good kid. So, do you want to tell me what's going on?'

'Not really.' Skye folded her arms, frowning. She'd recovered her attitude.

'Hey, Skye? I don't have to help here,' Tamara shot back. 'And I won't if you don't help me. I can't do anything unless you talk.'

Silence filled the room. Tamara watched as Skye weighed her options. Her attitude—defiant, but frightened—reminded Tamara of how her younger self had behaved. It wasn't an attitude she was proud of. But if she could say something to her fourteen-year-old self, what would it be? She'd seen letters in a magazine from famous people to their younger selves, giving them advice that they wished they'd had back then.

Skye got up and walked over to the wall, pressing her hands against it and bowing her head. 'Mum had an operation today,' she said finally. 'She's got a melanoma that they're cutting out. Dad's with her. It's not a big operation, but . . . I'm scared. Melanoma is really serious. She has to have tests to see if it's spread.' Skye sniffled. 'But Mum's in denial. They all are. And they don't care about what I think, anyway. They don't need me. Mum's never there for me.'

Tamara nodded. 'I see. That's a lot of baggage for you to be carrying around.'

Skye shrugged. 'Story of my life.'

Sympathy surged through Tamara. 'Look, love, I don't know what's going on in your life, but it sounds pretty stuffed up at the moment.' She paused, trying to gauge Skye's reaction. She took a chance. 'Mine was more than pretty stuffed up at your age, which is why I used to shoplift too.'

Skye didn't move, her hands still pressed hard against the wall. Her fingernails had gone white.

Tamara kept talking, soft and calm. 'I started shoplifting because I wanted someone to notice me. Get some boy's attention or look cool to my friends—you know, that sort of shit.' She didn't mention that later she'd done it to survive. Skye needed a story she could relate to. 'Were you doing that?' Tamara asked. 'Trying to get your mum's attention?' She sat back and waited, hoping like hell she was right.

Skye pushed off the wall and turned around, her eyes bright with unshed tears.

Tamara went over to the fridge and grabbed a bottle of water. 'Want one?' she offered, just as Skye's stomach let out a loud rumble. Her hands flew down to cover it, while her cheeks flamed red with embarrassment.

'You haven't eaten? It's nearly 3 pm.' Tamara glanced at her watch, then picked up the phone and dialled. Skye raised her head and looked at her, alarmed.

'Hi Paul, it's Tam at Angelic Threads. I'd like one large pizza with the lot.' She put her hand over the receiver and looked at Skye. 'Do you want olives and anchovies?'

Skye smiled weakly and shook her head.

'No thanks, Paul, just the basics.' She listened. 'Sure. I'll unlock the door, if you can just bring it in, yeah? Great, thanks. See you soon.' She banged the phone down and grinned. 'Pizza with the lot, on its way. When did you eat last?'

Skye shrugged. 'Last night.'

'Well, then it will taste even better.'

'Why are you being so nice to me?' Skye asked suspiciously.

'Like I said before, I *was* you, once,' Tamara answered simply, 'and someone gave me a chance. So, here's what we're going to do. You're going to write a letter of apology to Sarah, the owner of the surf shop, which I'll deliver since she won't let you in there. Then I want you to come and work for me on a trial basis for three months, twice a week. Outside school hours, of course, and you'll be paid a fair wage. You owe me, Skye, and I think you'll like working here. But we'll need your parents' permission.'

Skye nodded without hesitation, her smile wide.

'I also expect you to go home and talk to your parents about what happened today. Tell them everything.' Tamara paused. 'But if you're going to work here, you'll need some decent clothes—I'll give you a couple of shirts. And that earring will have to go.'

Skye looked anxious. 'I only just had it done. The woman who did it said it could get infected—'

'Oh,' said Tamara with a laugh, 'don't worry, I know the drill. We'll just cover it with a bandaid. Easy. Well, I'd better close the shop a bit early today.'

'My best friend dared me to shoplift,' Skye confessed as she took a bite of the steaming pizza. 'She said it would help take my mind off what was going on with Mum. That was a pretty stupid idea, wasn't it?'

Tamara chuckled. 'You can say that again.'

They were silent as they ate. Then Skye's mobile rang. Tamara watched as she froze, then dug it out of her pocket and checked the screen. 'My brother,' she said. 'Hello?'

Tamara heard an agitated voice radiating out from the phone. 'Where are you? You were supposed to be home by now. Are you really so selfish on the day Mum has her tests that you nick off and don't do what you're supposed to?'

'I . . .'

'Where the hell are you? Either get home now or I'll come and get you.'

When Skye bristled and opened her mouth, Tamara knew what was coming next. 'Get fucked, Stu. I don't have to tell you where I am. It's not like any of you care.' She took the phone away from her ear and went to hang up.

'Wait a sec,' Tamara said, 'let me talk to him.'

Stu was still talking, 'Don't you dare hang up on me, you selfish little bitch!'

Tam took the phone. 'What's his name?'

'Golden Boy.'

Tam gave her a 'come on' look.

'Stu.'

'Hello Stu? My name's Tamara. I'm the manager at Angelic Threads, a clothes store in the shopping centre. Skye's with me and I can drive her home soon if you'd like. Are your parents home yet?'

'Um, sorry, who are you?'

'A friend of Skye's. Look, get a pen and paper. I'll give you my details so you can look me up online.'

'Okay,' he said, sounding confused.

After Tamara heard the rustle of paper, she recited everything he might need to know. 'And are your parents home?' she repeated.

'Not yet. They're due after five, depending on how everything went today.'

'If you're comfortable with me driving Skye home, I'll make sure she's back before they get there.'

A silence. Then he said, 'Okay, sounds good. I can't stop you, anyway.'

Tamara handed the phone to Skye, who stabbed at the screen to end the call.

'Well, we'd better get going,' Tamara said, straightening up. 'I am going to speak with your parents, but today isn't the day. I'll call them late tomorrow morning—so you'd better have a word before then!'

❧

Tamara walked into her local pub and headed to the bar. God, she needed a drink. She ordered a Carlton Dry, then sat at a table in the darkest, quietest corner of the room. After taking a sip, she closed her eyes as the icy cold liquid slid down her throat, then she rested the cool glass against her forehead. *What a freaking twenty-four hours.*

She got out her phone and scrolled through Facebook, stopping to read a public post by Craig. A quote, printed on what looked like a very crinkled piece of paper, said: 'Please tell me I'm not as forgettable as your silence is making me feel.'

Something caught in her throat, and she couldn't take her eyes away from the screen. Her silence was making him feel forgotten.

Her behaviour towards her mum, who wasn't her mum at all, was probably making her feel forgotten as well. Two forgotten people who could be made happy by a single text or phone call.

Craig was the easier to deal with, so Tamara tapped out a quick message to him. 'Hi, sorry I haven't been in contact today. Crazy, weird things have happened. Just trying to find my feet.' She hesitated before adding 'xx'.

Straight away, Craig texted back: 'Like what? Want 2 talk?'

Did she? She wasn't sure. It was all so jumbled in her head, she didn't know if she could get it out so that it made sense.

'Maybe soon,' she finally typed. 'I've just found out I was adopted.'

The phone remained silent, and she guessed he was taking in the news as much as she was.

She took another mouthful of beer and opened the browser on her phone. After a deep breath, she typed: 'how to find your birth mother in Australia'.

A long list of results came up. She scrolled through them, trying to work out what information was relevant. How could she search if she had nothing to go on?

The night before, she hadn't told Angela she would return, but she hadn't said she wouldn't either. She'd left in the haze of fog that seemed to follow her wherever she went at the moment. Except for when she'd made the decision to help Skye—that had been in a moment of total clarity.

Now she had another eureka moment: she needed to start her search with Angela.

Draining the rest of her beer, Tamara left the glass on the table.

In the car, she wondered how Skye was getting on at home. The poor thing—she obviously wasn't feeling wanted or needed in her own home. Once again, Tamara was struck by the similarities between the two of them.

Chapter 18

Angela was holding the front door open as Tamara walked through the gate and up the path. 'Are you coming in?' Angela's voice sounded very frail, and her face was strained and resigned.

'If I can,' Tamara answered, feeling as if she was watching this scene from outside of her body. Then she realised that the Tam and the Tamperer had been quiet for a little while—maybe they'd been shocked into silence.

Tamara followed Angela into the kitchen.

'Would you like a cup of tea? Or one of your leftover beers?' Angela sounded as though she was entertaining a stranger. In a way, she was.

'No, thank you. Can I sit?'

'Yes, of course.'

In her hurry to pull out a chair from the kitchen table, Angela accidentally knocked it over. They bent down together and their hands brushed. Angela gazed straight into Tamara's eyes. The jolt that Tamara felt was powerful.

In those eyes, she saw remorse, apprehension and fearfulness. But she also saw love. She saw an old lady who was trying to put things right with the adopted daughter she had so badly wanted.

Tamara felt as if she should reach out and take Angela's hand. Maybe even give her a hug—it had been a long time since she'd done that.

But she couldn't. Not yet.

Instead, Tamara went around to the other side of the table and sat down.

Angela took her seat. Her chest was rising and falling with quick, short breaths. Tamara hoped she didn't have a heart problem.

The kitchen table was the same one that had been here when she was a child. An old faded Formica top with chrome around the edges. It was scratched and marked, but polished so that it shone.

Tamara took a breath. 'I'm really angry,' she said.

Angela didn't move.

'I'm really, really pissed off.' Although Tamara's voice was low, it held a great deal of power. She'd practised not letting emotion get the better of her. She didn't want to yell: quieter tones were much more forceful. Doctor Kerr had helped her with that.

But she found that she couldn't sit still. She pushed back her chair and started to pace around the kitchen. Glancing at Angela, she saw that her mother—no, she wasn't that anymore, was she?—had her head bowed and was staring at the table as if she was a naughty child being reprimanded.

'I can't believe you didn't tell me before now,' said Tamara. 'You let me think I was someone who I'm not. I could have searched for my birth mother—maybe even met her. Every year that goes

by means there's less likelihood of her being alive. If she's dead . . .'
Tamara's mouth dried up. Her tongue wouldn't work.

Come on, she coached herself. *Come* on.

'You know, when I was a kid, I always felt unseen. Unheard. Always, always unwanted.' She stopped and stared at Angela. 'Have you got any idea how that affects someone? You and Evan didn't love me, and now it turns out that my birth mother gave me up. Where does that leave me?'

Angela raised her head, tears on her wrinkled cheeks. 'Tam, that's not fair. I love you. I've always loved you. I just couldn't provide it in the way I wanted to.'

The words made Tamara's heart ache, but she still couldn't stop pacing, words pouring from her mouth. 'It took me years of therapy to work out I'm worthy of someone loving me. But even with that knowledge, I can't get over the fear that whoever it is will leave me. Everyone else has. And you've had a hand to play in that.' She felt as though she was getting rid of every resentment and bitterness she'd ever felt. Doctor Kerr would have told her this was a cleansing process.

Maybe it was. A weight had been taken from her shoulders.

Sitting back down opposite Angela, Tamara let out a huge sigh. Relief overcame her. She'd done it. She'd got her point across without yelling.

Now it was up to Angela.

Tamara looked down and saw her hands were shaking. Funny, she hadn't felt them doing that. Her nose began to run and she sniffed, not wanting to cry.

Angela seemed to realise her tirade had finished.

'I'm so sorry,' she said. 'I know your life has been very difficult.'

Her voice cracked. 'But you couldn't possibly have any idea what it was like to watch Evan treat you with contempt. I loved you—I didn't want him to be like that with the person I loved most in the world. But I was scared of him, of what he might do to us. The night he threw you out . . . After you'd gone, I couldn't hold it in, I screamed at him. Told him how much I hated him.' She dragged in a breath. 'Then he hit me.' She looked down. 'It was over for us from then on, but we kept up appearances.'

My assumption was right, Tamara thought with dull shock.

She wanted Angela to know they had this experience in common. There was a strong bond between people who'd experienced domestic violence.

'I used to live with a man who hit me,' she said.

'I'm so sorry,' Angela said, more tears spilling down her face.

Tamara lifted one shoulder. 'It's in the past.' She didn't want to say more about Matt now. It didn't feel like the right time.

Angela took the hint and dropped it. 'How about we sit in the lounge room? I'll make us a pot of tea.'

In a few minutes they were back in the cosy rockers beside the photos on the mantelpiece, with cups of tea and a plate of banana bread on the coffee table.

'So, why did you keep my adoption secret?' Tamara asked.

'Evan didn't want anyone to know he couldn't have children. He had such pride! I tried to get him to change his mind, but he wouldn't be swayed. Every time I suggested you might want to find your birth mother, he refused to agree.'

'So he hid it from everyone?' Tamara asked, astonished. 'How did you get away with not showing you were pregnant? Don't tell me you wore a fake belly!'

'I never went out much. Back then, I was a housewife. Other than shopping and church, there weren't many places for me to go, and you know that our families all live interstate. We lied to everyone. For a few months, at Evan's insistence, I pretended I had terrible morning sickness and stayed home from church.'

What a story! Tamara ran her hands over her face and leaned her head against the back of the chair. All this bloody emotion was exhausting.

'So, would you like to find your birth mother?' Angela asked. 'What you said in the kitchen—you're absolutely right. If you don't look soon, she might pass away.'

'Yes, but I'm still trying to wrap my head around everything. I don't know what I want yet. I need time to process all of this.'

Angela nodded. 'I completely understand. But for now, do you think . . . do you think we could be friends?'

Tamara closed her eyes and pinched the bridge of her nose. She didn't want to make any assurances. 'We can try. I need to take it day by day. Is that okay?'

Angela nodded, and they gave each other tentative smiles.

'So, tell me some more about you,' said Angela.

'What do you want to know?' Tamara asked, right before she bit into a piece of banana bread. 'Wow, this is really good. I don't remember you making things like this when I was a kid.'

'Evan didn't appreciate my cooking. It wasn't like his mum's.'

'Geez, he was a bloody control freak.'

Angela chuckled softly and rolled her eyes. 'That he was.'

Tamara wanted to keep their conversation light. 'So, what do you do for fun?'

'Fun? I'm a little too old for fun.'

'No, you're not! What are you, seventy?'

'Seventy-two next birthday.'

'Seventy-two is the new fifty-two. You must do something to celebrate!'

Angela looked sad. So much for keeping it light.

'Well, I don't have a lot of friends anymore,' she said. 'They faded out when you left, and I wasn't going to the school concerts and so forth. And Evan used to frighten people away. Occasionally we'd go to a movie or a bingo night at the bowling club, but not often. And then, when he wasn't well, he expected me to stay here with him all the time, waiting on him hand and foot. I had nowhere else to go.'

'That's awful,' said Tamara sympathetically, expecting to hear more about these tough times. She was relieved when Angela's mouth curved up in a smile.

'I intend to make up for it now, though!' Angela declared. 'The day after he died, I joined the bridge club at the community centre down the road. I don't know many of the other members yet, but you're right—maybe I should invite them to a birthday party.' Her smile widened. 'What about you? What do you do for fun?'

'Fun? Hmm.' Tamara had to stop and think. 'I take our dog Whiskey for walks in the park.' She stopped—Whiskey wasn't 'ours' anymore. *And he might never be again*, she thought sadly. She cleared her throat. 'I love to go shopping for beautiful clothes and shoes. And I love to sing, but I don't usually let anyone hear me, unless I've had a few and there's a karaoke machine nearby. And I love the movies!'

Angela nodded. 'Me too. I saw *The Dressmaker* the last time I went to the movies.' She leaned forward and whispered, 'I laughed so much I wet myself!' She raised her eyebrows in a comical way. 'Unfortunately, that's one of the downsides of getting old. But the movie was fabulous! Have you seen it?'

Tamara burst out laughing. 'I loved it too! Kate Winslet was so good.'

'And that Liam Hemsworth . . . is that his name? He's a twin, I think I've read? Well, he's just gorgeous! That chest!' Angela sighed theatrically.

Tamara couldn't stop giggling. 'I'll need a beer if we're going to have this conversation,' she said. She got up and started towards the kitchen. 'Liam's not a twin, by the way. He's got two brothers, and they're both actors.'

'Right! Well, I'll have to go to the video shop and see what other movies they're in. Are they all as handsome as each other? I'm sure I could watch the most boring of movies if Liam took his shirt off. Maybe he could just read the phonebook in a pair of undies or something.'

'Geez!' Tamara glanced over her shoulder in amazement at Angela's wicked smile. She fetched her beer and walked back into the lounge room. 'What else do you like to watch?' she asked Angela.

'I like most movies. One that stands out recently is *Bridge of Spies*. Have you seen it? Tom Hanks is in it, and the client he's representing calls him "Standing Man". He keeps getting knocked down, but he gets back up. I liked that analogy.'

'I tend to avoid the ones with guns and violence. I love comedy. Have you seen *Mrs Brown's Boys* on TV? You reckon you wet yourself over *The Dressmaker*—well, you'd better have a change of knickers handy when you watch that show!'

Before too much longer, the beers and the intensity of enjoying some time with Angela knocked Tamara sideways. 'I'd better go,' she said. 'I've got work tomorrow and I need some sleep.'

'But you've been drinking,' said Angela.

'Light beers. I'm fine to drive.'

'Where do you live?' The fear was back in Angela's voice. She was probably wondering if she'd ever see Tamara again.

'Well, right now, I'm staying in a motel.'

'What? I've got a few spare bedrooms. You can come and stay with me!'

'No. I can't.' Tamara's heart picked up speed. 'We're only beginning to get to know each other. I just can't.' She stood up. 'Look, I really have to go.'

'I'm sorry,' Angela said quickly. 'We've had a lovely evening, and I shouldn't have pushed you.'

Tamara's heart started to slow. 'It's okay. But I do have to go. I'll see you again soon.'

'When?' The longing in Angela's face was painful for Tamara to witness.

'I don't know. Please, don't rush this. There are twenty-odd years of making up and catching up to do. One night isn't going to fix everything.'

Take that Doctor Kerr, she thought. *I've got a handle on this!*

'Tam, if you want a room here, you're more than welcome,' Angela said, standing tall and straight. 'But I'll leave it for you to get in contact. The number's still the same.'

Chapter 19

Skye stood at the end of the couch and stared down at her mum. She was stretched out, one arm over her face, her eyes shut. She looked a bit like how Skye imagined someone dead would look—all grey and drawn.

'I've got to tell you something,' Skye said.

'What's that?' her mum asked.

Last night, Skye's mum and dad had told her that the small operation had gone according to plan, the CT scan had been done, and now they just had to wait on the test results. Skye had nodded, then taken herself back upstairs, stuck in her earbuds, and waited for Billy to Snapchat her. They had plans.

Meanwhile, Skye had been working up the courage to tell her mum about her new job—and the shoplifting. 'I'll call them late tomorrow morning,' Tam had told her. Plus her brother, being the arsehole he was, had threatened to tell their parents about her being driven home by some random stranger. Skye was shitting herself.

'It's best to be upfront and honest,' Tam had said in the car. 'It will make your parents respect you.'

Respect? I don't know what that is, Skye had thought.

Might as well dive right in.

'I got caught shoplifting yesterday,' she said.

Her mum took her arm away from her face and stared at her before sitting up. She was frowning and seemed really confused. 'What?'

Skye lifted her chin. She wasn't going to repeat it. Her mum had heard her.

'You got caught *shoplifting*?'

'Yeah. At the shopping centre. I took a pair of shorts and got caught. That lady from Angelic Threads—you know, the one where we've shopped sometimes—she stepped in and rescued me. It was so cool. And then she bought me a pizza and offered me a trial job.'

'When? Why?' Her mum looked panicky. 'Skye, why didn't you call us?'

Skye shrugged. First she felt ashamed, then angry. 'You were at the hospital.'

'You'd better talk to me, missy,' said Lauren, who was now standing. She tried to cross her arms, but Skye could tell from the pained look on her face that her bandage must have pulled. 'Tell me everything.'

'There's nothing to tell. I got caught. That's all. Now I want to work for Tamara. She says she'll pay me a fair wage. I'm starting after school today!'

Lauren was shaking her head as if to clear it. 'But Skye, why? You've got everything you could want here. Why would you steal something?'

Skye shrugged again. Why would she tell her mum that? 'Anyway, I'm just letting you know coz I won't be home. I have to go to work this afternoon.'

'Skye, I really don't understand. I wish you'd talk to me more. And this Tamara, is she the blonde lady? The one who's always bright and bubbly and remembers everything about everyone?'

'That's her. Oh, Mum, she's really great. She *gets* everything I told her yesterday.' Skye's words gushed from her before she remembered she wasn't supposed to be nice to her mother.

'You *talked* to this woman? Alone? About our private family matters?' Lauren's voice rose an octave.

Skye stopped, then said, 'Gotta go to school.' She ran out of the lounge room quickly, banging the door behind her. Her mum couldn't follow her and her dad had gone to work, so she hoped to be able to get to school and then to the shop. She didn't know much about Tamara, but she knew she'd protect her from her parents.

~

'Tamara?' Lauren asked the blonde woman at the glass-topped counter as she glanced around Angelic Threads. 'You're Tamara Thompson, aren't you?'

Dean stood beside Lauren, a frown on his face.

'Oh yes!' said Tamara. 'You're Skye's mum. Good to see you again. I was going to call you today.'

'I'm Lauren Ramsey, and this is my husband, Dean.'

Tamara smiled and shook their hands. 'So, how are you, Lauren, after your operation yesterday?'

'I'm fine. Thanks so much for your concern.'

God, aren't we all being polite? thought Lauren.

She felt Dean shift next to her. He had been wary when she'd rung him at work and asked for him to come home and drive her to the shop. 'Surely you can do this over the phone,' he'd said. 'And I think we should go when Skye's there. It's pretty average on her behalf. And you, my love, are supposed to be resting.'

'We can't leave it, Dean. This is a family emergency! Plus, it's only my arm, not anything major. I'm a bit tired, that's all. If you can't come, I'll ring Dad and see if he can pick me up, but I think we really have to.'

'I agree that we have to go,' Dean said. 'But how about once we've both talked to Skye? Tonight, maybe.'

'No. No, I need to find out what happened and how. God, I just don't understand it. We raised her well.' Her voice broke off. 'How is it that good kids go off the rails? All her friends are nice kids—none of them have been in any trouble.'

'They probably just haven't been caught. It seems that Skye doesn't have a future as a criminal mastermind.'

Dean always knew how to cheer her up. But now, in the brightly lit shop, Lauren felt off-kilter. Like the world wasn't lining up properly. *Tamara must think I've done a poor job of bringing up my daughter*, she thought. As parents, she and Dean had always led by example, making sure that both their kids understood the importance of honesty and integrity. It didn't seem to have worked for Skye.

Shame rose in Lauren's throat like bile. It made her think of Dirk and how Zoe must have been feeling after their meeting on Monday. But Dirk had needed her help—he wasn't able to look out for himself or tell his mother what he needed. Skye was fourteen, nearly fifteen. *She should know so much better than this!*

'Now, Lauren.' Her old mentor, Fran, flashed into her mind.

'She's a teenager. Testing the boundaries. Wanting to be noticed. Take a breath before you react.'

Tamara led Dean and Lauren into the storeroom at the back of her shop, and they all sat down on office chairs. 'I'm happy to talk now, but I'm the only one in the shop at the moment,' said Tamara, 'so if a customer comes in, you'll have to understand that I need to go out and serve them.'

'Of course we do,' Dean said. 'We don't want to hold you up from your job. We're just not sure, ah—'

'Look, it's pretty simple,' Tamara cut in briskly, with her usual bright, friendly smile. 'I've seen Skye around a fair bit. Obviously, we all sort of know each other by sight and we've chatted whenever you've been in to buy clothes or Skye's been in with Adele. Yesterday, I heard the alarm go off from across the hall.' Tamara described what had happened next, then shook her head with a rueful smile. 'I felt I had to do something to help. I've never had the impression that your daughter is the sort of girl to do this type of thing—and, believe me, when you've been in this industry as long as I have, you get an instinct about people.'

Lauren felt herself relax. This wasn't something Skye had been doing for a long time before getting caught. Well, that was one small mercy.

Tamara continued. 'I've asked Skye to come in and work for me, on Thursday evenings and Saturday mornings for three months, out of school hours. It's just a trial to see how she goes. I thought it might give her a sense of responsibility and make her think about her actions more. That's if you're agreeable, of course.'

Lauren frowned. She felt as though Tamara was taking over— but at the same time she *was* asking for their opinion.

So, how did Lauren feel about Skye having a job? It might be good for her work ethic, but what about her studies? There needed to be some accountability and punishment for what she'd done, but Lauren and Dean were her parents, not Tamara.

'This is all very nice of you,' said Dean, 'but why are you going to so much trouble for our daughter?' He sounded suspicious. 'What's in this for you?'

'I totally understand why you're both concerned—believe me, I've never intervened in something like this before. It's just that Skye reminds me of my teenage self. The short story is, someone gave me a chance when I mucked up, and I'd like to do that for your daughter. I reckon the theft was a bit of a cry for help.'

'Cry for help?' repeated Lauren, baffled.

'I bought Skye a pizza last night because she hadn't eaten all day, and we had a chat. She seemed very upset and worried. I understand that your melanoma diagnosis is recent. And, like all teenage girls, she's obviously got loads going on in her head already. But I don't know exactly what's bothering her.'

Dean nodded slowly. 'You're right, I'm sure the melanoma has got a bit to do with it. God knows I've tried to talk to her, as has Lauren, over the past couple of days, but it's been like talking to a wall. If you can get her to open up, we'd certainly appreciate it. As much as I'd like her to talk to us, just so long as she's talking to a responsible adult, well—' he held up his hands '—that's probably all that matters.'

'Talking is always good, especially for a teenager,' Lauren agreed, although she still felt unsure. Then she realised she hadn't asked an important question. 'Which shop did Skye steal from? We should apologise to the owner.'

'The surf shop straight across from here. But Skye already wrote a letter to apologise, which I delivered this morning. The owner told Skye yesterday that she was banned for life, but softened up a little when she read that letter.'

Tamara's smile was a bright lightbulb in Lauren's face. She wanted to squint and turn away.

The buzzer sounded. 'Excuse me,' Tamara said, walking out to her customer.

Dean and Lauren stared at each other.

'What sort of punishment does this deserve?' Dean asked her, looking lost.

'I've got no idea,' Lauren said, rubbing her eyes. 'I'm devastated.'

Then they waited in silence until Tamara returned.

Lauren licked her lips. 'We've got to impose a punishment,' she said, more to herself than to anyone else. 'Something more than Skye doing a trial job here.'

'Well . . . I'm not looking at this job as punishment.' Tamara pursed her lips. 'More as a learning experience. Skye seemed to show genuine guilt and regret. If you're happy with our arrangement, she starts here this afternoon. I can even drop her home afterwards. If you're not keen, can you let her know?'

Anger started to trickle through Lauren. Or was it panic? First the melanoma, now Skye—everything was out of her control.

I know how to raise my own child, she thought. But she couldn't think of a rational reason to turn down Tamara's offer.

The buzzer sounded again. 'Perfect timing!' said Tamara. 'I was about to suggest that the two of you have a word in private.' She slipped out of the room.

'How do you feel about all of this?' Lauren asked Dean.

'Tamara's trying to help us, that's for sure.'

Lauren lowered her voice. 'You don't think she was telling us how to raise our own kid?'

'Yes and no. But ultimately, I reckon she's got Skye's best interests at heart. Can you imagine if security had been called?'

Lauren shuddered at the thought.

'Obviously, Tamara had some sort of a similar incident when she was younger and someone helped her. I understand her reasoning: one good turn deserves another. Skye might be able to help someone else in the same situation one day.'

'Maybe. But, Dean, where have we mucked up?' Lauren was appalled to find tears in her eyes. She only ever cried after having the nightmare. It must be the drugs she'd had yesterday, making her more emotional than normal.

'Oh, honey, I don't think we've mucked up,' Dean said. 'Skye is a teenager who's experienced a huge upheaval in her life and is having trouble coping. She's testing the boundaries. What's important is the way we handle her from now on.'

'It might be a good thing that I've got a bit of time off,' Lauren mused. 'If I'm around a bit more, she might talk to me.' *And not just Tamara.*

'We have to get Skye talking,' Dean agreed.

Lauren reached out, grabbed hold of Dean's hand and squeezed it tightly. They looked at each other and a silent agreement passed between them: they would do whatever it took to keep their daughter on the straight and narrow.

When Tamara walked back into the storeroom, she seemed a little nervous.

'We're very appreciative of your offer, Tamara,' Dean said, 'and we're very happy to support your plan to have Skye work with you. If there's anything we can do—'

Tamara beamed and shook their hands again. 'Nope, Skye and I will be fine. I'm looking forward to seeing her this afternoon. Thanks for coming in!'

~

'How are you feeling?' Holly asked. She sat in the chair Lauren had indicated, then started fossicking in her handbag. 'I've brought you a few things,' she said, drawing out a box of chocolates and a book. 'Here you go, the latest Liane Moriarty. Thought it would help you stay on that couch—where you should be, recovering!'

'Oh, thanks so much, Holly! I can't wait to read it.' Lauren glanced at the blurb before setting it down next to her. 'I'm fine. Tired, but fine.'

'Good. Any results back yet?'

'No, although apparently we'll hear something later this afternoon. It's the waiting that kills me, you know? I just wish we could start planning ahead.'

'I can understand that.'

'Can you?' Lauren asked, more sharply than she'd intended. She sighed. 'Sorry, I'm being a bitch.'

Holly laughed. 'You're allowed to be. You've got a lot to contend with. How are Stu and Skye?'

'Oh my God, Holly! Skye's been caught shoplifting. Dean and I haven't been home long—we just went to see the woman who "saved" her.'

'Shoplifting? What? That doesn't sound like Skye . . . Wait, hold on. Saved?'

Lauren explained about Tamara. 'Now, instead of Skye having a caution, or whatever they do to kids these days, she has a job. Tamara's put her to work!'

'A remarkable way of dealing with things.' Holly sounded intrigued.

'Not sure how I feel about it.' Lauren put her hands to her face and let out a groan. 'I guess I should just be pleased that Skye told me. She could have tried to hide it or lie about it, I suppose. I'll talk to her later, when she gets home from the shop. Although, I probably should wait until Dean's here too—he seems to act as a buffer between us. She doesn't hate him quite as much as she hates me.'

'She doesn't hate you,' Holly said. 'She's trying to find out who she is, as well as processing your diagnosis. Don't forget how crappy it is to be stuck between being a girl and a woman. Adults treating you like a young girl, because you still are, while your brain tells you they should treat you like an adult. Anyway, you know all about biological, emotional and psychosocial conflicts—I don't need to explain.'

'*Now* you're talking like a psychologist.'

'Probably because I am one.' Holly grinned. Then, more seriously, she said, 'It's hard on you all. Do you want me to talk to her? I offered yesterday.'

'I don't know,' Lauren said, feeling defeated. 'I really don't know. But there's one thing I do know—I'm embarrassed. Mortified. There's no way I ever would have thought that either of my children could do something like this. I can't imagine what Mum and Dad will say when I tell them. Or Dean's parents.'

'Kids make their own decisions,' Holly reminded her. 'Not all the choices they make have anything to do with the way they've been brought up.'

'There's no way Stu would have shoplifted.' Lauren frowned. 'I'm just so angry with Skye. And I feel indebted to Tamara, when I don't want to be.'

'It's okay to feel all of that, Lauren,' said Holly, sounding every inch the psychologist again. 'All emotions are valid.'

'Any more news on Dirk?' Lauren asked, wanting to change the subject.

'His mother did as she promised and took him to the doctor yesterday. They're running some tests. We'll hear more soon enough, I would imagine.'

'Poor kid.'

'Poor family,' Holly said.

'I still can't believe his mum wouldn't take him to the doctor.' Lauren felt the prickle of tears again. Good God, what was wrong with her?

Under Holly's silent, observant gaze, Lauren felt as though she was being assessed. She got up from the couch and went to look out at the sunny afternoon.

'Maybe you shouldn't worry about Dirk right now,' Holly said. 'There's more than enough going on in your life. Skye needs you, and you need your family.'

Lauren nodded. 'That's very true. I was curious.'

She decided not to admit that after her surgery, in the car on the way home, she'd picked up her phone to call Zoe, just to check that she was taking Dirk to the doctor. That was all—nothing unprofessional about it. Of course, Holly wouldn't see it that way. Which was why Lauren had put the phone down without dialling.

Another change of subject was needed.

'Do you think it would be worthwhile getting Skye in to see a counsellor? One that specialises in teenagers and cancer?' Lauren asked, leaving the window and walking back to her couch.

'It would be a great thing! I can write a referral if you like.'

'Thanks, Holly.' Lauren lifted her hands in despair. 'I wish I understood her, but her shoplifting has really thrown me.'

Holly stood up and gave Lauren a hug. 'Never rains but it pours, huh? I'd better head off.'

'Thanks for keeping me company. And for the gifts.'

Holly let herself out, and Lauren lay on the couch for a bit longer, willing herself to sleep. But her mind wouldn't stop. Every time she shut her eyes, she had images of the dream: the dark walls, the hands holding her down, the claustrophobia.

'Stuff that,' Lauren muttered and got up. She went into the study, turned on the computer and checked her emails, hoping there might be something about her adoption. But she'd posted the letter on Saturday—it had probably only just arrived.

Then she started to google. 'Adoption in the 1960s,' she typed. From the first page of results, she clicked on one headline that screamed at her: 'Stories from mothers who had their babies taken from them.' According to the article, approximately 150,000 babies were given up for adoption between 1951 and 1975. Most of these were forced adoptions.

Lauren was struck by one woman's story.

I asked to see my baby, but the midwives told me that wouldn't be possible because I was a BFA. 'What is that?' I asked. 'Baby for adoption,' they said. I told them: 'My baby is not for adoption.' Then the nurses said to me that I didn't have a choice. They handed me papers and said I was to sign them. I couldn't read, but I just knew they were about me giving my baby up. I refused. They told me it was so they could register the birth, so I ended up signing. I never saw the baby again. I don't even know if it was a boy or a girl. I lie in bed every night, forty-five years later, and pretend to hold him or her in my arms before I go to sleep. Every day I pray for the child, and promise I'll find them. But I haven't yet, no matter how I've tried. I never got to see that child take its first step or lose its first tooth. I might have grandchildren. I resent not knowing.

Lauren finished reading the story, tears running down her face. It must have been horrific for that birth mother, forced to give up a child, especially if he or she had been created in love. Constrained by a society that dictated women had no choices—no rights.

What did my mother go through? Lauren wondered. *Could this story be hers?*

Chapter 20

After the school bell signalled the end of classes, Skye rushed to the toilets and changed into one of the shirts Tam had given her. She brushed her hair and pulled it back into a ponytail, then realised she'd forgotten the bandaid for her earring. *Damn it*. She hoped she could get one off Tam.

'Where are you off to?' Adele asked, dropping her bag next to Skye's and pulling out her lipstick. 'Hot date?'

'I've got work,' Skye said proudly.

'Work?' Adele looked appalled. 'What for?'

'At Angelic Threads. For three months. I'm gonna get a staff discount on the clothes, get first pick of the new stuff that comes in, and maybe even run the store when the manager goes away,' she bragged. There was no way she'd be telling Adele the truth.

'Bullshit, you are not.' Adele smoothed her hair down then shook it out, trying to add a little body to it. She applied her lipstick and eyeliner while Skye watched.

'I am.' Skye didn't care what Adele thought—Tam believed in

her and that made her feel like she was walking on air. Adele could say what she liked, but today it would bounce right off.

'Did you do what I dared?' Adele asked sharply. 'I thought you said you were going to text me when you'd done it. I never heard from you yesterday. Guess you wussed out.'

'It was a stupid dare, anyway.' Standing up to Adele felt good. What she didn't know wouldn't hurt her.

Skye dreaded going home after her shift, though. God knows what her parents would say to her; she was sure she hadn't heard the last of it from them.

'Oh well, your loss.' Adele shrugged. 'Best way to get clothes or booze but.'

Or a criminal record, Skye thought. Then she noticed Adele scratching her elbow. 'So, you've done it heaps of times?' she asked.

'Oh yeah.' Scratch, scratch, scratch.

'Which shop?'

'Almost every shop in the centre.' Adele made a kissing sound as she looked at herself in the mirror, checking her makeup.

Yeah, right. 'What have you lifted?'

'What haven't I taken? Bags, shirts, a bottle of Baileys. I've got a whole box full of clothes in my cupboard that Mum and Dad don't know about. I sell them on. Make money, you know?' Scratch, scratch, scratch.

Skye shook her head. What a load of bullshit. And this girl was supposed to be her best friend. But Adele wasn't a friend anymore. Not a real one. Her nana, Connie, had once told her that friends need to be 'true in confidence and character'. Adele wasn't being that, and it hit Skye like a force between the eyes. Adele was just someone she spent time with—a means to an end. So she didn't have to sit by herself at lunchtime.

What had Skye seen in her? All Adele did was tell lies and bag people out. No, Skye didn't want to be around this sort of person anymore. Jasmine was much nicer: she stood up for Skye, talked to her, asked how her mum was.

'Doesn't your mum ask where you get the extra money from?' Skye asked. One last question to see if her 'bestie' would tell the truth.

'Nah, she wouldn't even know I've got it.'

Skye struggled not to roll her eyes. 'I gotta go. Don't want to be late.'

'Sure, see you tomorrow,' Adele said, but Skye could tell she was giving her the cold shoulder.

Skye hoisted her backpack onto her shoulder and started to walk out of the bathrooms. 'Oh.' She stopped. 'Did you ever hear from Neil?'

'Nope. Told you, didn't expect to.'

'Doesn't that make you feel weird after everything you did?' Skye couldn't imagine how awful it would be to share something like that with a boy, then never hear from him again. It was such a relief to know Billy wouldn't be like that.

'Fuck, you're naive,' Adele said. 'You're so sheltered, Skye. It was a one-nighter. Nothing weird about it.'

That doesn't make you any different to the guys you keep calling fuckboys, Skye thought. *And that's not someone I want to be.*

'But you lost your—'

'So?' Adele raised her eyebrows as if daring Skye to finish her sentence.

Skye shrugged and walked out.

∽

'Good day?' Tam asked as Skye dropped her bag in the Angelic Threads storeroom.

'It was okay,' Skye answered in a flat voice, then realised she sounded like a typical whiny teenager. 'Actually, it was a brilliant day! I got top marks in a maths test, but I only just passed my English essay.'

Cocking her head to the side, Tam waited.

'Okay, school sucked,' Skye said, laughing.

'Good to hear things are normal. So . . . I had a visit from your parents today.'

Skye's face went hot. 'Oh. I bet that was fun.' *Is she going to tell me they won't let me work here?*

'It was fine.' Tam told her what had happened. 'They seemed okay, although I reckon you might be in for a bit more punishment when you get home.'

'Yeah, well, they'll have to think about it,' Skye said, pouting. 'Golden Boy hasn't ever done anything like this, so it will all be new to them.'

'You are *so* jaded for a fourteen-year-old.' Tam shook her head. 'You do realise that not everyone is out to make your life hell, don't you?'

'Maybe not, but those two are.' She changed the subject. 'Hey, do you have a bandaid I could borrow to cover my earring?'

If Tam had been her mum, she would have told Skye off for forgetting. But Tam just said, 'On the bottom shelf over there. Now, I'd like you to go into the shop and check that all the sizing is in the right order and garments haven't been put back on the incorrect racks. You should be able to do that?'

'Yeah, sure.' Skye went off and started at the front of the store, flicking through each item of clothing and checking the sizes. A couple of times she had to rearrange something, but mostly everything was where it should be.

'Skye! Hey, Skye!'

She looked up. Standing in the doorway was Adele and a couple of girls from Year Eleven. Skye didn't know their names. *What is Adele doing with them?*

'What?' she called back.

'Thought we'd see what you were doing. Been walking around trying to work out which shop you were in. Thought it might have been Target or Kmart. You know, something appropriately lower class.' Adele and her new friends sniggered.

What? Adele had known Skye had a job at Angelic Threads.

Then Skye understood: this was for questioning her in the toilets about Neil. Adele hadn't liked it, so she'd come here to be a bitch.

'Everything alright?' Tam came to the front of the store.

'Fine,' Skye muttered.

'What are you girls up to?' Tamara asked, leaving the confines of the shop. 'Hello, Adele, have you come for some new clothes?'

'Nope, I came to check up on Skye. Didn't think she'd be working here.'

'Well, she is and can't be distracted, so you'd better keep going, okay?'

They started to drift away, still giggling, but Adele turned back to stare before they'd gone too far. There was envy in her face. Envy? Then Skye clicked: she was working in the cool shop, with the cool-aunty type chick. That made Skye smile.

Tam turned to her. 'I'll take over here. How are the change

rooms looking? Any clothes in them or dirty mirrors? We need to make them sparkle!'

'Okay,' said Skye, relieved that Tam had sent her away from the shopfront.

❧

Bloody girls, Tamara thought. *What's got into Adele? God, I'm glad I'm not a teenager anymore.*

She watched Skye walk towards the back of the shop and then checked outside to make sure the others had gone. They had. Little shits.

She turned her thoughts back to Skye. Lauren's illness was obviously a huge concern to the girl, but there was more going on for her—those girls were proof of that. Was Skye being bullied? Maybe this was something to ask her parents.

❧

In Tam's car, Skye looked at her phone. A text from Billy: 'Can you meet me tonight?' Sliding a sideways glance at Tamara, she locked her phone, put it back in her pocket and stared ahead at the road.

It was bothering her that she had to go home. She really didn't want to. What mood would her parents be in? At least her dad would be there by the time they arrived. He usually smoothed things over a bit.

'You nervous?' Tam asked.

Skye watched her long red fingernails tapping the steering wheel in time to the music and thought how different her life would have been if she'd got Tam as a mother.

Maybe I'm adopted too! The thought suddenly occurred to Skye.

Maybe that was why she didn't get along with her mum. But if that was true, how did they have the same colouring? Maybe you could pick a baby that looked like you.

Then Skye realised that she hadn't answered Tam's question. 'Yeah. I'm a bit nervous.' Skye felt that she could be honest with Tam. She didn't feel that way about anyone else. Well, except Billy.

'What punishment do you think they might give you?'

With a *whoosh*, Skye let her breath out. 'Imprison me for the rest of my life.'

Tam smirked. 'That's a bit OTT, don't you think?'

'I really don't know. They can't do anything that's going to upset me too much. Unless... unless they take my music away.' She chewed her lip. 'I wonder if they're going to tell my grandparents. That would suck.'

'All your grandparents are still alive?'

'Yeah, both lots. Plus I might have two more out there. Mum's adopted—'

'Adopted?' The word burst from Tam.

What a weird reaction. 'Yeah. What's wrong with that?'

'Nothing. I don't reckon I know anyone who's adopted, that's all.'

Skye nodded. 'Yeah, I don't know anyone else except Mum. I heard her talking a few days ago—saying how much she wanted to find her birth mother now she's got cancer. I think she's worried about her family's medical history, in case it affects me and Stu.'

'What are your grandparents like? Your adoptive ones, I mean.'

'They're a bit older so, you know, there's no way they can be too cool, but they're alright. Mum always says they weren't just her parents—they were like her guardian angels.'

'What a beautiful way of looking at it. They must be very special people.'

'I suppose they are,' Skye said. 'They must be, to have put up with Mum!'

Skye grinned, expecting Tam to laugh at that one, but she frowned instead.

Tamara remembered Lauren's face when she'd come into the shop earlier that day. So many swirling emotions—love, anger, confusion, sadness. Clearly Lauren wasn't a terrible parent like Evan. But this didn't fit with what Skye had said, that her mum was never there for her. And why had Skye just put Lauren down so harshly? What was going on? Maybe she was just afraid and confused in the wake of her mother's diagnosis.

'So, you said some things about your mum yesterday. It sounds pretty rough.' Tamara glanced at Skye, who was staring out the passenger window.

'Mum's too busy to talk to me,' Skye said. 'She's always thinking about the kids in her class. I don't think she ever wanted me, really. There are five years between me and Stu. Maybe I was a mistake. Anyway, it's obvious that she loves Golden Boy more than me.' Skye's voice was tinged with pain.

Silence filled the car.

Tamara's heart hurt. Such a little girl in an adult body, with so much pain and sadness inside of her.

All too soon they drove down Skye's quiet street and pulled up in front of her house.

As Skye grabbed her schoolbag, Tamara was struck by an idea. 'Have you ever thought about trying to find your mum's parents?'

'Who, me?' Skye laughed. 'Why would I want to do that?'

'Well, your mum is probably preoccupied with her health right now, and you kids are so good at using the internet and social media. And you never know, you might just make your mum sit up and take notice.'

Skye's eyes went wide. She looked as though Tamara had just blown her mind. 'Yeah, well, maybe.' She didn't say anything for a few seconds, staring into space. 'But how would I do that, anyway?'

Tamara shrugged, wanting to seem casual. 'I have no idea! Just a thought that jumped into my mind. There'd have to be internet adoption forums or something, right?'

'I suppose.' Skye reached for her schoolbag again. 'Anyway, I gotta go.'

'Ready to face the music?' Tamara asked.

'Guess so.' She gave a rueful smile. 'If I don't turn up at work next time, you'll know I'm being held prisoner!'

Skye walked to her front door, paused to wave goodbye, then went inside. The lights were on but the house was quiet. Maybe they weren't all home yet? She dropped her bag in the hallway. When she got into the kitchen, she saw her mum, dad and Stu sitting at the table with solemn faces.

'Hi,' she said, unsure what to do.

'Skye, come and sit down,' her dad said. He got up to pull out a chair for her.

Skye stayed where she was. 'What's going on?'

Lauren patted the chair. 'Come and sit, darling.'

Darling? Shit, something was very wrong. Skye couldn't

remember the last time she'd been called that. This wasn't about her, she realised. It was about her mum.

'No,' she whispered. 'No, I've got to go to my room.'

Stu stood up and went to her—tried to put his arm around her protectively. 'It's okay, Skye, just come and sit.'

'Come on, it won't take long,' her dad said, but he sucked at sounding normal.

She kept standing, looking at them all.

Lauren got up and walked towards her. 'Skye, the results aren't what we hoped they'd be. I've got to go into hospital tomorrow.'

Skye jammed her hands over her ears and ran upstairs, her heart thudding.

The stars were shining out of a clear, black sky. All Skye could hear was Billy's heavy breathing and the tick of the engine, cooling. Lying on the backseat of his car, she gazed out of the window and tried to work out what had just happened.

Well, she knew what had happened. It *had* hurt, and now she was all sticky and wet. She hoped there wasn't any blood that Billy would see when he turned the light back on. That would be embarrassing.

She'd texted him the minute she'd run upstairs, needing someone to hug her, to love her. He was her someone.

The banging on her door had stopped after a while. Then low murmurings through the wall told her that her parents were in their bedroom. Weird thoughts kept popping into her head, like: *On the upside, at least you haven't been punished yet.*

Billy texted her back to say he was coming straight over.

See, Adele? she thought. *Billy loves me. You were just someone's plaything for one night. We're forever.*

She waited for their signal: a text message saying that Billy was parked around the corner. Then she locked her door and snuck down the stairs, stepping over the third one from the top because it squeaked. Silently, she opened the door and locked it behind her, then slipped out into the warm summer night.

As soon as she'd got into the car, Billy pulled her to him and kissed her.

'You make me so hot,' he whispered between passionate kisses.

Desire curled in her stomach and crept down and down and down, until she felt wetness between her legs. 'Can we go to the quarry?' she asked.

Now it was over. She had finally done it. She wanted to think that Billy had been kind and gentle and caring—but it hadn't been like that at all. Once they'd got into the back seat, there was no more kissing. No affection. It was all speed—like he was scared she'd change her mind. One hand went straight between her legs and the other to her breast. Breathing heavily in her ear, he shoved down his jeans and pushed himself on top of her and finally inside her.

The sex wasn't like the Mills & Boon novels. She hadn't expected it to be, but it wasn't even like the porn she'd watched. It was quick, hard and sweaty. She hadn't been able to explore him and do the things she'd read about. Drive him to distraction like the books had talked about. It had been about Billy and his need only.

And now she didn't feel anything.

Dear Diary,

We landed in Fremantle two weeks ago. I was so pleased to be off the ship. For a large ship, it suddenly seemed very small, with nowhere to hide.

Mummy and Daddy didn't understand why I didn't want to be with my friends anymore. I preferred to lie in my bunk and hide from the world.

I want to wash myself clean from what he did to me that night, but it doesn't matter how many times I scrub, he's still there. I'm so ashamed.

I feel his breath on my ear and the strength in his arms as he held me down.

'Don't scream,' he said.

I don't think anyone would have guessed what he's capable of. He's the life of the party, the joker, the charmer. He has money and status. Maybe that's why he thinks he can take what he likes, no matter the consequences.

He'd known where to go and how to keep any night owls from seeing us. No, not us. There is no us. He'd known how to avoid being seen.

I can't help but wonder if I'm the only one he's done this to. After all, it's a long voyage; he can't have kept his desires hidden for all that time. Perhaps I was the only one who didn't agree to what he wanted from me.

He took it anyway. I hate him for that.

Now I'm dirty and tarnished. Old goods, as Mummy calls loose women.

It was freeing to walk off the boat and away from anything to do with him. I never have to see him again, and I'm very grateful for that.

We now have a house in Fremantle. The sky is so blue but the heat is awful. It burns like fire. Daddy has been in bed with headaches since we arrived. The doctor says it's the heat. The air makes me sweat with each breath.

This new start isn't what we imagined. And we don't have a puppy.

Chapter 21

Lauren finished packing her bag with the last of the toiletries, then zipped it up and sat on the bed, her head in her hands.

Without a word, Dean hugged her and then carried the bag downstairs to put it in the car.

She picked up the phone and dialled her parents. 'Hi, Dad, it's me,' she said when George answered.

'Ah, so you've got the results. Should I be breaking open a bottle of champagne?'

'Um, not quite.'

'Oh.' So much surprise, dismay and uncertainty all in that one, short sound.

'The doctors found cancer in my sentinel node, so I have to go into hospital very early tomorrow morning. Turns out someone had to be taken off the list so they fitted me in.' Lauren sat on the bed and leaned her back against the wall.

'Right. Sorry to hear that, love. Well . . . Here's your mother.'

There was a bumping sound as George handed the phone to

Connie. In the background, his voice a murmur, he repeated what Lauren had told him, and she heard Connie's sharp intake of breath and whispered, 'No.'

'Hello, darling,' she said into the phone, clearly trying to keep her emotions under control. 'The results not so good?'

At the sound of her mum's voice, Lauren's throat closed over. She only just managed to say no.

'Oh, my darling girl, I'm so sorry this has happened.'

Static crackled over the line as Lauren struggled to get herself together. 'I'm scared, Mum,' she managed to say. 'Scared and worried. What if it's spread?'

'Of course you're scared, Laurie,' her mum said soothingly.

Lauren took another shuddering breath. Her mum hadn't called her 'Laurie' since she was a teenager. Somewhere, somehow, that pet name had been lost as she'd grown older. How comforting to hear it again.

'This is a horribly frightening time for you,' her mum said. 'So many unanswered questions. You'll have to trust that the doctors know what's best.'

'Yes, that's true. I'm trying to do that.'

Dean came back into the bedroom and grabbed his towel, heading for the shower. When he saw Lauren's tears, he leaned down to kiss her on the head and handed her a couple of tissues.

'How did the children take the news?' Connie asked.

'As you would expect. Stu was stoic and practical, and Skye . . . well, she didn't want to listen. I don't think she wanted to hear any bad news. Mum, she put her hands over her ears so she didn't have to listen. It was so awful.'

'Poor pet. And Dean?'

'He's accepting. Does it sound strange, Mum, if I tell you I've sort of always seemed to know that this was going to happen?'

'No, not at all. You've known for a long time you're at risk of skin cancer. I had a friend once, she'd been diagnosed with breast cancer. She told me it was almost a relief, because her family history had indicated that she might be. And, once it happened, she just got on with making sure she got well again. And she did. Lived another thirty-two years and died in her sleep when she was eighty-five. God rest her soul.'

Lauren smiled. 'You always seem to know what to say.'

'I wouldn't be so sure about that,' said Connie. 'Now, where are the kids? Do you want them to come here, or can we bring some dinner to them tomorrow?'

'Stu will be here, so he can look after Skye. I'm glad I taught him to cook.'

'An attractive man is one who can cook *and* do the washing.'

There was a muffled male voice in the background.

Lauren actually laughed. Not that she felt like it, but it was nice to hear her dad teasing her mum. It brought back lovely childhood memories of them working in the garden or sitting together talking. Connie had a beautiful laugh; Lauren had always thought it sounded like chimes. Not like her own raucous, loud laugh.

'I'd better go. There's still lots to do. Dean will ring you when I'm out of surgery.'

'We love you, our darling girl. Be brave.'

Lauren pressed the end button and shut her eyes. Her mum was right: she had good doctors and she needed to trust them. And now she knew part of what the state of play was, she could go about getting better as of right now.

She wanted to talk to Skye—to hug her tight and tell her everything would be okay. Well, she couldn't promise that. But she could hug her daughter.

Walking out into the hallway, Lauren went to stand outside Skye's door. The need to talk to her was so strong. She tapped a few times. Was the door still locked? She didn't want to try the handle in case Skye yelled out at her to go away.

'Skye?' Lauren called. No answer. 'Skye. I don't know if you can hear me or not, but I want to tell you that I love you. I'm sorry we've been arguing lately. I'm not sure why. We've always been good friends, haven't we? What's happened to get us so off track?' She took a breath. 'I know you've got all sorts of horrible emotions going through you right now. But please know I love you so very, very much.'

Skye still didn't say anything. Perhaps she was asleep. Perhaps she was wearing her earbuds with her music on full blast.

Or she might just not want to talk, no matter what Lauren said.

With a sigh, Lauren padded back to her bedroom.

Chapter 22

'You can stay for as long as you like,' Angela said to Tamara.

'Thanks, but it's only going to be for a couple of nights,' Tamara insisted as she walked down the path to the front door, holding her suitcase.

Living in a motel room with paper-thin walls had had its drawbacks. Namely, neighbours who thought that screaming at each other, then having noisy sex, then screaming again was a fun way to spend an evening together.

Tamara had thought hard about asking her mother if she could come over for a night or two. Well, she'd tried to think hard while using a pillow to muffle the moans of 'harder, harder, harder!' being shouted from the room next door.

'It's only for a couple of nights,' she kept telling Angela, 'until I find a new motel.' But Angela was obviously still hopeful. And, if Tamara was totally honest with herself, she was feeling positive too. She wanted to give the possibility of a friendship with her mother a chance. If she was truly going to heal, she needed to mend her fences.

Then she and Craig could start afresh. Maybe their relationship would be even better than before.

Tamara lugged her suitcase down the passage to her old bedroom. She found it difficult—frightening, even—to walk down there for the first time in so many years. As she sat on the edge of the bed, so many memories crowded around her. She remembered lying there, listening for the sounds of her parents heading to bed; she would sneak out of the laundry door when she heard Evan's snoring.

Thankful that Angela was giving her the space she needed to unpack by herself, Tamara shut the door and began with the box containing her shoes.

Soon, everything was in its place. She flopped onto the bed and stared at the ceiling. The long crack in the plaster had grown a bit wider, and the shadows from the tree outside the window cast the same shade on the dirty white walls. As a child she'd slept in this bed with her arm tucked around a ragamuffin doll.

Oh, the doll! She'd forgotten about it. What had happened to it?

There was a gentle knock on the door. Tamara rolled her eyes but smiled at the same time. 'Come in!' she called.

'Do you need anything?' Angela asked, opening the door just a crack and putting her head through.

'No, I'm all good,' said Tamara, patting the bed. 'Come and sit for a moment.'

Angela hesitated before walking into the room and glancing around. 'Looks like you're pretty settled,' she said.

'Yep, just about there.' Tamara paused. 'Do you know what happened to that doll I used to have? A ragamuffin, with red wool for hair.'

Angela smiled. 'Wait right there.'

Tamara swung her legs over the edge of the bed. She felt as though she was six again, waiting for her mum to come and check on her. But without the fear.

Angela walked in with a box and held it out. 'I kept quite a lot. After you'd gone, Evan wanted to throw all of your belongings out. But while he was at work one day, I snuck in and packed up the things of yours I wanted to keep. I'd always hoped I'd see you again.'

After opening the box, Tamara saw the doll. She picked it up and held it out, like a mother holding a child. Then she sat it on her knee and hugged it close.

'Raggedy Ann,' she said, awed. 'Where did she come from?'

'I gave her to you the Christmas you turned three. I'd found her in a second-hand store and brought her home. She needed a good wash, but by the time I'd finished with her, she was as good as new. You loved her.'

'I remember.'

Tamara noticed something else in the box. She reached in and pulled out a book. 'Oh, *Tilly and Tessa*! I loved this story.'

Angela nodded, her smile shaky.

Tamara put the book on the bed and checked again. There was a plastic sleeve with documents inside. Now, *that* wasn't something she'd loved as a kid!

'Last night,' Angela said, 'you told me you weren't sure if you wanted to look for your birth mum, so I didn't say anything about these documents. But here they are. I want you to have the option to read them, whenever you wish. Over the years, when it's been possible, I've done some research. I wanted to bring it to you, but I just didn't know how to approach you until Evan died.'

Tamara's heartbeat sped up. Now that it was here before her, she couldn't wait to read everything. Slowly, she pulled out the ageing paper from the plastic. The words swam in front of her eyes. Blinking, she refocused and started to read.

Dear Mrs Thompson,

Thank you for your enquiry. We have provided the following information.

The Departmental records have been searched and the following information was recorded:

Name: Tamara Grace Thompson

Born: King Edward Memorial Hospital, Subiaco, Western Australia

Date of birth: 1 March 1973

Records state that the child was born without complications at 2:56am and weighed 3628.74gm. Length was 46cm and her Apgar scores were 7 and 8.

Birth mother was twenty, single and studying at the University of Western Australia. She had been in a long-term relationship with the birth father. He didn't want to continue the relationship when informed about the pregnancy.

It was the birth mother's wish, at the time, not to have any contact.

As of today, the ninth of May 1997, the birth mother hasn't requested to be put on the Contact Register.

Yours sincerely,

Flora Dune

Tamara let the letter fall to her chest, taking another piece of paper from the file.

<u>Non-identifying particulars of mother:</u>

Age: Twenty

Birth place: England

Marital Status: Single

Education: Completed Year 12

Occupation: Student

Health: No known hereditary diseases. Wears glasses.

Family: One of three children. Parents are both deceased. Father had a stroke when he was 56. Mother died of natural causes.

Physical description:

Height: Five foot nine

Hair: Red

Eyes: Blue

Build: Medium frame

Complexion: Very fair

Tamara turned the page over, searching for more information, but there was nothing. She re-read it, drinking it in like a woman dying of thirst.

'I'm sorry I couldn't get more information, Tam,' said Angela. 'The agency is very strict.'

Tamara swallowed. 'I just think it's amazing you went to this much effort. And I've learned more about her tonight than I thought I'd ever know.'

'Do you think you'll keep looking?'

'I don't know. Doesn't seem like she wants to find me, does it? Otherwise she would have put her name on the contact register. She's what? Sixty-three? She might be dead. Anyway, she's not going to want some long-lost daughter turning up. I reckon I'll leave it.'

'I'm happy to answer any questions you have,' Angela said softly.

Tamara gazed at the shadows of leaves on her bedroom wall. The wind outside was tossing them around, and they looked like long fingers trying to reach out and hold on to something. *A bit like Angela*, she thought.

'I wonder what was it like to give up a baby back then?' said Tamara.

Drawing in a deep breath, Angela thought for a moment before saying, 'I've read quite a bit about this in recent years. For a while I didn't care why your mother had given you up. I was just pleased we had you and I had the option of keeping you. But after you'd left, I understood more of what she might have been feeling—if she was made to give you up. I've read horrific stories of unwed mothers back then being forced to sign adoption papers while they were still in labour. One woman was deprived of sleep until she signed them. Sleep deprivation is a form of torture!' Angela placed a hand on Tamara's shoulder. 'I have the books in the spare room if you'd like to read them. They're hidden under the bed.'

Swallowing hard, Tamara tried to organise her feelings.

'Thank you,' she said softly.

A few seconds later, her phone beeped with a text, and Angela got up from the bed. 'I'll leave you to finish what you've still got to do tonight. Sleep well. See you at breakfast.'

'Good night,' said Tamara. 'It means a lot to me that you kept some of my things.'

Picking up her phone, Tamara saw that the text was from Craig. He'd asked her out for a drink on Sunday. Smiling, she didn't have to think about the answer: 'Yes.'

Chapter 23

'Oh. My. God. Skye, you did it!' Adele cried, running from the bus and falling into step beside her.

Skye's stomach constricted. How does she know? How could she know? Nah, she couldn't know. *Don't be ridiculous! Play it down.*

'What do you mean?' Skye asked, trying hard to make her voice sound neutral.

'Um, what do you think I mean? Can't believe you did it with a fuckboy, but you've done it. What was it like?'

Skye stopped and looked at her, devasted. 'How the fuck do you know that?'

'It's all over school! Billy told Kirk, Kirk told Trent, Trent told Paige, and she told me.' Adele looked really happy to be delivering the news.

'You're wrong,' Skye said.

'What? No, I'm not. I know you did it.'

Skye shook her head. 'Billy wouldn't have told anyone.'

'How the fuck do I know then, you dickhead?'

Skye silently turned her back on Adele and walked off, her heart beating fast.

'What's wrong with you?' Adele called.

Ignoring her, Skye kept her head down and went straight to the toilets. Sitting on the loo, she got her phone out. 'You told people?' she texted him.

She waited for an answer. The screen remained blank.

Not wanting to leave the cubicle, Skye weighed up her options. She could go to class and pretend nothing had happened—or she could wag school. She wanted to run home, hide in her room and never come out.

How could Billy do this to her? He'd said that he loved her.

Adele's voice echoed in her ears. 'Fuck, you're naive.'

Tears slipped down her cheeks. 'Billy,' she whispered.

When the bell rang, Skye knew she didn't have a choice. She needed to go to class. Swallowing hard, she picked up her bag and headed into the bright sunlight.

A group of girls walked past and stared at her curiously. She ignored them, keeping her head down as she walked towards her English classroom. The sound of laughter was coming from there, but Skye felt as if she'd never be able to laugh again. What a betrayal. It had all been a lie. Every little misgiving she'd had, every little fear that it had all been a joke—they'd all been right. He'd used her.

She walked into the classroom and the laughter stopped instantly.

'So the teacher's daughter isn't such a *good girl* after all,' one of the boys called from the back row.

Skye stared at him. What the hell was he on about?

'Truth or dare, Princess.'

'What?'

He started up a cruel chant: 'Skye and Billy, pashing in his car, Snapchat, Snapchat! Ah! Ah! Ah!'

Skye's mouth dropped open. She turned and ran, her long plait thumping behind her. She raced to the school gates and then kept running. She had no idea where she was going, but she wasn't staying at that school.

∾

'Shit, Skye, what's wrong?' Tamara stared in horror at the girl in front of her. She dropped the hangers she'd been holding and rushed from behind the counter to get to Skye, who stood weeping in the shop doorway.

'Billy,' she sobbed.

Tamara reached for her. 'Come on, come back to the storeroom. It's okay. We'll sort something out.' She had no idea what had happened, but it must be bad for Skye to turn up here, out of the blue. Why wasn't she at school? And who was Billy? Probably some lowlife scumbag who'd rejected Skye. God, the shit that teenagers had to go through.

'Calm down,' Tamara said in a soothing voice. 'It's all okay. What happened?'

Skye hiccupped and tried to talk, but a fresh flood of tears started.

'Billy . . . Photo . . . Everyone will know,' she wailed.

Tamara realised that she wasn't going to understand anything until Skye had stopped crying, so she held her tightly against her chest and stroked her hair. Soon, the crying subsided and Skye pulled away, rubbing her swollen eyes.

'Start at the beginning,' Tamara said.

Skye told her everything, starting from the bad news about her mum's results and ending with Billy showing the Snapchat photo to his mates.

Tamara stared at her, fury burning in her chest. 'Oh, Skye,' she said, keeping her voice very soft, 'that's the most despicable thing I've ever heard. Billy's in serious trouble.'

Shaking her head, Skye waved her hands. 'It's too late, Tam. And it's all my fault, anyway.'

'Now, you listen to me and you listen well, Skye. This is *not* your fault. It's a terrible form of bullying. A normal person wouldn't do anything like this.'

'Yeah, they do,' Skye interrupted. 'It happens all the time. I just didn't think he'd do it to me. He told me he loved me.' A fresh round of tears started.

'You can stay here for the day, okay? You'll be safe. I won't let anyone in to see you. But we'll need to tell your dad what's happened, once you've heard from him about your mum, then he can call the school. Okay?'

'Tam?'

'Yes, sweetie?'

'I wish Mum wasn't sick.'

Tamara's heart broke. 'Of course you do, sweetie.' She gathered Skye into her arms again and hugged her until the tears stopped.

Hiding in the Angelic Threads storeroom, Skye kept going over everything, every tiny detail, about Billy. How could she have been so stupid? All her senses, right from the start, were telling her something wasn't right—that he was pretending.

That's why I couldn't believe he was interested in me, she thought. *I wish I'd trusted my instincts.*

She lay on the floor and looked up at the ceiling. She could hear Tamara's happy voice talking with customers, bringing them the clothes they wanted and ringing purchases up on the till.

Skye wished that time travel was possible. But she couldn't rewind to her mother being well, or un-take that photo. She couldn't un-sleep with Billy. There was no turning back from here.

Chapter 24

Lauren was propped up on the couch, watching some mindless daytime TV show that made no sense to her. Five days had passed since the operation to remove the lymph nodes in her armpit. Each one would be biopsied. The wait for more results was on again.

She was sick of waiting. Her family was sick of waiting. She couldn't even imagine how it would have felt to have waited longer for the surgery.

Skye sat on the armchair opposite, her earbuds in, staring into space, one leg swung over the arm of the chair. For nearly an hour she'd barely moved.

Lauren's heart ached every time she looked at her daughter. If she could change what Skye was going through, she would. Youth and innocence had been taken away from her daughter because of a couple of silly decisions. What Lauren wouldn't do to be alone with that boy for thirty seconds: she'd make him wish he'd never been born.

Dean had taken the horrifying phone call from Tamara, only an hour after Lauren had been talking to her surgeon about how the procedure had gone.

Not wanting to leave Lauren at the hospital by herself, Dean had rung the school principal, Hamilton, and demanded an explanation. Hamilton had been caught on the back foot because no one had made him aware of the situation. Dean wanted to go to the school and talk to the boy—but, of course, Hamilton hadn't allowed it.

A day later, Hamilton had rung Dean. On speaker phone in the hospital, he and Lauren had listened to the principal's report.

'It seems that Skye sent Billy a Snapchat photo of herself in a rather compromising position,' he said. 'From there, Billy showed it to other kids—didn't send it on via text messages or social media, but physically held his phone up for his mates to see. They just happened to be with him at the time. From the boys I've talked to, Skye's face was very visible. Billy isn't admitting to anything.'

Lauren's breathing had become strange when he said that.

'All I can do is suspend him for bad behaviour for two weeks,' the principal had said apologetically. 'Other than hearsay, there's no evidence. I'm sorry, Lauren. I wish I had better news.'

After that, Dean had decided to ring the police, to see if they could press charges. Lauren thought the answer might be the same as the one Hamilton had given—and she was right. Dean spoke to an officer on the phone, getting increasingly frustrated, before finally hanging up. He turned to Lauren with a look of absolute disgust. 'That little bastard has got away with it. If he'd sent the photos to others, via text message or social media, they could charge him with distributing child pornography. Or if he'd saved it to his phone, that would mean he was in possession of child pornography. But because the photo was on Snapchat, it's gone. It's Skye who'd be charged with "distributing child pornography", because she sent the Snapchat.'

Lauren had thought about ringing Billy's parents. In the end, she'd decided against it, but she felt so bloody helpless.

'I'm not going back to that school,' Skye had said dully, the first night Lauren was home.

'You don't need to,' Dean said. 'We'll find you another one.' He and Lauren had already discussed this.

Today, Lauren had made a couple of phone calls to schools in the city. She thought she might have found a good one.

The doorbell rang. Lauren went to answer it and found Holly standing there, a grim look on her face. 'Hey, how are you going?' she asked, after Lauren said hi.

'Getting there. It's uncomfortable.' She pointed to the lumpiness under her arm where the drain was inserted.

'It looks it. What does that do, exactly?'

'Keeps the fluid away. Lymph nodes usually do that, but there aren't any left in that armpit. It settles down in time. Anyway, come in. What's news?'

'Not great, unfortunately. I wanted to come and tell you in person.'

Skye appeared at the doorway. Lauren glanced over at her and noticed how pale she was.

'Hi, Skye,' Holly said with a large smile. 'I hear you haven't been well. How are you feeling?'

'Not too bad, thanks.'

'We're looking forward to seeing you back at school.'

Skye turned and disappeared up the stairs without another word.

Holly watched her go with a slight frown on her face, and Lauren wondered how much gossip there had been at the Goose. Schools were like those small country towns on TV—everyone wanted to know everything about everybody. And if they didn't, they made it up.

'So, what's this bad news?' Lauren asked as she led the way into the lounge.

'It's about Dirk. He has a form of childhood leukaemia.'

'Oh no,' Lauren said softly. She let out a sigh. 'That's so unfair.'

'It's horrible. The family are distraught.'

Lauren felt a surge of dejection. 'Why should this happen to a beautiful little boy who has his whole life in front of him? To a family that can't have any more kids?' Her voice rose in frustration as she sank onto the couch. 'Is there a prognosis?'

Holly sat in an armchair. 'I'm not sure. I just know that Dirk's in hospital—he's had to have a couple of blood transfusions, but they'll start chemo as soon as possible.'

Lauren's mind started buzzing with ideas. 'Okay, well, we need to get the kids to make cards, so we can take them in when we visit him. If his parents are okay with that, of course. But however we do it, we should involve his classmates somehow.'

'I agree. It's important that they understand.' Holly gave Lauren a long look. 'How's Skye going?'

'Looking in from the outside . . . not good. What's the word around school?'

'Do you really want to know everything?'

Lauren thought about that. Of course, she didn't. She wanted her daughter to be a happy girl who had fun with her friends. Not the butt of gossip and innuendo.

'Not really,' she said. 'But you'd better tell me. I can't help her if I don't know the full story.'

'Alright. According to what I've heard, Billy asked her out at the beginning of term. A few of the older girls have told me that he'd been dared to date Skye by one of his mates. You know, because she's a teacher's daughter.'

Lauren took a short, sharp breath through her nose.

Holly kept talking. 'The night you found out you had to go to hospital, Skye must have snuck out and met him somewhere. Apparently they had sex, and then his part of the dare was done. He was able to discredit her straight after that.'

'Oh my God.' Lauren stared at Holly. 'She's *fourteen*!'

'And he's seventeen, so he's underage as well.'

'I'll kill him. Dean will kill him.' Lauren pressed her hands to her chest.

'I'm sorry, Lauren. I know this is awful to hear. As for Billy showing the Snapchat photo to his mates—unfortunately, it happens regularly, but we never think it will be our own child.'

'Does it really happen regularly?'

'Oh yeah. More often than you'd realise. Snapchat, in particular, is a horrible medium for this type of thing, because the photo disappears so quickly. The kids make the mistake of thinking that no one but the sender will see it.'

Lauren nodded and sighed. 'I wish we had more control over what technology the kids use. It's impossible to monitor.'

'Do you know if she's had any contact with Billy since?'

'I certainly hope not. Dean and I talked about stopping her from going online, but we need to build trust with her again. We can't keep her away from the internet forever. Anyway, Jasmine has called the landline a couple of times—of course, Skye says she doesn't want to talk to anyone from school. But because Jasmine's never done that before, I'm guessing that Skye is off social media.'

'That's a good thing.' Holly paused, took a breath, then seemed to make a decision. 'Lauren, can I recommend a service to you? You mentioned counselling, but this might be even better.'

'Of course, what kind of service?'

'Skye might really benefit from a kids' youth group. There are a couple of options—if you and Dean are keen, give me a call and we'll discuss it. I've seen these groups do a lot of good for several kids at the Goose.'

A youth group? Lauren couldn't imagine Skye going to anything like that, unless she was dragged there kicking and screaming. But Lauren didn't want to seem rude. 'Sounds interesting. I'll think about it.'

She got the feeling Holly could see right through her, because her friend nodded and then immediately changed the subject. 'So, have you had any word back about your adoption?'

'No, but that's okay—it's only been a week.'

Holly tilted her head to one side thoughtfully. 'Did you know you can send your DNA in to Ancestry.com and they match it with swabs that others have sent in?'

Lauren had read about that on the site, but for some reason it had never crossed her mind to do it—maybe because it sounded like something from a science-fiction movie, too complicated for her tired brain to handle right now. But why not try it when she was ready? 'That's a really good idea. It'll give me something to do while I'm waiting for the government to get back to me.'

After Holly had headed back to work, Lauren lay there on the couch, staring at the ceiling. She thought about Skye. About Dirk. About her birth mum. Holly was an excellent psychologist, because suddenly everything seemed to click into place.

Lauren needed to talk to Skye.

∽

'Skye!' Lauren called.

Her daughter was lying listlessly on the old couch on the back verandah, earbuds in, while she tapped her foot in time to some music.

'Skye?' This time Lauren waved her arms about to get her attention.

She looked up and took her earbuds out. 'Do you need something?' she asked.

'Yeah, to talk to you.'

Skye frowned. Then she slowly swung her legs onto the wooden floorboards and sat up, as though she'd been expecting it.

'Look,' said Lauren, 'I don't even know how to start this conversation. Uncomfortable ones are always hard to have, but we need to do this.' She paused. 'You're going through a dreadful time, and I wish I could take that away from you. It breaks my heart when I see how sad and mixed-up you are.' She took a breath and paused. She didn't know what else to say.

Skye sat there, her hands folded in her lap, staring down at them. Somehow Lauren had to get some eye contact.

'Skye, please look at me, darling.'

Slowly she raised her eyes—they were filled with tears.

'Come here.' Lauren sat down and held out her arms, and Skye leaned into her. 'I love you. Dad loves you. We hate seeing you like this.'

Skye's shoulders heaved as she sobbed into her mother's chest, while Lauren stroked her hair and let her cry. It would be good for her to get it all out.

A little while later, Skye lifted her face. 'Why didn't you want me, Mum?'

Lauren was stunned. 'Not want you? What on earth do you mean?'

'The age gap between me and Stu. Adele told me she thinks it means I'm an accident. Plus, you're always saying how good he is and how I'm so disorganised and can't be trusted.'

'Oh, Skye, that's not how it is at all.' Lauren smoothed Skye's hair back from her face and held her face in her hands. 'Sweetie, I had four miscarriages before I managed to stay pregnant with you. We were so excited when you went to term and thrilled when you were born healthy. You were very much wanted. I would have had you sooner if I could have.'

'But . . .' Skye sniffled. 'But you're always picking on me! Telling people I don't do the right things. You don't do that to Stu.'

Lauren was silent, absorbing this. 'I'm sorry,' she said after a while. 'You're right that I do that sometimes. I just didn't think about it. You're both so different, but not in a bad way! The world would be very boring if we were all the same. Perhaps you don't remember, but Stu got a little—how should I say?—guidance from your father and me when he was your age.' She smiled, and Skye gave her a watery smile back.

'Look, I want to be the best mum I can be, and I'm sorry that you think I'm not. Because I didn't know my birth mum, I always swore I wouldn't let any child of mine feel like they weren't wanted. I can't tell you how sorry I am that you've been feeling like this. I know I get so busy with the kids at school, especially at report time, but those kids could never replace you and Stu. You're the most important people in the world to me and your father.'

Lauren could see that Skye was digesting everything she'd just said. There had been enough talking for the time being. She just sat there with her arm around Skye, making sure her daughter knew how much she loved her.

∾

'Why do you want to find your birth mum so much?' Skye asked Lauren. They were still on the couch together, drinking lemon cordial, Lauren's arm wrapped around her daughter's shoulders. 'It's because you're going to die, isn't it?'

'No! The melanoma was just . . . what they call a catalyst. A wake-up call. It's not because I think I'm going to get sicker—you must understand that, Skye. Michelle is really positive I won't even need chemo. There are just so many pieces of me missing. I often look in the mirror and wonder where my eyes came from. Are they my biological mum's or dad's? Who do I look like more? What about my nose?'

Skye smiled, nodding. 'Yeah, I think things like that sometimes too.'

'The thing is, searching for my biological parents is risky. It could disrupt so many lives—and until now I wasn't sure I wanted that for everyone involved. I guess I've been thinking about how everyone else will react and not my own feelings or needs. And I'll still tread very carefully in doing this, but I would like to know who my birth mum was and what she looked like. And my dad too, if that's ever possible.'

'I thought maybe you wanted a whole new family,' said Skye.

'No,' Lauren said immediately. 'I love your grandparents and the life they gave me. When I was younger, I worried that my birth mum hadn't wanted me, but now I understand there may have been circumstances in her life that prevented her from keeping me. I don't need her to be my mother now.' Lauren sipped her lemon cordial. She was exhausted talking about all this emotional stuff, but it needed to be done. 'Did you want to talk to me about Billy?'

Skye stiffened. 'No.'

Lauren nodded. 'You lied to us, though, didn't you? You snuck out of the house? Please don't lie to me again, Skye.'

'Yes, I snuck out.' Her voice was low. 'He told *everyone*, didn't he?'

'That's got to be addressed at some stage, Skye. Soon, but not now.'

'Okay.' She paused. 'Have the doctors told you that your melanoma is genetic?'

'Possibly. Another reason to find my birth mum is to learn more about our medical history. If other family members have melanoma, then your and Stu's chance of getting it is higher too—it's called Familial Malignant Melanoma. But we've always known that we need to keep an eye on your skin.' Lauren watched Skye processing that. 'Don't panic about it, just be wary.' She smiled and sang, 'Slip! Slop! Slap!'

'*Mum!*' Skye answered with a wide grin, rolling her eyes.

'Look, sweetie, I'd love to keep talking but my eyes are about to shut. I really need a sleep. Do you mind? We can keep chatting later.'

'All good, I'll watch TV. I'm getting addicted to *Days of Our Lives!*'

They both laughed, then Lauren got up from the couch and kissed Skye's head. 'It's really good to talk to you properly again, darling. I've missed the real you.'

Chapter 25

In her room, Skye went on her iPad. She realised how much her mum loved and cared for her. And she'd remembered Tam's suggestion about going online to look for her mum's birth mother. Imagine if Skye actually found her! That would make her mum so proud and grateful. Stu would eat his heart out.

First Skye went to Google and looked up her mum's birthday plus 'adoption', but nothing came up and she didn't know what else to put in.

Her fingers hovered above the Facebook icon. She didn't want to go on there—she knew what would be waiting: heaps of notifications, messages and tags. Things that would remind her of that fuckboy Billy and what he'd done to her, and her stupid fuck-up in sending him that photo.

Just ignore all of that, she told herself. *You can't never go on Facebook again. And there's got to be a group with adopted people looking for their families.*

There would be public groups, though, so maybe she didn't need to log on to see them? But then if she wanted to post something or reply to a post, she'd be stuck. And she wouldn't be able to log back in—she'd forgotten her password again.

She stabbed at the blue icon and saw what she was expecting: two hundred and ninety-three notifications. She didn't bother to touch the world symbol and see who'd tried to contact her. In the search area she typed 'adoption'.

The first in a long list of hits said: 'Adoption and Family Reunions within Australia'. That looked pretty useful. Skye clicked it and read some of the posts.

Looking for my brother. Born Kyle Dugan in 1987 in Royal Adelaide Hospital, Adelaide. Please PM with any details you might have.

My sister has stage four bowel cancer. We are desperately searching for a brother we have only just found exists, before she dies. The information we have is that he was born Peter Wheeler, on the 9th of July 1968. His birth mother's name was Jeanette Mary Darkin. If you have any information, please PM us as soon as possible. We would like to reunite our family.

This looks like the perfect spot, Skye thought, scrolling through all the messages. There were so many! She read about desperate mums who were searching for the babies they'd given up, and people who'd spent their whole lives wanting to meet their biological parents. There were even missing persons reports. Some people posted photos in the hope that someone would recognise them.

How should Skye word her own post? Into the heading bar, she typed: 'Wanting to find my mum's birth mother.'

My mum has been diagnosed with melanoma and would like to find her mother. Mum is forty-seven and was born at King Edward Memorial Hospital, Perth, in 1969. Her adoptive parents are George and Connie Ramsey. She has red hair, blue eyes and very fair skin with freckles. If you have any information, please PM me.

Skye re-read it and hit 'update'.

Then she decided to clear all the notifications so that she'd know if someone commented on her post. There were also seven private messages waiting for her to look at—she'd need to clear them too.

She checked out the names of the people who'd tried to contact her. Adele: no surprise there. She'd be wanting to gloat. Skye felt sick just looking at her name. Then there were five names that Skye didn't recognise: all older boys asking if she was keen on being their fuck buddy. That made her feel even sicker.

The last PM was from Jasmine. Skye held her breath and clicked on it, then kept holding her breath while she read it: 'Hey, this sucks, but you're going to be okay. Call me when you want to talk. xx'

Skye smiled slightly.

Glancing at the time on the iPad, she realised she needed to go have a shower. Her shift at Angelic Threads started in an hour, and she had a lot to tell Tam.

'Can you hang these up at the sale rack, please?' Tamara asked.

Skye took the armful of clothes and walked to the front of the shop. Tamara watched her start to hang them with the efficiency of an old hand.

She's a fast learner, Tamara thought.

'Hey, Skye?' a loud voice called out from the throng of people walking past the shops, and Tamara's stomach dropped. She walked to the front of Angelic Threads and saw two girls in uniform jeering at Skye.

'That's enough!' Tamara gestured for Skye to go back into the depths of the shop, then she went over to the girls. 'If I see you two around here again, I'll be finding out your names and calling your parents.'

'Ooh, we're so scared,' one of them said with a laugh.

'Come on,' said the other, looking a bit more worried. 'Let's get out of here.'

Tamara watched them go, her arms crossed. When they turned back to look at her, she indicated for them to keep going. A safe distance away, the one who'd laughed gave Tamara the finger.

'Brave of you,' Tamara muttered. She stomped back inside. 'Right, we're not even wasting any breath on those girls,' she said. 'I'm going to get you to start counting the float for me.'

Skye's red eyes widened. 'What?'

'I think you're trustworthy enough to do that, aren't you?'

Tamara was relying on a technique that Doctor Kerr had told her about once: if you give a child responsibility when they least expect it, they're more likely to respond positively towards you because they feel as if you believe in them. Right now, Skye needed to feel that someone believed in her.

'Have any of the results come back for your mum?'

'Yeah, there was a call just before I left,' Skye said as she opened the till and took out the fifty-dollar notes.

'And . . . ?'

'The scans are saying it isn't anywhere else. So if they can biopsy the nodes, and if the scans that Mum has next week show nothing, she won't even need treatment. Just regular check-ups.'

'That's so positive! Great news.'

'I'm still worried,' Skye admitted. 'Melanoma can appear anywhere, even when you've had all the tests. It just comes back.'

'Hmm, I don't know a lot about it, but I think that can happen with most cancers. People can be in remission for a while, then it comes back or it doesn't. That's not something to worry yourself over. Just celebrate the good results for now.'

Skye nodded as she kept counting the money. Then she flashed Tamara a pleased-with-herself grin. 'Guess what I've done?' she said, a glimmer of her old self appearing.

'Dare I ask?'

'I'm looking for Mum's birth mother, just like you suggested.'

'Are you?' Tamara was surprised, considering what Skye had said about it before. 'What made you want to do that?'

'It came up in a talk we had today. Mum wants to find her, but I don't reckon she really knows where to start or has the energy to look much online, especially with her sore arm, so I thought I'd have a go. I mightn't get anywhere, but you never know.

'Actually I did try looking about a year ago. Mum was really pissing me off and I thought I might like to live with another family.' Skye shrugged. 'Stupid of me really. And I never got any interest at all. I think trying to find someone's birth family is a lot harder than anyone realises. Especially if they don't want to be found, or worry that it will upset the people in their lives. I guess there must be women who've had babies and their husbands don't even know about it. That could put their whole relationship in jeopardy, couldn't it?'

Tam nodded. 'Sure could. The fallout is certainly something you need to consider carefully. And searching the whole of Australia for one person is like looking for a needle in a haystack.'

'Totally. There's so many people looking for family. It's just as likely that the person I'm looking for has posted their ad, but I haven't seen it coz I haven't gone back far enough in the timeline. Anyway, like I said, I'll have a go and see what happens.'

Tamara smiled. Finally, Skye had found a positive way to get her mum's attention! 'That's a really nice thing for you to do. Now, while I'm thinking about it, a girl dropped this letter off for you yesterday. Jasmine, she said her name was.'

Skye grinned and reached out for it. *How nice to see that she can still trust one of her friends,* Tamara thought. Of course, Tamara didn't say that she'd already opened and read the letter: no way would she have passed it on if it had been cruel. She was so glad and relieved that there were still nice kids around Skye.

Checking Facebook later that night, Skye was disappointed, but not surprised, that no one had responded to her post. She knew it could take months, even years, to get a useful lead. Still, she'd hoped there would be a couple. She hadn't been sure what she would do if she got three or four people responding—some of them might be genuine, but she expected there would be fakers too. Actually, maybe she shouldn't have put in as many details as she had. But it was too late now. At least she hadn't put in her mother's birthdate.

She set down her iPad and opened the letter from Jasmine. She'd already read it five times because it made her feel so good.

Hey Skye,

I miss you at school. Just wanted you to know that. I PMed you on Facebook but then I realised you're not checking it. I tried calling your house too.

The other thing I wanted to tell you is there's a lot of us who think Billy's a loser fuckboy. It's not you we're all talking about—it's him. I think he's going to find it a bit hard when he comes back here after his suspension.

Would love to chat if you want to, but I understand if you don't.

Love Jas xx

Skye swallowed and wiped her runny nose. Her eyes were a bit teary too.

Her iPad dinged with a Facebook notification. Someone had commented on her post! Why were her hands shaking? Tapping the notification, she read: 'Good luck in finding your biological grandmother. I've been searching for ten years for mine. I've come to the conclusion sometimes people don't want to be found.'

Skye let her breath out. Well, that was positive. Not.

She scrolled through again, looking at the new posts, flicking over adverts and photos for hours. Then, suddenly, a photo flew by with a flash of orange-red. *Red hair?* When she scrolled back up, she felt like she was moving underwater.

There it was. A photo that had been posted by 'Todd Atkinson'.

Of a woman who looked like an older version of herself. Well, with a bigger nose. It couldn't be that easy, could it? She enlarged the photo and stared. Nah, it couldn't be anything to do with her mum. It was too easy. Tam reckoned nothing in life came easy. And this picture, of a woman so like herself? Way too easy.

She flicked back to Atkinson's profile.

Todd didn't have his own photo up on Facebook, so he'd probably created his account just so he could post this one thing. He'd written that it was a photo of his late wife and that she'd given two babies up for adoption.

Nothing else. Nothing! It was so frustrating. Old people were totally useless with Facebook—Skye's gran called it 'the face book'. He hadn't included any contact details or even said where he lived. Skye could respond publicly or PM him, but the photo had been posted nine months ago. It had only shown up in her Facebook feed now because the admin of the page had given it a bump. What if he never replied?

Or worse, what if he was an arsehole, and he replied but her mum hated him? What if he was a child molester or a serial killer or something? *Oh my God.* What if he'd killed his wife and he was coming after her children next? Or he might want their money. And could Skye tell her mum that her birth mother was probably dead? Her hands were shaking again. *Why didn't you think about this more, you idiot?*

Her mum had been right—this was risky.

Skye went to Google and typed: 'Todd Atkinson, Western Australia'.

Chapter 26

Skye burst into the kitchen. 'Mum! You know how you were talking about some type of punishment for me sneaking out of the house?'

'Yeah.' Lauren was trying to chop veggies for dinner with only one arm fully useful and the other not even half helpful. What was Skye talking about? Had she just brought up her own punishment? *Wonders will never cease.*

Skye was bouncing on the balls of her feet. 'I found this place called Walk This Way—it's sort of like a youth group thing. They have camps and stuff. Um . . . Jas told me about it. She wrote me a really nice letter that she gave to Tam. Anyway, her friend from church went to Walk This Way. She said it was cool.'

That was strange. Lauren knew Jasmine's parents quite well, and she didn't think they attended church.

A carrot slipped from under her knife and smacked onto the tiles. 'Damn it,' she muttered, stooping to pick it up. 'Skye, can you give me some help here, please?'

For once, Skye didn't roll her eyes or complain that Lauren

would criticise her chopping technique. She just bounced over, picked up the knife and went to work on a potato, while Lauren washed the carrot and brought out another chopping board.

'So, will you let me go to Walk This Way?' Skye asked brightly. 'It sounds so good. They help change the way you think. Make positive decisions instead of negative ones.' She finished with the potato, then went to Lauren and took over chopping the carrot. 'You'll cut yourself if you're not careful.'

Lauren grinned. 'Yes, Mum,' she said.

This is a miracle, she thought. *Holly would be so proud of me. Who knew that one talk would change Skye's outlook so much?*

But why was Skye suddenly so interested in a youth group? Lauren had just been thinking that Skye would only attend something like that if she was dragged there. What was it that Skye had just said about Jasmine's friend liking this group?

'Does Walk This Way have a website?' Lauren asked.

'Yeah, it's up on the computer. I left it there so you could have a look at it. You'll love it. And, Mum?' Skye said, as Lauren started to leave the room. 'Please don't take this the wrong way, but can Tam take me? Please?'

The hurt was sudden and sharp, but then Lauren tried to think about it from Skye's point of view. One, she'd made the effort to find something she thought would help her—a very mature decision. And, two, there were probably some issues that Skye still didn't feel comfortable talking about in front of Lauren.

After all, Lauren thought, *who wants to talk to their parents about sex?*

'Let me read that website first and talk to Dad,' she said, 'but I'm sure that will be fine.'

As if on cue, the front door slammed and Dean walked in. He stopped to kiss Lauren and then went to hug Skye. 'Good?' he asked her.

'Really good,' she answered, staring up at him with a smile.

Dean pulled back, his hands on her shoulders. 'You look like the cat who's got the cream, Skye. What's going on?'

'Nothing,' Skye said, her smile widening. 'I just feel a lot better. Jasmine sent me a nice letter, and I sort of reckon things are getting back on track.'

'The track was a bit boggy there for a bit,' admitted Dean. 'It's great to hear that.'

'Speaking of that,' Lauren interjected. 'Dean, can you come into the study and have a look at this website Skye brought up for us? She's had an intriguing idea.'

'Ah, a mystery in the making,' he said, wiggling his eyebrows. 'Where's Stu?'

'Not home yet,' said Skye.

Lauren pulled at his arm and he followed her into the study.

'This is a little weird, but it doesn't seem bad,' Lauren said in a quiet tone, so Skye didn't hear. 'When Holly dropped by today, she suggested that Skye might benefit from a youth group. Of course, I thought it would only happen if hell froze over . . . but then Skye came into the kitchen, all bubbly, and told me that she wants to try a place called Walk This Way. Something about Jasmine saying it was cool.'

Together they read through the information. Pastor Connor was in charge of the group and there were two other counsellors: Todd Atkinson and Sasha Collins.

'This sounds perfect for Skye,' said Dean. 'What do you reckon?'

'I agree.' Lauren shook her head in amazement. 'I'm just a bit concerned, honey, that our daughter's been replaced with an alien.'

⁓

'Welcome to Walk This Way,' said a man with tattoos on his knuckles as he ushered Skye and Tam in through the front door of the church. 'I'm Pastor Connor. We're pleased to have you here. It's great that you've taken the first step to come and see us.'

This wasn't how it was supposed to be. Skye wanted to see Todd Atkinson, not this pastor guy. She frowned and looked around the church. From the stained-glass windows overhead, small streams of sunlight hit the pews and floor. It was pretty cold, and Skye reckoned it would be the perfect spot to visit on the hottest days; the thick stone walls would keep the fierce heat from getting in.

'We'll do our best to help you in whatever way we can, Skye,' said Pastor Connor, 'but it needs to be a joint venture. Are you willing to do that? And your parents?'

'Uh, yeah. Mum and Dad have signed all the papers. Tam's my friend, but she's a support network-type person too.'

'Wonderful, you can never have enough support people. Come through and let's talk a little a bit about you, Skye.' He led the way to his office and they all sat down on comfy leather chairs. *This isn't so bad*, Skye thought, just as the pastor asked, 'How do you think you got off the rails? Why have you made some of the decisions you have?' He folded his hands on his desk and stared at her expectantly.

Skye gulped. This wasn't going according to plan. *Being a spy is hard!*

Finally, Tam spoke up. 'Pastor Connor, I don't think Skye is that off track. She was caught shoplifting a little while ago, but we've established that it was more about getting some attention than starting a career as a criminal. She's had some pretty hard knocks lately. Her mum's being treated for melanoma. She just needs help figuring out a few things.'

'Is that right, Skye?'

Skye nodded quickly. 'I suppose.'

'You tell me, then. What would you like to get out of Walk This Way?'

'I dunno. Can you change my life?'

Pastor Connor smiled and looked a lot nicer. 'We can sure have a good go at it. So, what I would usually do is assign you a counsellor—'

'Can I work with Todd, please?' The question just burst out of her.

The pastor stopped talking. He looked totally confused. *Oops.*

Tam glanced over at Skye, surprised. 'How do you know who you want to work with?' she asked slowly.

'A friend,' Skye rushed on. 'Well, not really a friend, but someone's friend I know at school . . . anyway, they worked with him and said he was, um, like, really cool.' Her hands were shaking a bit, so she slid them under her thighs. Then she worried that they might leave sweat stains. *Just keep smiling*, she told herself.

Pastor Connor smiled again and spread his hands out. 'Todd it is, then.'

The next day, Tam pulled up in front of the church, gave Skye a hug and then had to rush off to work. Skye stood outside, hanging back, watching all the kids walk in. They were all about her age or a bit older: some with tatts, some with heaps of piercings, and others dressed just as neatly as her. Such a weird mix.

She walked into the church to find it empty. Where had all the kids gone? Aside from Skye, the only person there was Todd Atkinson, standing up near the altar. She recognised him from his photo on the Walk This Way website.

Todd gave her a welcoming smile. 'Hello, young lady.' He glanced down at his clipboard, squinting. 'Sorry, love, my eyesight's not what it used to be. Let's see . . . looks like you're lucky last. Skye Ramsey, is it?'

'Yep, that's me.' She was trying hard not to seem like a weird stalker. *You are a weird stalker*, she reminded herself.

Todd seemed like a really normal old guy. Skye had no idea how old he was—everyone looked a bit the same after fifty. Todd had grey hair and wrinkles, and he wore a boring flannel shirt tucked into jeans that looked like they'd time-travelled from last century. And jeans with white runners! The worst fashion crime imaginable.

'Through here,' Todd said, ushering Skye into a narrow hall that led out to a courtyard. Trees grew through broken pavers, filtering the sunlight. Wooden tables and chairs, painted in mismatched bright colours, were scattered around. High walls kept out prying eyes, and one wall was covered in graffiti. It was almost cool.

A lone wisteria wound its way up an iron frame; it was covered in pretty purple-blue flowers. Skye noticed that Todd put his hand on the wisteria as he passed by. He looked like he was remembering something sad. 'I love wisterias,' he explained, noticing her curious glance. 'They were my late wife's favourite flower.'

Really? Skye thought. *What else did she like?*

'I'm sorry to hear that your wife passed away,' she said politely.

Maybe now would be a good time for her to mention the Facebook post. Except, what if he wasn't the right Todd Atkinson? It would be so embarrassing. She'd never live it down, and her mum would kill her. She had to find out more about him and his dead wife.

From somewhere deep in the brown-brick building next to the church courtyard, loud hip-hop music started thumping. Skye recognised the song—she had it on her iPhone. She'd downloaded it because Billy liked it. Hip-hop wasn't usually her thing, but she'd wanted to seem cool.

Billy. Arsehole. Fuckboy. Coward.

'Come and meet the crew,' said Todd. 'We've got quite a few kids here.' He led her through a door into the building, towards the music. 'Fifteen in the program at the moment, but there's room for twenty. We're planning a camping trip to the wheatbelt. Would you be interested?'

'Camping?' She'd never been camping.

'Yep, it's a lot of fun,' he said with a grin. 'We take tents and put them up in the paddocks, cook over barbecues and go bush-walking.'

Skye didn't say anything. She couldn't even imagine what that would be like. She'd seen the big paddocks on the way to Margaret River before and there always seemed to be so much nothingness out in the country. Emptiness. Only cows and grass and horses. And dirt and bugs. And limited phone reception.

'Well, you can think about it,' Todd said. 'We don't go until next week.' He pushed open a door and hip-hop pulsed out. When he waved at a couple of kids, they grabbed a remote to turn the music down. 'Not all of the crew are here right now. Some have sport or community work. Everyone comes and goes. In and out. This is

Skye,' he said, without any other introduction. 'This is Grant, Dave, Paige, Cassie—' he listed a few more, but Skye tuned out, thinking, *Who cares?* 'You've already met Pastor Connor—he's over there, pretending he knows how to shoot pool. And this is our one and only Sasha. She makes the best chocolate cake in the world.'

Sasha laughed. 'Hi, Skye, it's lovely to meet you. Come on in, we're just setting up what we need for our camp next week. Do you like camping?'

'Not sure.'

'You're missing out,' said Dave, a guy with those massive earlobe plugs that looked really painful. 'Best fun, dude.'

'Where do you go?'

'I've got two thousand acres at Cadoux,' Todd said. 'It's about two and a half hours north from here. We take the bus, head up there and kick you all out to commune with nature for a couple of days.'

Skye thought it over. Maybe Todd would have family photos up all over his house. 'Sounds fun.'

Chapter 27

After the kids had all gone, Todd packed up the rest of the pool table and wiped down the bench. Connor and Sasha had left too, so he was on his own, getting ready for the next day. He was happy to do this every night—it stopped him from going home.

He thought about Skye, their newest member. He hoped they'd be able to help her. She was yet to tell him anything, but it was only the first day. He'd learned not to expect anything to happen quickly.

Joining Walk This Way had been the best thing he'd done since he moved to Perth two years ago. And the first conversation he'd had with Pastor Connor had been in this very room during an interview for the volunteer role as a counsellor.

'Have you got any children, Todd?' Pastor Connor had asked.

'No, no, I haven't. My wife and I tried for years, but it never happened. We didn't try IVF—figured if it was supposed to happen, it would. We owned a farm near Cadoux, which kept us pretty busy, and I coached the local under-sixteen footy team and helped out during the cricket season. Worked with boys more than girls. I've got a "working with children" clearance if that helps.'

'Yes, you'll certainly need one of them,' Connor replied.

Todd had decided to be straight with Connor. 'Look, this is going to sound strange, and I can't explain it myself. I decided that today would be the turning point since my wife died. I've spent a year grieving for her. Sitting around the house, staring at walls.' He cleared his throat. 'My wife and the farm were my world for so long, and within the past two years I've sold the farm, save for two thousand acres and the farmhouse, lost my wife and moved into a completely foreign environment. I need to do something, help out somehow. I was driving past here a couple of days ago and saw these kids walking into the church, and I thought, *What the hell, I'll go and take a gander*. I don't need paid work—I made enough money from the sale of the farm to keep me for the rest of my life, but I still have to do something.'

This was the most Todd had said out loud since before his wife's death. He glanced down at his hands and saw they were knotted together the same way as his dad's used to be when he'd been worried about something. Todd had said far more than he'd intended to, and Connor was a good listener—still, he probably had to be.

'You've had a tough few years,' Connor said after a brief silence.

Shrugging, Todd looked away. 'It's life, isn't it? Can't change it— just got to keep on keeping on.'

'But why are you so keen to work with troubled young adults? It's not like coaching a footy team—some of these teenagers have had very hard lives. And there are plenty of other options out there. Volunteer activities that don't need you to commit for a long period of time—Rotary, Lions, Apex. They all do great things.'

'There was a boy I knew.' Todd stopped. The hum of traffic outside seemed to grow louder in the silence. The heat, almost non-existent when he first arrived, now seemed to intensify. A bead of sweat trickled between his shoulder blades.

The baked, dry earth from his memories appeared to creep over the room. Covering everything and thrusting his mind back to the funeral.

Wheat-coloured grass rustled in the country cemetery. Dust flicked up with every footfall—and there were many that day. The whole community had turned out to mourn the loss of Darren O'Grady. Lines of people, two at time, walked behind the hearse. Couples holding hands, the wives clutching at hankies, the men stony-faced, knowing that this could easily have been their son. Groups of teenagers clung together, their shock, confusion and grief spilling out as they wrapped their arms around each other and held on; for most it was their first brush with death.

A suicide.

All too quickly, the coffin was lowered and it was all over. A young man, sixteen, who'd had the world at his feet, was in the ground, never to return. The community was left in shock, fearing for the rest of their children left behind. It seemed that no one was safe from the power of a tortured mind.

The song 'Wish You Were Here' by Pink Floyd rang out across the graveyard. As it ended, all that could be heard were the sounds of grief.

Todd looked up at the bright blue sky and watched a crow flying over the procession. Was Darren's soul free of torment? What had those last few minutes been like, before he slipped into a heavy sleep, never to wake again? Who had he thought of, and had he suddenly wished he could change his actions? Questions his parents would ask, Todd assumed, for the rest of their lives.

The hum of traffic grew loud as he came back to the present and realised where he was. Clearing his throat again, he grunted an apology and took a sip of water from a cup Connor had placed in front of him.

'Darren was a good kid, from a good family,' Todd continued. 'I coached him at footy, knew his family quite well—they lived on a farm not that far from us. We'd see them at the local community events. From all accounts, he was going places. Talented enough to have a crack at the AFL, brains enough to study whatever he wanted at uni, and he had the makings of a great farmer. Darren could have done anything.' Staring into the distance, Todd sighed, then brought his gaze back to Connor. 'He lost his way. Then he got depressed, and it killed him. So if I can stop something like that happening to another family . . .' The words died in Todd's throat.

That conversation with Connor had been a bit over a year ago. One year and twenty-three kids later. Twenty-three kids whose lives he'd made an impact on. It was a good feeling. He had a natural ability to bond with these kids. To draw them out and get them talking. Talking was always the first step.

He was sure he could support Skye too. He knew a little of what had happened to her. Kids could be very cruel.

Chapter 28

When Skye came home from the youth group, Lauren was sitting in front of the computer. She shifted uncomfortably and waved at her daughter through the doorway. Skye threw down her bag and bounced into the study, perching on the desk corner.

'Hey, how was it?' Lauren asked.

'It was good. Really good.' She sounded happy.

'Did you meet anyone nice?'

'Um . . . yeah. My counsellor, Todd, is pretty cool. But I've only been there one day. I didn't really get to know the others that well.'

'What did you do?'

'Just sat around and chatted. There's going to be a camp next week. Sounds awesome. I'd really like to go.'

Camping? Skye had never shown any interest in camping. But they'd never been, so she was probably curious. 'Hmm. Tell me a bit about it. Is it on a weekend?' Lauren turned back to the computer.

'I guess so, coz they're big on encouraging us to go to school—they give us, like, rewards, if we have one hundred percent attendance.

Anyway, the camp's in the wheatbelt somewhere. Just a couple of days. We do all these positive programs and stuff. Supposed to help with our social interaction, learning and employment opportunities.'

Skye had changed her tone to sound like a newsreader, and Lauren smiled. 'Well, if it's part of the program, you should definitely go!'

'What are you reading?'

'Working on the family history. I've taken some DNA samples and I'm going to send them off to Ancestory.com to see if they match with anyone on the system.'

Skye ducked her head and nodded, fiddling with her necklace. 'Cool. Well, I've got stuff to do.' She left the study and headed up to her room.

Lauren watched her go. What a difference a conversation made!

And look at what had happened in such a short time. They'd been a happy, healthy and normal family. Now, Lauren was about twenty lymph nodes lighter, her daughter seemed to be getting back on track after a terrible time, and she'd been given the all-clear for three months. After that, she'd go back to Michelle and have all the tests again, but the signs were positive.

She smiled. Life was good.

Of course, she'd always have that fear in the back of her mind that the melanoma would turn up again at some point. From what she'd read in a few online cancer support forums, that was normal. But she wouldn't let it control her or take her over. Not like she had with Dirk.

Ah, Dirk. At least he was getting help because of her intervention. That was good. However, she could see that she'd taken it a bit too far. Become too invested in what was going on with him to the detriment of her own family. 'I've told you before,' Fran would have said to her. 'It's all about balance—and balance, my dear, is something you're not very good at!'

Leaning back in the chair, Lauren wanted to stretch. But the drain stopped her. Fluid was still dripping into a thick plastic bag under her arm, and she couldn't wait to get it out. Michelle had told her that it might only be for another few days. *That would be more than wonderful*, Lauren thought.

A car sounded in the driveway, and she smiled. She always looked forward to that time of the evening when Dean got home and they had a quiet drink together and talked about the day. It had been a long time since they'd done that. Tonight was the night.

She grabbed a beer from the fridge and met him in the doorway. He looked so tired. 'Drinks?' She held up the bottle and waggled it at him.

'Ha! Here's my lifesaver. Great idea.' He bent to give her a kiss.

They headed to the backyard. After they'd sunk into the cushioned outdoor chairs, Lauren took Dean's hand and rested her head back. The sun was still high and it was hot, but she felt good sitting beside him, even if they didn't say anything.

'Skye's back from Walk This Way,' Lauren told him.

'How did it go?' He loosened his tie and took a few gulps of beer.

Lauren repeated what Skye had told her, then mentioned the camp, which he thought was a great idea.

He touched Lauren's cheek. 'I thought we should go out to celebrate your results tonight, if you're feeling up to it. What do you say?'

'How about we celebrate here? I'm probably not quite up to going out yet.'

Dean grinned. 'Excellent! I'll cook. What type of takeaway do you want?'

'Oh, that's your cooking, is it?'

'The best kind!'

Stu knocked on Skye's door. 'The takeaway is here!' he called.

There was no answer.

'Skye?' He pushed the door open.

The room was empty.

He went in a little further and looked around. There was no way of knowing if anything was gone, because he hadn't been in here for so long.

He went downstairs. 'Seen Skye?' he asked his dad.

'No . . . that's why I asked you to call her. Isn't she in her room?'

'Um, no. Mum?'

'Hmm,' Lauren answered from the study.

'You seen Skye?'

'Not since she came home. Try out the back.'

Dean went out to the front yard, while Stu went to the open back door. 'Skye?' It was dark and the outside light didn't reach the far corners of the yard. 'Skye?' he called again. He thought he heard a movement near the fence. Walking down the path and ducking under the clothesline, he stopped and looked around.

There she was, lying on the grass near the biggest tree, gazing at the stars.

He didn't say anything, just dropped down beside her and stared up too.

'There's so many of them,' Skye whispered, after a while.

'And a lot more we can't see coz of the lights,' Stu said.

'Do you think anyone is looking back at us?'

He chuckled. 'Nah, I don't think there're any perverts up there.'

Rolling over, Skye gave him a smile. 'Funny.'

'How you doing, really?' Stu asked.

'Shithouse. But okay at the same time. It's weird.' She flipped back over.

'Yeah. Thought so.' He paused. 'I feel like that too, sometimes, you know.'

In companionable silence, they lay there for a while.

'I could always cut Billy's legs off, or maybe his hands,' Stu offered. 'Yeah, actually, his hands. Then he wouldn't be able to text anymore.'

Skye giggled. 'Good idea. Start with his thumbs and then go onto his fingers and finally get to his wrists.'

'You're a sadist!'

'Nah, it would be too good for him.'

'Hey Skye?' Stu said.

'Yeah?'

'As much as you're a pain in the arse, we all love you.'

Chapter 29

'Here's cheers,' Tamara said, clinking her glass against Craig's.

'Cheers.'

They both took a long sip and looked at each other. A bubble of happiness rose in Tamara's chest and she smiled at him. 'I've missed you,' she said honestly. 'I really have. Seeing you tonight . . . well, it's very good.'

'Seeing you is better than very good,' said Craig. He cleared his throat, and Tamara knew this meant that he didn't want to talk about anything emotional.

'How's your week been?' she asked.

'Busy. It's no fun pouring slabs for houses in summer. I reckon I should shut the business down when it's really hot. I drank five litres of water today and there's not been much come out!'

Tamara giggled. She put her chin on the palm of her hand and watched him.

'What?' He frowned. 'Have I got something in my beard?' His hand went automatically to the bushy hair.

'No,' she said. 'Just looking at you.'

'And how's your week gone?'

'Not bad. Mum and I are getting on so well now. I'm going round there after work every few nights.'

'You're not staying with her?' asked Craig.

Tamara shook her head. 'No, I couldn't do that. We've been talking a lot, and there's so much more I understand now. She's getting old and, you know, I never thought I'd ever get the chance to have a friendship with her.'

'What's she like?'

'Well, she's been pretty downtrodden. Dad was overbearing and controlling—sometimes violent, I found out. But she's also very different from what I remember. She's reminded me of so many things that I'd blocked out. I'd only remembered the bad stuff. My brain just couldn't recall anything that would make me want to go back there. But a lot of good stuff has come back.' She smiled. 'And last night, I dreamed I was standing in the kitchen, stirring a bowl of chocolate cake mixture. Mum was beside me, and we were laughing. I'd been eating it when I wasn't supposed to. Anyway, turns out it wasn't a dream. I told Mum and she got out a photo album and showed me a picture of myself with chocolate cake mix all over my face.'

'I bet you looked cute,' Craig said, smiling too.

'You know, I thought there'd be nothing left of my childhood. No pictures or mementos or anything. But there were. Mum took photos, had them developed on the sly and kept them all. She's had this huge trunk in the garage, hidden away all these years. Evan probably would have burned it.' She sipped her drink. 'He must have hated me.'

'Hate is a pretty strong word,' Craig said. 'I don't think you can say that about your dad. I'm a bloke, right?'

'Hadn't noticed.' A grin played around her mouth.

'I've chosen not to have kids—never met the right chick to have them with, I suppose is more accurate—and now I really think I'm too old . . .'

'Got that bit right, buddy! *I'm* sure not having any kids.'

Craig smiled and raised his glass to that. 'I just reckon it would be real hard to know you were firing blanks and then have to face up every day to a kid at the kitchen table that isn't yours. It would do your head in if you were a small-minded fella. Which obviously your dad was.' Craig drained his glass. 'You back at a motel now?'

Tamara nodded. 'Yeah.'

'Do you, um . . . Have you had any thoughts about . . . ?'

A cheer went up at the bar. There was a loud clinking of glasses. 'Barbecue at your place on Sunday!' someone yelled.

'Look out, Jimbo's won the meat raffle!' said Craig, glancing over at one of his employees. 'He always wins. It's gotta be rigged!' "It's all about luck, Craig, me boy," he tells me.' Craig pretended to tip the tatty old gangster hat that Jimbo always wore. '"Nothing to do with the way you hold your tongue or pray. It's just luck!"' He made his voice the deep baritone of Jimbo's—a voice that would have been more at home on a radio program than a building site.

Tamara snorted. Craig had just taken off his employee perfectly.

'How's Whiskey?' she asked, ignoring the question that Craig hadn't finished asking. She knew he'd been going to ask if she had any thoughts about moving back in. Well, she did. Maybe sometime in the next few weeks, but there was still a need to take things slowly.

'Whiskey's fine. Missing his walks with you, though.'

Tamara toyed with her drink, wiping at the condensation on the glass. 'Want to take him for a walk soon? Maybe up in the Perth Hills near the quarry?'

Craig didn't hesitate. 'Yeah,' he said. 'That'd be great.'

Chapter 30

Skye loaded her bag into the storage area of the bus and turned back to face her parents. They seemed very excited for her. And, weirdly, she felt excited too. Not just because of Todd and her top-secret mission—she actually wanted to know what camping would be like. How embarrassing! But she couldn't seem to help herself.

'Make the most of it,' Dean said, pulling her into a hug.

'I hope you have a really great time,' said Lauren.

Skye could tell her mum wasn't sure whether to hug her or not, so Skye leaned closer, then Lauren grabbed her and held her as tightly as she could.

Tam had been telling Skye that she should keep making an effort with her mum and how relationships needed work and good communication. 'I'm not saying you've caused it all, Skye,' Tam had said, 'and I'm not saying your mum has either, but these things never happen without a bit of help from both sides. I should know! It's great that everything is going so well for you both now, but keep it like that. Be open, talk.'

Now, Skye was pleased that she had. She felt her mum shake against her as if she was crying; when she pulled back, her eyes were damp.

What was she going to think when Skye told her about Todd? Then again, maybe he wasn't the Todd she hoped he was, and then Skye's mum would never know.

Skye ducked her head and got onto the small bus. She was the only one whose parents were there to see her off. The other kids had just drifted in like they always did, bags slung over their shoulders. Pastor Connor started the engine and climbed into the driver's seat, waiting for everyone to board. Skye found a seat by herself at the front, wondering if anyone would ask to sit next to her. But the others were all scattered throughout the bus, none of them sitting together. That was pretty strange—the Walk This Way kids all seemed to get along well.

'Righto!' called Sasha. 'That's everyone, right? We're just waiting for Todd—he's putting the eskies in the storage hold. Now, I wanted to let you know that this camp will be a bit different from the others. Todd will be staying in his house when we get there, and Pastor Connor and I will be in charge of you lot during the nights, because Todd has work to do in the house. Understood?'

Everyone was nodding and saying 'yeah', so Skye did too. She watched as a couple of the other kids put in their earbuds.

Why do you care whether they're friendly? You're on a mission!

When Todd boarded the bus, Skye felt it tilt towards the ground. He wasn't a large man, but he was tall and beefy. Solid.

'Can I sit with you?' he asked Skye.

She glanced around. There were heaps of spare seats. He could sit anywhere. Did he want to talk to her because she seemed familiar?

Nah, probably just because she was the newest kid in the group.

'Yep,' she said, shifting over.

'Excited?' he asked, as the bus pulled out into the traffic.

'Sort of. Bit scared.'

'Why?'

She shrugged. 'Dunno. Never done anything like this before, I guess.'

She definitely hadn't. This was the weirdest thing she'd ever done.

'What does your family do for holidays?'

'Um, we go to see my grandparents in Margaret River. One year we drove across the Nullarbor to Adelaide. I dunno, mostly we hang out in Perth and do things there. Movies, zoo, plays. Mum's always tired from the end of term.'

'My wife used to teach. She still teach, your mum?' he asked, and Skye nodded. 'You've got a brother or sister? Both?'

'A brother. The Gold . . . I mean, his name's Stu.'

'Older, younger?'

'Older.' Skye turned and looked out of the window. Were these normal counsellor questions, or was Todd weirdly curious? 'Um, have you got any kids?'

'No. Unfortunately my wife and I weren't able to have any.'

Not able to have kids? Shit, that wasn't something she was expecting to hear. Maybe he really wasn't the right Todd Atkinson. Disappointment surged through her.

Soon the traffic thinned and they were on the Great Northern Highway. Skye hadn't been out this way much before.

'I always find this drive very strange,' Todd said. 'So familiar but so different.'

FLEUR McDONALD

'What do you mean?' Skye asked.

'I lived on the farm for a very long time. Only moved to Perth after my wife got too sick to be nursed at home on the farm. So whenever I come back, it drags up a lot of tough memories. In some ways, I can't wait to see how the place looks, how the horses are, what the season is doing. In other ways—' he locked his fingers together until his knuckles went white '—I don't like being there at all.'

He sounded so sad. Skye didn't know what to say next. 'So . . . you've got a couple of horses? That's pretty cool.'

Todd nodded. 'Five of them, actually.'

Skye didn't say anything, but she felt another butterfly of excitement in her belly.

She decided to try a more serious question, since he seemed very keen to talk. 'How did your wife die?' she asked, then instantly felt uncomfortable. 'I mean, you don't have to tell me . . .'

'She had cancer.'

'Oh.' Skye looked down at her hands. 'My mum has just had cancer treatment.'

'I'm sorry,' said Todd. 'Though I don't know why we say that. It never means anything or helps, does it?'

'No.'

'How's your mum?'

Skye shrugged. 'They say she's okay at the moment. See, the thing is, I've read a lot about melanoma, and it can come back any time.' She told him all about what she'd learned online.

She noticed that Todd had gone very still as he listened. He'd linked his hands together and was staring at them, like he was concentrating on what she said.

'They say that melanoma is a difficult cancer to understand,' he said. 'But, Skye, any cancer can do just what you've said melanoma can. It's unpredictable and, as much as we try to understand it, cancer still manages to outsmart the cleverest of doctors and scientists.' He took a breath and seemed about to say more, then stopped. 'But I'm sure your mum has very good doctors.'

Skye leaned her head against the window, watching the white lines disappear with each wheel turn. She realised there was something she could ask him about his wife. 'You said your wife was a teacher. Did she ever put the kids she taught above you and her family?'

Todd steepled his fingers and tapped them against his mouth. 'That's an interesting question. At times, she certainly got caught up in the lives of her students and was very busy with them. But I never begrudged her that, because sometimes my job overtook our life too. Seeding and harvest are always the busiest times of the year for farmers. And then there's shearing and lamb marking. Farming is always dependent on the weather so we have to work long hours when it's good. I hardly saw my wife for two or three days at a time. Sometimes life does get in the way of family, but it evens itself out at other times. Have you felt like your mum is too busy with other kids for you?'

To her embarrassment, even though she'd been getting along okay with her mum and they'd worked so much out, Skye's eyes filled with tears. She couldn't say anything, so she nodded her head.

'Ah. That's a nasty feeling. Anything in particular that happened to make you think that, or is it how you've felt for a long time?'

'Dunno,' she said. 'I don't like report time. She's always busy then. And sometimes she focuses on her students' dramas more than us.'

Loud country music broke out over the speakers, the kind that only really old people liked, and Todd whooped with happiness.

'What the hell is that?' yelled Grant.

'This, my friend,' said Todd, 'is called an education. Welcome to the legendary music of Slim Dusty.'

'Oh my God, you're not serious?' cried Paige. 'Make it stop.' She put her hands over her ears, her brow crinkling like she was in pain.

'Are you sure?' Todd asked, laughing.

'Yeah!' said Paige and a few others.

Todd nodded at Pastor Connor, who stabbed at the audio player. The music changed to something with a *doof-doof* beat that was so much better.

'Now my friends, if you don't behave, Slim Dusty will be your punishment!'

After that, all the kids started chatting, and Todd and Skye joined in. She realised that the other kids were pretty cool.

Eventually the bus turned into a dirt driveway and trundled down the two-wheel track towards a glimmering silver structure in the distance.

'What's that?' Skye asked Todd, pointing at it.

'My shearing shed. It's not used anymore. I used to run eight thousand sheep when I was in my prime.' He sounded wistful again.

'Do you miss it?'

'Oh, yeah. But, you know, I like what I do now. Walk This Way has been a godsend for me. I get to meet great kids like you. Keeps me young.' He smiled.

Skye found herself smiling back. Even if it turned out he hadn't been married to her biological grandmother, she was glad she'd met him.

'Where are we camping?'

'You'll set up in the shearing shed. Roll the swags out there. Tents would be too hot . . . and you never know what might be crawling along the ground.'

Had he just said 'crawling'? 'What do you mean?' she asked.

'Snakes and spiders.'

'Oh shit!' She shuddered. 'Are there a lot of them?'

'I don't have all their names and numbers,' he said seriously. 'They don't tend to introduce themselves, they just turn up. Quite bad-mannered, really.'

'That's not even funny,' she said.

He just grinned at her and raised an eyebrow.

When the bus pulled up, Skye got off very gingerly, keeping a sharp eye out for any creepy-crawlies. It was hot. The air seemed to shimmer and it was completely silent. No engine noise, no chatter of people on the streets, no horns. Just a long, long silence, broken only by the occasional bird call. She shivered despite the heat. There was a lot of nothingness out here.

Dear Diary,

The baby has gone. I'm glad. I never wanted it. I'm glad that I don't know what sex it was or who it's gone to. The way that child came into being means it's most likely cursed.

The last nine months have been awful. Mummy and Daddy were so angry with me. It took them a long time to understand that this wasn't my fault. When they did, they wanted to track him down. I didn't want them to and finally managed to talk them around.

It's better this way. I gave up the child and no other lives were ruined in the process. The treatment at the hospital was terrible, though. Single mothers are regarded as second-class citizens. We had no rights at all.

I met a girl there, Lizzie. She wanted to keep her baby, but the hospital staff wouldn't let her. They tricked her into signing adoption papers by saying they were for registering the birth. Lizzie kept saying that she wouldn't let them take the child, but they sedated her. When she came to, the baby was gone. It should be a public scandal.

The nurses said we couldn't see the adoptive parents, but some of the girls snuck down to the offices within the hospital and watched through the windows. They would come back and tell stories of well-dressed young couples with expectation on their faces. Happily taking babies who weren't theirs.

I feel so much older than my sixteen years. I've seen a business that preys on young women.

Some of the girls, like me, couldn't wait to be rid of the child. A time in their lives they never wanted to remember. For others, like Lizzie, I suspect the whole sorry saga will destroy them. By the time Lizzie left the hospital, she wasn't eating and hadn't stopped crying for days. I often wonder about her. I wish I'd thought to get her address so that I could at least write to her.

Lizzie asked me once how I could give my baby up so easily. I told her I felt as though I had a foreign being inside of me; one I couldn't relate to. I didn't ask for it to be put there; it was through force and terror that it came into being.

The one thing I am certain of is that I will never tell anyone, my family will never tell anyone, and I don't ever want to see or know of that child again. I hope that wherever it is, the child is well looked after and never learns the circumstances behind its creation.

Now that it's gone, I can join my family in focusing on our new life in Australia. We do have the house with the back-yard. And a puppy, although he's not really a puppy anymore.

Chapter 31

Todd woke in his old bed, in his old home, and stared at the paint peeling on the ceiling. He could hear the generator going. Pastor Connor would have started it so they could have hot water in the showers. It wouldn't be long until they'd be eating their breakfast and walking to the pocket of bush on the eastern boundary, where they'd fish for yabbies in the lake.

Skye would be Todd's priority today. Then, tonight, he would have to start sorting out his wife's study. If he was going to rent out the house, he had to do it. There was no way around it.

He threw back the covers, got out of bed and went to put the kettle on. Then his eyes caught on the last picture he'd taken of Jacqui, and he fell into a reverie. Only the whistling of the kettle made him tear his gaze away.

Sunlight streamed through the kitchen window, glinting off the granite speckles in the benchtop as he put a spoonful of powdered coffee into the cup and added a teaspoon of sugar. A pecking noise caused him to look up, and a fleeting smile crossed his face.

'I'm coming. Be patient. It was a hard night and I'm a little slow this morning,' he said to the magpie at the window. 'I'm glad you're still here. Keep thinking that one day I'll come back and you won't be.'

Todd opened the fridge. When Jacqui was alive, it had always been full of fruit and veggies, and leftover casseroles or quiches. Even though he had just arrived, its almost empty shelves were another reminder that she was gone. As he reached in, he saw only the tub of butter, the litre of milk and the packet of processed ham he had brought with him from Perth. And the mince for the magpie.

He'd never have touched processed meat when Jacqui was alive. She'd always made sure that cold meat from their own animals was tucked away in a Tupperware container. He'd never even tasted the salty rubbish in packets. But these days he only cooked for himself, so making a proper dinner seemed like a waste of effort.

He grabbed half a handful of the meat, picked up his coffee and went through the French doors onto the balcony. Stepping out into the warmth of the early morning, he found the magpie waiting for him on the table. 'Going to be hot today,' he said to the old bird as he set his cup on the glass tabletop and held out the mince.

Then he glanced around and sighed. The green of the gum trees gave the illusion of coolness, but he knew better. By nine, the sun would be a fiery ball in the cloudless sky.

Jacqui had been diagnosed with melanoma three years before. By the time it had been found, it was stage four and she'd gone straight into a palliative care program at home. They'd had to act fast and make decisions, *big* decisions they knew would change everything.

At first she'd been against selling the farm; leasing it had been her preferred option, so after she was gone Todd could go back to something he knew and loved. Todd, on the other hand, couldn't imagine coming back here without Jacqui. Just the thought of returning to their old life without her made him want to curl up and die. What was left out there for a man on the wrong side of fifty, who perhaps had only another ten years of farming in him? And he didn't have anyone left to leave the farm to. So they'd compromised and sold most of their fifteen thousand acres, keeping two thousand and the farmhouse on in case he wanted to come home.

In the Perth Hills, they'd found a large house on five acres and the property had enough of a rural atmosphere for them both to feel comfortable. But Jacqui had survived only another six months after they'd bought that place.

Now, he was pleased he'd kept the two thousand acres. The kids from Walk This Way always loved it up here, away from the temptations of their daily lives. It had become their sanctuary.

The magpie warbled and crept closer, craning his neck to see if there was still meat in Todd's hand. 'Being greedy?' He laughed as he held out another small amount. The magpie looked up at him before plucking the mince from Todd's fingers, then flew to the edge of the railing. He set down the meat before eating daintily.

'Is he your pet?'

Skye had come up the path. After their chat on the bus yesterday, she'd sought him out. He smiled at her, and she grinned back.

'He's been here for eight years,' Todd explained. 'Got a nest just up there in that tree. Brings his babies in every year to meet us, but none have ever stayed as friendly as this guy. My late wife, Jacqui, used to feed him too.'

'Can I try?'

'Course.' He handed her some mince, then showed her how to place it in the palm of her hand and hold it out.

The magpie looked at her warily but hopped closer. Todd watched, smiling, as the bird cocked his head to one side and gave Skye a beady stare, then hopped closer again.

'Just don't move,' Todd murmured.

With a flutter of wings, the magpie half flew and half walked, grabbed the meat and took off into the tree to the sound of Skye's short, sharp squeal.

'What?' Todd asked, bemused.

'I thought he was going to peck me!'

'He wants the mince, not your hand.'

Skye laughed. Then her expression turned serious. 'Can I ask you something?'

'No worries, go right ahead.'

'You seemed to know a bit about melanoma, when we were talking on the bus. Why's that?'

Three years, and Todd still had trouble saying it. He stared out over the country. The golden stubble paddocks were the only sign that there had been a crop in them not more than three months ago. Along the fences grew statice wildflowers, mingling with wild oats and brome grass. Jacqui would go along the fences and cut the purple-and-white flowers to put on the table during summer. It was so hot and dry and dusty; she used to say that she 'needed the colour'. He could almost hear her saying it now.

'Did your wife have melanoma like my mum?'

Todd dragged himself back to Skye. 'Yes. Yes, she did.'

Skye nodded, something bright in her eyes that he thought was sympathy. 'What was she like?'

'Jacqui was from England and had very fair skin. It didn't stand up well to our Australian summers, unfortunately. Her closest friend was a large-brimmed straw hat that she never went anywhere without.'

'Mum always makes me wear sun cream and a hat whenever I go out. I'm just like her with my skin. There's every chance I'll get melanoma too.'

'And there's every chance you won't. Come on, miss, I think we need to have some breakfast and then go and catch those horses, don't you?' Todd stood up and grabbed a couple of apples before leading the way out of the house.

That evening, Todd let himself into Jacqui's study. It was the same as the day they'd driven away to face whatever the future held for them in Perth. Of course, he'd been back in once or twice, on the times he'd come back to visit, but he'd never thought about clearing it out. He liked to be able to feel her presence.

The first time he'd gone into her study, he'd opened her filing cabinet and looked through. He'd been wanting to get hold of credit card details that would bring memories back, written in black and white. Such as the time they went to Fremantle and ate fish and chips on the beach. Or their trip to Darwin in the wet season.

But memories weren't the only things he'd discovered. There were doctors' reports he'd never seen and adoption papers he didn't know about.

The first doctor's letter he found was dated 1982.

Dear Doctor Gerard,

Thank you for seeing Jacquelyn Emma Atkinson. She has presented to me with fertility problems. I believe they may have been caused by complications during two previous pregnancies. The birth in 1973 resulted in damaged fallopian tubes, through a retained placenta. Mrs Atkinson has recently married and is keen to have children. Would you please discuss options with her?

Doctor H. Van de Hoover

After reading this letter for the first time, Todd stared at the page. His hands started to shake.

Jacqui had given birth to not one, but two children, and he knew about neither of them?

On his hands and knees, he riffled through the file, searching for answers, for questions he hadn't formed yet. He found more fertility reports from before they were married. Why hadn't she told him? His breathing was shallow. A sob escaped him—he didn't know how, because it felt as if his throat had closed over. She'd kept secrets from him? He couldn't understand; they'd always agreed there would be no secrets.

The shock had never really worn off, but the sadness in his heart had been patched somewhat by the kids from Walk This Way.

Now, sitting in Jacqui's study, he could hear laughter from the kids as they sat around a lantern near the shearing shed. He thanked his wife again for having the foresight to make sure he got involved in volunteer work.

'You're going to need something to do after I'm gone,' she'd said gently as Todd lay alongside her, holding her as tightly as he dared.

Towards the end, she had become cold so easily; she loved his body heat on her skin.

'I'm not thinking about the future,' he told her. 'I'm concentrating on you and every day we have together.'

'Face facts, Todd.' Jacqui tightened her grip with surprising strength. 'Sit up. Look at me.' Doing as she said, Todd saw the intensity in her eyes: something he'd rarely seen in the thirty-nine years they'd been together. 'I'm going to die. Sooner rather than later. I'm sorry. I've fought as long as I can, and I'm tired.'

'But—' he began.

She shook her head. 'Be realistic. That's what you've always been so good at. It's why you were so successful at running the farm. You can't just waste away in this house. You need to keep busy: get a job, volunteer, make a difference. Don't wallow around here and wait to die. You need to keep living.'

'What's there to live for?' he said, his voice gravelly. 'You're not going to be here soon. We haven't got kids.' He'd looked away so she hadn't seen his tears before grasping her hand and wishing, with all his might, that he could make everything better. But he couldn't.

'Face facts,' she'd told him.

Well, one fact was that Jacqui was dead. Another fact was that he'd lived in isolation for a long time after she died, in a city where he hadn't known anyone and hadn't understood the culture. And a third fact was that now he had all the kids he'd helped through Walk This Way. He had Connor and Sasha and a few other friends.

But he didn't have any family.

It had been Connor's idea that Todd search for those two adopted babies. At first he'd resisted—what would be the point? He couldn't give those now-adults their mother anymore. But slowly he'd come around. He could offer them stories and memories of their mother. Show them photos and tell them what she was like. It would be another way to keep her alive in his memory. How to contact them, though?

He'd put some information about Jacqui onto a Facebook page with a photo. He still didn't understand how Facebook worked—he'd needed a lot of help from one of the Walk This Way kids. Jacqui had always been the one who'd dealt with computers and all those other gadgets, and he hadn't wanted to put too many details online because he'd read an article in the paper about identity theft. When no one had responded for months, he'd stopped checking. What were the odds, anyway?

Perhaps there was a better way to search. Or, if he was completely honest with himself, perhaps he wasn't ready. Intellectually he'd known it was a good idea; emotionally was another story.

Tonight, he certainly didn't feel ready to keep prying through her study. He wondered what else he might find; what else she'd kept hidden. But he needed to get someone living in here before the place went to rack and ruin; he'd already noticed mouse droppings in the kitchen. This clean-up couldn't be avoided any longer.

He sat in Jacqui's chair and spun around once, then looked at her desk. Her laptop sat there untouched, surrounded by pens and pencils; he wasn't even sure how to turn it on. There was a photo of them at a fundraiser for the Royal Flying Doctor Service three years before she was diagnosed. They both looked so happy. There had been no indication of what was about to happen in their lives.

From the desk drawer, he pulled out her yearly diary. He put it into one of the storage boxes he'd brought with him and flicked through the next drawer down: cheque books, envelopes and the stationery she'd written her thank-you letters on. The third drawer held the most recent receipts and statements of the credit card bills. Looking at a couple of them, he was thrust back into memories of hospitals and chemo. The credit card payments for specialists and scans jumped out at him.

God, what he wouldn't give to have her back. To talk to her. To understand.

He leaned back in the chair, not sure he could go on. Maybe he could send a packing company in to put it all into boxes. No, that wasn't an option. There were too many personal things in here. No one except him could touch them.

Taking a deep breath, he stood up and started on the filing cabinet in the corner of the room. The files labelled 'Household', 'Telephone', 'Power', 'Statements', he stacked into small boxes. The next drawer was teaching aides and lesson plans. The last drawer was personal items—things Todd didn't recognise.

Shoved under the last file, at the back, was a well-worn book. He looked at it for a long time before reaching in and picking it up slowly. Did this hold more information about the adopted babies? Did he want to know? They'd had thirty-four great years together as husband and wife, and all of this had happened beforehand. Did it really matter?

Dear Diary,

I've met the most wonderful man. His name is Todd Atkinson and he's a farmer. He is quite a big cropper—I think that means he grows a lot of crops! He said he has sheep as well.

I didn't think I could fall in love again, after Angus. I

was scared of going down that path and opening myself up to any more hurt. To love someone can give them the power to destroy you.

Todd isn't like that. He's gentle and kind. Thoughtful and considerate. Very handsome.

He's asked me to marry him, and I've said yes. I shouldn't have, though. I carry too many secrets. However, I have and I want to and I will.

Todd stared at the familiar handwriting, the elegant cursive that Jacqui had been so proud of. *Taught by the best in England*, she used to say. *The teachers would crack our knuckles if our writing wasn't neat.*

'Too many secrets,' he whispered, continuing to read.

Dear Diary,

Devastation reigns in our house today. Or at least in my heart. The doctor has confirmed what I think I already knew. I can't have any more children.

I have many emotions: anger, denial, confusion. Of course, none of these will help, but it feels good to get them out onto the page.

When I told him, Todd was his usual, understanding self. 'Then so be it, my love,' he said. 'We'll be okay. We've got each other.'

And he's right. But I will allow myself a few days to grieve what could have been. If I had met Todd sooner, if circum-stances had been different, if previous wrongs were righted. If I had told Todd. I'm too afraid to tell him now.

Mother's Day is torture, as are the birthdays. My first thought in the morning is that I hope both children are happy, wherever they are. They'd be eleven and seven now; I often imagine what the younger one looks like—if he has Angus's black hair and deep, almost black eyes. Or is he more like me? Is his hair combed short and are his knees knobbly like his father's?

It's best not to think about these things. That's what the hospital staff told me. They said to cast all thoughts aside as though neither baby ever happened.

But they did. My babies can't be forgotten, and my heart aches. And so it must continue to be that no one knows.

She had a son, then. Oh, he'd longed for a son. Someone to take with him in the ute, to teach about crops and grain; someone to pass the farm on to. 'I would have loved him as if he were mine, Jacqui,' Todd whispered.

Dear Diary

Today I caught myself looking at children on the streets of Perth. Trying to see if they had any similarities to the children I bore.

I watched little ones playing on the swings, delight on their faces. They're younger than what mine would be, but it didn't stop me from searching their faces.

Teaching fills a small gap—I'm so glad I chose it as a profession.

Read an article today; it suggested I write a diary to the children. Then if one of them ever comes looking for me and I'm not alive, they'll know they were loved.

It was almost too much to take in. Now that he'd seen her thoughts written down, her pain and despair, it broke his heart.

He looked around this house that he'd called home. How different it would have been with two children within its walls. The laughter and noise. The love!

How could he blame Jacqui for not telling him? It wasn't his place to judge the woman he'd loved to distraction. But how different their lives could have been.

Once he'd glanced through the diary, he searched through the drawer again. In a plastic sheath, he found a two-page letter.

Dear children,

Where to start? Firstly, you both need to know you are loved. There isn't a day that passes in which I don't think about you. You both are my first thought in the morning and my last at night.

I wonder what you're doing at the very moment I'm writing this letter. It's strange to think that you both might be eating, or talking, or laughing right now. Or even writing something at the same time that I'm composing this letter to you.

My life has been complicated; many things have happened.

Baby One, I have no idea whether you're a boy or a girl. At the time I didn't care. The circumstances around your conception were traumatic. I'm not sure you need to know about them—or maybe you do? Maybe I'll write it down for you one day, but not now. Suffice to say, it took me a long time to even think about you. It was a time I needed to forget in order to start a new life. It's taken me this long to come to terms with what happened, and now I think about you every day.

Baby Two, I'm almost certain you're a boy. Before they took you from me, I saw a large amount of blond hair, but nothing else. Not your little fingers and toes or your eyes. I hope you have Angus's dark eyes; I always felt I could drown in them. Still, with the fair hair, your eyes will probably be blue like mine.

I attended teachers' college with your father, Angus. We had a romance for a year, and I was so in love with him. The night I told him I was pregnant, he broke off the relationship and I never saw him again. I was so distraught.

Again, I had to go through the process of putting another baby of mine up for adoption. Giving you away was the hardest decision I've ever made.

Baby Two, your birth was harrowing. A retained placenta and haemorrhaging damaged my fallopian tubes and as a result I am infertile.

Fortunately my husband, Todd, is a wonderful man. Without realising it, he put my pieces back together and made me whole again. Well, I'm as whole as I can be without knowing that the two of you are safe, well and happy.

And now I am sick—with only a few months to live. My body is full of melanoma. I had plans of trying to find you both, but now it's impossible. I can only hope that one day you'll find me, or at least what's left of me—this letter and my diary—and know that you both were loved.

Here's what I know about you.

Baby One, you were born on 12 May 1969 at King Edward Memorial Hospital. You were taken from me straight away. I never saw you, held you or knew who you were being adopted by.

Baby Two, you were born on 1 March 1973, also at King Edward Memorial. I heard you cry, saw your blond hair and then they bundled you away. The nurse took pity on me and told me I'd had a son.

It's very odd to think that I have given birth to two children, but the things I know about you can fill only one paragraph each. A short one at that.

So, let me tell you a little about myself. I was born in London. My parents were good, honest, hard-working people who chose to come to Australia as part of the Ten Pound Pom scheme. We travelled by ship, landing in early 1968 at Fremantle.

After Baby One was born, I threw myself into my studies, then went straight to teachers' college, where I met Baby Two's father. After you were born, working hard during my teaching diploma helped me with my grief. I graduated near the top of the class. Cadoux was my first and only school: I met Todd and never left.

He doesn't know about you yet. I'm trying to find the right time to tell him. That may never come and, if it does, it will be a shock to him. Be kind to Todd if you meet him. He would have made a wonderful father to you both.

I love reading and sewing. Cool weather and wildflowers. I love Todd. Children, teaching them and being around them, are my life.

There you have it, my lovely ones. It's been strange writing a letter when I've got no idea if it will ever be read.

Todd and I move to Perth next week. I don't have much time left.

I have left this letter in a drawer. I hope that Todd will find it after my death. I hope that if you ever come looking for me, he will be there to give it to you.

With every ounce of love I hold, Your Mother xxxx

Chapter 32

The clock in the hall chimed three o'clock in the morning. Todd had no idea how long he'd been sitting on the floor, tears running down his cheeks.

It was still dark outside, but if he looked hard enough he would see a glimmer of the approaching dawn on the horizon.

'Why didn't you just tell me?' he begged answers from the empty study.

Torn and grief-stricken, he made himself get up off the floor and go into the lounge. Something was niggling at him.

He tried five photo albums before he found the right one. Jacqui had brought them from her parents' home, after they'd died. It was full of black-and-white photos of her family when they'd first arrived in Perth. Jacqui in bathers at the beach. Jacqui smiling at the camera, ice-cream in one hand and a tissue in the other. Jacqui with her parents flanking either side of her, dressed in her graduation gown.

Todd looked carefully. He could see it now: under a bulky

jumper, as she smiled slightly, was a slight swelling of her stomach. And in this one, the graduation photo, even though she was smiling, her eyes were dead and dull. Not holding the excitement of a new teacher ready to go out and take on the world.

On winter evenings they'd sat in front of the fire, flicking through old photos. Jacqui had told him stories of her childhood, and he'd told her stories of his. Not once had he noticed there was anything different about the woman sitting beside him from the girl in the photos.

He went back to the diary. 'The circumstances around your conception were traumatic,' she'd written of Baby One. What did that mean? Frustrated, he got up and paced the perimeter of the room. Had she been raped?

Now that he knew when the first baby had been born, Todd assumed that Jacqui's parents had been aware of all the details, although perhaps they hadn't found out about baby number two. Jacqui's relationship with them had been close, and he'd got along well with them too—but apparently not well enough for anyone to tell him the truth.

Taking a colour portrait out of the plastic pocket, Todd held it close to his eyes, examining every detail of her sixteen-year-old face. The familiar curve of her chin, her pensive smile and the freckles on her nose. Her red hair. Her eyes were light—in real life, a sapphire blue, deep and rich.

Much like Skye's colouring, in fact. His stomach flipped. *Don't be stupid*, he told himself. Hundreds of babies are adopted out every day. There is no chance in the world that Skye could be Jacqui's granddaughter.

Todd didn't think he'd be able to sleep, but he must have because the sun was high when he finally opened his eyes. His friend the magpie was outside, warbling and pecking at the window, waiting for his morning feed. Somehow Todd managed to go through the motions of showering, still turning over everything in his mind.

When he ran the razor down his cheek, he swore as he nicked a pimple and it started to bleed. With shaking hands, he grabbed a towel and held it over the spot.

'I still don't understand,' he said, staring at his reflection in the mirror.

A knock at the door echoed through the house, and Todd dabbed at his face, taking one last glance at himself before he went to answer it.

Skye. It was very strange. To his eyes, she now seemed to look just like sixteen-year-old Jacqui. He had to remind himself that it was just a coincidence.

'You're late,' she said, with raised eyebrows. 'I thought we were going riding. I had so much fun yesterday, but, oh my God, my arse and legs are so sore. There are muscles in places I didn't know! Geez, what did you do to your face?'

He cleared his throat. 'Oh, shaving accident.' He dabbed at the wet spot with his finger—must have nicked it worse than he'd thought. 'I didn't sleep that well. I'm coming now. Just wait while I make a coffee to go.'

'Have you fed the magpie?' Skye asked.

'No, not today. I heard him earlier this morning, but he seems to have got impatient and gone home.' He beckoned to Skye and gave her a small smile. 'Come in and make yourself at home while I get ready.'

They walked into the kitchen, where he started making his coffee.

Then he realised that Skye was staring at the photo of his wife and shifting from foot to foot. He knew enough about teenage girls now to know that she was extremely nervous.

'I need to tell you something,' she said.

'What would that be?'

She took a deep breath, then the words rushed out of her without pause. 'I wanted you to be my counsellor because I saw your post on Facebook about looking for babies that been adopted out and the photo you put up looked like me.'

Todd stared at her. 'Slow down. You saw the post? But I put that up months ago. How . . . ?

Skye nodded. She was trembling, as though she was afraid that he'd be angry with her. 'I want to make my mum happy by finding her birth mum. I don't know if Jacqui is her, but they look so alike. And I didn't want to just contact you and put you in touch with Mum. I wanted to know who you were, in case you were, you know, some psycho or whatever. When you said that Jacqui had melanoma, I nearly told you . . . but I just couldn't. I was still scared that I was wrong.'

So it hadn't been a wild goose chase after all. Todd knew he wasn't angry with Skye for deceiving him, but otherwise he didn't know how to think or feel. He just stood there for a moment as they both gazed at Jacqui's photo.

'You look like her too,' he said finally. 'I thought you reminded me of someone, but it took me until I was looking at photos of a young Jacqui last night to realise who it was. Of course, until now I thought it was impossible.'

They stared at each other, both realising the enormity of the situation.

'Skye, what's your mum's birthday?'

'May twelfth. Oh, and she was born in 1969.'

Todd nodded solemnly. 'You mustn't say anything to your mum yet. This type of thing has to be handled very carefully. Will you leave it to me?'

They didn't go horseriding that day. Todd and Skye explained everything to Pastor Connor, who at first was incredulous and shocked, but soon burst out laughing and told Skye that she would make an excellent super-spy for the Australian government. She grinned and thanked him. Todd assured Connor that he would handle this issue with Skye's parents. Of course, it would no longer be appropriate for him to counsel Skye under the Walk This Way program; something that made him a little sad.

When Todd got up the nerve a couple of hours later, he dialled Lauren Ramsey's number with shaky hands. In his experience, kids didn't always know exactly what was going on in their parents' lives, even if they thought they did. Perhaps Lauren wouldn't be as interested in this information as Skye had led him to believe. And he didn't know what he was going to say. He'd rehearsed a few lines in his head but nothing had sounded right.

'Hello?' she said. Was he fooling himself, or did she sound a lot like Jacqui?

'Is that Lauren?'

'Yes.'

'It's Todd Atkinson, from Walk This Way.'

'Is Skye alright?' she asked immediately.

'She's fine. In fact, I'm happy with her. She seems much more content within herself, and that's the aim of these types of camps.' He paused and gave a little laugh. 'She very much likes my horses and they seem to love her.'

'She's been riding?' The surprise in Lauren's voice was obvious. 'I'm ashamed to say, I didn't know she liked animals. We've never even had a goldfish!'

'Well, I've led her around the yard a few times on horseback. She's been learning more about the responsibility of keeping an animal—grooming, feeding and so on. Responsibility is a good tool to have. Animals teach that very well.'

'Of course.'

Todd took a breath. 'But I'm ringing with something else on my mind, Lauren, and you'll have to bear with me. This information is very new and I'm not sure what to make of it all.'

'Right?' Lauren's tone was surprised and curious. Surely there was something reminiscent of Jacqui in the upward lilt of Lauren's questions.

'Skye and I have spent a bit of time talking, and she told me you've recently had an operation for melanoma?'

'Yes, I have.'

'My wife had melanoma too. Look . . .' What should he say about Skye's involvement in this? 'I've been cleaning out a few of Jacqui's things while I've been visiting the farm. We used to live here, you see. It's my property.' He coughed. 'Skye also told me you were adopted and have been trying to find your birth mother.'

'Well, yes,' Lauren replied, 'I've tried the government agencies and an online DNA test, but no results as yet.'

'I don't want to get your hopes up, but in my wife's study last night, I found a diary as well as a letter written to the two children she gave up for adoption. I want to find Jacqui's kids, so I can bring them stories of her—'

'What did the diary say?' Lauren broke in over the top of him.

'I found out that her first baby was born on the twelfth of May in 1969. I understand that's your birthday?'

On the other end of the line, Todd heard Lauren gasp. 'Yes,' she said, faintly.

'Lauren, Skye looks like my wife at sixteen. The resemblance is uncanny.'

A long pause. 'You said Jacqui was sick. Is she still alive?'

Todd swallowed. 'No, no, I'm sorry. She died from her melanoma.'

Chapter 33

'You just wouldn't believe it,' Skye said to Tam. She was sitting on the glass-topped counter after closing time, swinging her legs. She couldn't wait to tell Tam the whole story, but she wanted to do it right. 'The horses were so cool. Their noses are so soft and smell amazing. I think I want to be a jockey now.'

'A jockey?' Tam asked. 'Why can't you just have a horse and ride it? Jockeys need to get up early to train and they can never eat.'

Skye's eyes widened. 'Really? Good point.'

'How did you get on with all the others?'

'They're cool. Especially Paige—she knows all of Rihanna's songs off by heart! But I didn't spend the first day with the kids. Todd and I mostly mucked around with the horses that day. He said that's what he likes to do with the first-timers. "Teaches responsibility,"' Skye chanted. 'You just have to fall in love with them.'

'And what were Todd and Pastor Connor like?'

'Todd is *awesome*. He's like this great big bear. He and I talked heaps. His wife died from melanoma too.'

'Hang on, your mum isn't dead!' Tam cut in, looking really exasperated. 'You exaggerate so much!'

Skye shrugged. 'You know what I mean. Anyway, Todd knew a lot about melanoma. We talked heaps about it and what it meant. It's possible I have the gene because of my fairness. Anyway, the thing is—'

'Everyone has to be careful,' said Tam. 'It's not only fair-skinned, red-haired beauties who can get melanoma!' She wagged a finger at Skye with a smile.

'Yeah, that's true.' Skye leaned forward. 'Listen, I've got a secret . . .'

Raising her eyebrows skyward, Tam said, 'And what's that?'

As dramatically as she could, Skye told Tam all about seeing Todd's post on Facebook and how she'd become a super-spy at Walk This Way, and all the rest of what happened on her adventure.

'I'm a hundred percent positive that Jacqui's my biological grandmother. Todd thinks so too. See, the birth dates are the same, and Mum has the same hair colour, eye colour as his wife had. All that's left to do is the DNA testing.'

'Okay,' said Tam, who was looking a bit stunned. 'So, does your mum know about this?'

'Yeah, totally. Todd called her. It's all good.'

Coming home on the bus, Skye had imagined what it would be like to have Todd as a grandfather. She'd be able to go to the farm and ride the horses whenever she wanted. And now that she knew him, she knew she'd always be able to go to him in a crisis. The thought made her really happy.

'So, anyway, Jacqui gave up two babies,' Skye said. 'The other one we still don't know anything about, except that it was probably a boy. So I might have an uncle out there somewhere! How cool is that?'

Tam had been folding a stack of black pants, but now she stopped.

'You know, I was adopted,' she said, without looking up.

Skye stared at her, eyes wide. 'Really? Wow.'

'Mmm, yeah. I only found out a few weeks ago when I reunited with Mum. I don't have a lot of information yet. Just a confirmation of my birthday and a few other details.'

Skye was hit with an idea. In her mind, she went back to the letter that Lauren had let her read, the one Jacqui had written when she was dying.

'Hey, when's your birthday?' Skye asked. 'I want to put it in my phone.'

'The first of March.'

'And the year?'

Tam gave her a look. 'Let's just say I'm very old.'

'Come on, I need to know how many candles to put on your cake! And Mum says that ageing is nothing to be ashamed of. Should *I* be ashamed of getting older?'

Rolling her eyes and chuckling, Tam said, 'Alright. I was born in 1973.'

Skye grinned in pure delight, and Tam gave her a questioning look.

Suddenly, Skye was positive that the nurses had lied to Jacqui about the baby being a boy. It had been a girl! And that girl, now a woman, was standing right in front of her. How had she not realised before? Their mannerisms, the way they laughed, even the way they sneezed. The shape of their eyes and how they walked. How was it that two half-sisters could be brought up in different houses by different families, but still have so many things in common? Genes were incredible. And how amazing that they lived not far from each other!

Now that Skye really thought about it, it was all so clear. She supposed that after all the failed efforts she'd made when she was a little kid to randomly find her blood relatives, with her mum telling her over and over to stop doing it, she'd switched off that bit of her brain and kept ignoring what it was telling her about Tam. But some part of her had known. She hadn't only wanted her mum's attention—she'd wanted Tam's as well. She'd wanted to chat with Tam like they were chatting now.

My cool aunty!

'So, anyway,' Skye said, 'are you going to try and find your birth mum?'

'I don't know. It's not a high priority for me, but that might change.'

Skye studied the woman she was now sure was her aunty. 'How'd it make you feel, finding out?'

'Oh, now that's a loaded question. There was so much other stuff going on at the time. A fair bit to process. But in some ways it helped me make sense of a lot of things. My father wasn't very nice to me when I was growing up. When I found out I'd been brought into the family as a baby, I understood him a lot more.'

'But . . . aren't you curious about where you came from?'

'I know where I came from,' Tam answered. 'I was raised in Whitfield Street with my mum and dad.'

'You might have a whole other family out there who's really cool!' Skye gushed. 'You might have a father and mother, sister . . . or a brother. Though they can be a bit boring at times.

But you might even have a really smart, pretty, wicked niece—just like me!'

'And modest too. God help us all if that's the case!' Tam said, snorting. 'Have you counted that float yet? And can I ask why you're putting your bum prints all over my nice shiny counter? You're going to need to polish that before we go home.'

'Uh, no. Sorry.' Skye jumped down and opened the till.

Chapter 34

Three weeks later, when Lauren's arm had healed and she felt well enough, she appeared at the door of the kindy classroom and was met with shrieks of delight. She smiled and bent down to greet each and every child. The pure joy on their faces made her catch her breath. They loved her, and she loved them.

'There must be so much news to tell,' she said to them all as they came inside.

Joy had been setting up the room just as Lauren had asked the previous day. There was butcher's paper spread over the tables next to colourful pencils and crayons. Today they'd start working on a large drawing for Dirk's hospital wall.

'Now, children, first I've got some big news to share with you. Shall we all sit down and I'll tell you about it?'

Once she and Joy had the kids settled, she sat down with them. 'I guess some of you have noticed that Dirk hasn't been at school very much,' she said.

'Is he sick?' asked one child.

'Yes, he is. He's in a hospital especially for children and the doctors are doing all they can to make him get better. His mum says he's missing all of you so much!'

'Is he going to die?' A pair of large hazel eyes looked at Lauren.

That was the question she'd hoped not to be asked.

When Zoe had rung Lauren out of the blue, she had given her the news in a low, flat tone. 'We don't know what's going to happen. It's not looking good at this stage, but the doctor says that things often get worse before they get better. Dirk's neutrophils—that's a type of white blood cell—are very low, which means he's got to be on a special diet. White blood cells help fight infection, so the doctors are worried about him catching something that could kill him. It's a whole new language to learn: neutrophils, white blood cells, red blood cells, platelets. Blood transfusions. God!' Zoe sounded exhausted. 'Did you know, he has to have a white cell injection in his stomach every week? He's covered in bruises. Nothing like the ones you saw—these are deep and purple. I'm sure they go through to the other side.'

'I'm *so* sorry,' Lauren said. 'Would he like to see the other children? I can organise a visit. Or would it be too much?'

'The doctors won't let them in, I don't think. It's the risk of infection. And he's so tired, just sleeps all the time. The chemo is making him sick.'

'That's terrible,' said Lauren. 'I'll organise something. And let me know if there's anything—I don't care how small it is, just anything, we can do here from the school.'

'Thank you. And, Lauren . . . I need to thank you. When we had that meeting, I was a bit taken aback. But you also helped me see that I was being so stupid.'

Lauren had felt empty when she'd hung up the phone. She hadn't been sure whether to cry or just sit and stare.

'Mrs Ramsey?'

She blinked and saw the children looking up at her, waiting for her to answer their difficult question. 'Well, the doctors are doing their very best to make Dirk well again, but he'll be away from kindy for a while. I think it might be nice if we draw a great big picture to go on his hospital wall, don't you?'

Smiling at them, she reached around her arm to touch the spot where the lesion had been. She was beginning to get nervous about her check-up, but she had to get used to the idea of these three-monthly check-ups, always with the risk of finding something again. It was just how she had to live from now on.

Guiding the kids over to the tables, she watched as they all started to draw. Some drew love hearts; others, green grass and sunshine. But they all took turns at tracing the letters: 'To Dirk, love from the kindy class of the Goose.'

Later that day, Lauren stood in front of her letterbox and stared at the envelope with the government symbol in the corner.

Dear Mrs Ramsey,

Thank you for your enquiry. The Departmental records have been searched and the following information was recorded:

Name: Lauren Connie Jenkins

Born: King Edward Memorial Hospital, Subiaco, Western Australia

Date of birth: 12 May 1969

Records state that the child was born without complications at 2:56am and weighed 3778.75gm. Length was 48cm and her Apgar scores were 6 and 7.

Birth mother was sixteen, single and a student.

It was the birth mother's wish, at the time, not to have any contact.

As of today, the first of April 2016, the birth mother has not requested to be put on the Contact Register.

Yours sincerely,

Flora Dune

This was all what she'd expected. The letter fell to her chest as she took out another piece of paper from the file.

<u>Non-identifying particulars of mother</u>:

Age: Sixteen

Birth place: England

Marital Status: Single

Education: Completing Year 12 at the time of the birth

Occupation: Student

Health: No known hereditary diseases. Wears glasses.

Family: One of three children. Parents are both deceased. Father had a stroke when he was 56. Mother died of natural causes.

Physical description:

Height: Five foot nine

Hair: Red

Eyes: Blue

Build: Medium frame

Complexion: Very fair

Well, that was it, then. One more piece of evidence that she was Jacqui's biological daughter—and that she and Tamara Thompson were half-sisters, a revelation from Skye that at first had left her reeling. When Lauren had spoken to Tamara about it, she tried to laugh it off until she'd seen her own birthday in Jacqui's letter, along with the other details. Tamara had then shared the information that her adoptive mum, Angela, had given her.

There was something about Tamara that Lauren still hadn't warmed to, even though Skye thought she was the best thing ever. But Lauren knew this was quite normal. Obviously, siblings didn't always get along! Plus, Lauren and Tamara had been brought up in such different ways. Lauren wasn't sure how Tamara felt, so she'd just been very nice and cordial to her, wondering if her feelings would ever change.

Now, all that was left to do was the DNA test. Perhaps it wasn't strictly necessary, but Lauren and Tamara had agreed to do it as a final confirmation. A form of closure. Todd had agreed to give them a sample of Jacqui's DNA as well.

Lauren had been making sure not to let these discoveries take over her life. She'd been enjoying time with Dean and laughing with Stu. And she'd been taking walks with Skye every afternoon. They would put their new puppy, Tinker, on the lead and take him to the park. Somehow Skye had managed to talk them into getting a small Jack Russell who had so much attitude that Lauren was sure the dog thought he was six foot tall, when in fact his tummy nearly scraped on the ground. Owning Tinker had been part of Skye's change for the better—she seemed to come to life around animals. A yappy, bouncing, small dog was a small price to pay for making Skye happy. And it was certainly cheaper than the horse

Skye craved. She was now telling everyone that she wanted to be a vet.

On their walks, Skye and Lauren talked about their days. Skye seemed much more settled in her new school, although her friends were few and far between. At least she'd made a good friend at the Walk This Way camp—a girl called Paige. She'd cut loose everyone from the Goose, although a few days ago she'd said she missed Jasmine. Maybe Lauren would try to track her down next week while she was at school and see if she wanted to catch up with Skye. First she'd have to check that this was okay with Skye. They'd made a promise never to let the lines of communication be cut again.

Lauren felt like a new person. Her sleeping had become much better since her nightmare had all but disappeared. For some reason, it had hardly bothered her since she'd learned her birth mother's identity.

Lauren looked at Tamara and smiled. They put the small sticks in their mouths and ran them over the insides of their cheeks. Skye held the plastic bag out for Lauren, and she placed the stick in there. Tamara did the same as Todd held another bag for her. Sitting on the kitchen table, in a plastic bag, was Jacqui's hairbrush; DNA could be sourced from the roots of loose hair. Todd had said to them, more than once, that he was so pleased he hadn't cleaned Jacqui's things out yet.

'I'll post them, if you like?' Stu offered, as they started to package them up.

Lauren shook her head. 'Thanks, darling, but this is something I need to do.'

Dean nodded his agreement, squeezing her shoulder supportively.

'Do you want to come?' Lauren asked Tamara.

'No, that's okay,' Tamara said, glancing at her watch. 'I've got to go and meet Angela for a drink, then get home in time to cook Craig's dinner. He's been gone since five this morning, so he'll be tired.' She kissed Todd and hugged Skye before saying goodbye to Dean, Stu, Connie and George.

Lauren's parents each gave her a big hug before she followed Tamara out the front door. 'Good luck, my darling girl,' Connie said, with just the hint of a quaver in her voice.

The two younger women faced each other in the driveway.

'You ready for this?' Tamara asked.

'More than. What about you?' said Lauren.

Tamara gave a short laugh. 'It's so out of the blue. I wasn't even sure I needed to find my birth mum, and now here we are!'

Chapter 35

'It's here!' Lauren said, waving the envelope at the small gathering of people.

They were all sitting in the Ramseys' lounge room, drinking champagne, eating nibbles and getting to know one another better. Tamara, her partner Craig and her adoptive mother Angela, who seemed to go everywhere with her. Lauren's parents and Dean's. Todd. They were a varied crowd and, mostly, they all got along. Lauren still held Tamara at arm's length. But to Lauren's surprise, Craig and Dean had found common ground and were talking about motorbikes. Lauren knew her husband was building up to talk to her about buying one—he'd left the pamphlets in the toilet. Still, she'd cross that bridge when it happened.

When Lauren flourished the envelope in the air, a cry of excitement went up from everyone, and Stu rushed to top up their glasses with champagne.

Dean, Todd, Connie and George came over to stand next to her. Skye hung at her shoulder, bouncing on her feet with excitement.

'We already know what it says,' Skye said. 'Come on, hurry up!'

Lauren took a breath and ripped open the envelope.

There was a silence. Everyone waiting. Everyone watching. Lauren scanned the page.

Dear Mrs Ramsey,

Thank you for supplying a sample of DNA (saliva sample) to be matched to Tamara Grace Thompson (saliva sample) and the DNA supplied by Mr Todd Atkinson on behalf of Mrs Jacquelyn Atkinson (hair sample).

It is my conclusion that Jacquelyn Emma Atkinson is both Lauren Connie Ramsey's and Tamara Grace Thompson's mother. There are five DNA markers we compare and they all match . . .

Lauren broke off. 'It's a match,' she whispered, tears filling her eyes. She turned and looked at Todd. 'We've found our missing pieces.'

A cheer broke out, and Todd swept her up in a hug. Skye jumped on top of them with a yell of delight: 'I knew it! I knew it!'

'I've gone from having no family to having all of you,' Todd said, choked with emotion. He turned and held up his glass. 'Here's to a new family!'

'A new family!' Everyone shouted happily.

But then sadness swept over Lauren. She wished that Jacqui was here so she could hug her too. What was important, Lauren reminded herself, were the stories Todd could tell about Lauren's birth mother and his life with her.

Tamara listened to Lauren read the letter, one hand holding Craig's tightly, the other gripping Angela's. Goosebumps broke out over her skin and she froze. A match. Just as they'd expected. But she was still having trouble believing it. She still didn't know what to say to Lauren or Todd. Or to Angela. She turned and saw tears in her mother's eyes, and that she was smiling.

Then Skye threw herself against her and hugged her tightly. 'I knew it,' she whispered in her ear. 'Now you've got that really smart, pretty, wicked niece we talked about!'

As she hugged Skye back, Tamara suddenly felt very grateful.

Skye slipped outside and called Tinker to her. He gave a bark of delight and licked her face, before curling up and falling asleep on her lap. She stared out into the blackness. The clouds that danced along to the Fremantle Doctor—the sea breeze—were blocking the stars tonight. It didn't matter. She knew they were there.

It felt like everything was falling into place.

Moving to a new school and letting Adele go as a friend had been the best thing she'd ever done. No one knew her down in the city. The bus ride was a bit longer, but that was okay. Sometimes Stu dropped her off on his way to uni. She still teased him about being the Golden Boy, but two days ago he'd said, in all seriousness, that he'd lost the title: now she was the Golden Girl!

Then there were Tinker and horses and the farm.

And the best thing was, she had two new family members.

It didn't matter that Todd wasn't related by blood. He needed a family, and they were linked. She hadn't needed another grandparent, but it turned out that it didn't hurt to have a third grandfather.

'Skye? Where are you?' her mum called. 'It's time to cut the cake.'

'New beginnings, Tinker,' Skye said, picking up the pup and tucking him against her chest as she walked back into her home. 'New beginnings.'

Author's note

Listed below are the websites I found particularly useful when I was researching the adoption process in Australia.

www.findandconnect.gov.au/guide/nsw/NE00524

www.ozreunion.com.au/adoption_register.asp? listingtype=14 http://au.reachout.com/finding-your-birth-parents

www.dcp.wa.gov.au/FosteringandAdoption/Pages/ PastAdoptionInfo.aspx

www.facebook.com/ReunionsAustralia/?fref=ts

I'd like to thank my friend Belinda, who willingly shared her adoption story, along with all the documentation and information surrounding her adoption and her search for her mother.

While researching melanoma, I consulted Carrie, a melanoma nurse, and the following websites:

www.melanoma.org.au/understanding-melanoma/ stages-of-melanoma/

www.cancercouncil.com.au/835/b1000/melanoma-24 melanoma-diagnosis/

Any mistakes in the book are mine.

Acknowledgements

All my love and appreciation to my gentle soul, Garry, who somehow loves me amid my chaos and craziness, of which there is plenty. Thank you for loving me, for keeping everything going while I'm under pressure with deadlines and for bringing peace when I need it most.

Rochelle and Hayden, you continue to make me proud, and bring light and happiness to our home. I love you both very much.

To my clan, who get a mention in every book: Cal and Aaron, Em and Pete, Heather, Jan and Pete, Robyn, Scottish, Tiffany. I love it when you all tell me off or point out something that is so clear to you all, but never to me. Thank you all for loving me enough to do that. And to all my family.

Kelly Waight, I'm sure this book would never have been finished without your input. Thanks for the numerous hours spent pouring over white boards, dreaming up ideas and swearing with me. That always made me feel better.

Sarah Baker, you seriously are my rock. Thanks also to editors Virginia Lloyd and Kate Goldsworthy for polishing something so very raw.

Louise Thurtell, again, thanks for every opportunity you send my way. And for your patience and support.

Appreciation and love to Gaby Naher, agent *extraordinaire*, for guiding my career. Without doubt, you are the greatest!

Everyone at Allen & Unwin. A book is such a team effort and I can't thank you all enough for your carefully considered approach to all my novels. I'm with the best publishing house!

Once again, to all my readers, heartfelt thanks and appreciation. I wouldn't be here without you all.

If you'd like to contact me, please do. I always do my best to respond! You can follow me on social media:

www.facebook.com/FleurMcDonaldAuthor/

Twitter @fleurmcdonald

Instagram fleurmcdonald

I also write a blog at http://fleurmcdonald.com/blog/

With love,
Fleur x